WINNING

BY

DAVID O'NEIL

W & B Publishers
USA

W & B Publishers

For information:
W & B Publishers
Post Office Box 193
Colfax, NC 27235
www.a-argusbooks.com

ISBN: 9781942981121
ISBN: 1942981120

Book Cover designed by Dubya
Printed in the United States of America

Winning

Part One

July 1812

Chapter One

Independent Command

The deck felt right beneath Martin's feet, although it had only been a matter of twelve weeks since he was last on board HMS Vixen. Back on board a ship he felt comfortable, where he belonged. He confessed to himself, he was still a little uncomfortable with his land-based title as Sir Martin Forest-Bowers, Bart.

Lady Jennifer, his wife, accepted her place without any problem. As the daughter of a naval captain, now a titled Vice-Admiral, and a noble Lady in her own right, she had been groomed for the part since she was a child.

There was a clatter and a shout, disturbing his train of thought. He turned to see Peters, his cox'n, directing two men to bring a cupboard for glassware aboard. It was to be secured in his cabin alongside his new wine cabinet. Constructed to match, the two units made a handsome contrast to the rather spartan furnishings which Martin had lived with up to now.

He ran his hand over the length of new timber replacing the rail, which had been shattered in the engagement with the French on his return from America. First Lieutenant Patrick Brooks joined him. "The remainder of your furniture has been delivered and installed, sir."

Martin looked up and grinned. "I suppose it is something I must learn to live with now. I always liked the way the cabin was before our French friends re-arranged it."

Brooks smiled grimly, "A fair exchange if I might put it that way, sir, one frigate-captain's cabin for one 74-gun ship of the line!"

Martin smiled. "I suppose, put that way, I cannot complain." He straightened up and looked with affection over the ship, his command. The raw-looking replacement timber where the enemy cannon had ripped and torn the fabric stood out against the weathered appearance of the rest of the woodwork. A few weeks at sea and the scars would disappear. The Atlantic weather soon took care of that. "She is a good ship!" He said almost under his breath.

Brooks heard. "She is that," he agreed.

The arrival of a carriage on the quayside interrupted Martin's train of thought. He turned to see Peters, his Cox'n, already assisting Jennifer to the gangway, followed by his nine year old daughter, Jane, pretty in her summer dress. As Jennifer approached, Jane put her hands up to Peters, who swept her up high in his arms, causing her to laugh happily.

"Good day to you, Patrick. Will I be introduced to your fiancée before you sail?"

Without pausing, she raised her cheek for her husband's kiss, and held her hand out to the blushing Lieutenant.

Patrick bent over her hand, cleared his throat and managed, "It would be my pleasure to introduce you as soon as it can be arranged, my lady."

"We will expect you, if it is agreeable, on Wednesday, at Eastney, just a small private gathering of family and friends only. Your departure at the end of the week allows little time for social activities, so we must make the most of the time we have."

With a smile she turned and took Martin's arm. "Now, my dear, show me your refurnished cabin. I trust it is an improvement on the 'monk's cell' you used to occupy." Their daughter, Jane, was by this time sitting cross-legged on the deck looking at an array of small knick-knacks which McLean, the former poacher, had laid out on deck to show her. James Woods, now Midshipman, looked on with interest.

***

The house at Eastney was alive with activity when Martin arrived on Wednesday afternoon, having spent the morning in the office of the Admiral-in-Command of the shipyard at Portsmouth. It was Admiral Hope's task, one he took most seriously, to see that the ships passing through his hands, were in the best possible condition before they were allowed back to sea. Martin had always tried to spend time with the Admiral who was now well into his declining years, though as his friends observed, in body alone. He was still as keen-minded, and astute as ever.

Lady Jane Bowers, Martin's adoptive mother, greeted him, presenting her cheek for a kiss. "My dear, we are in turmoil because we are fourteen at table instead of twelve." She smiled. Martin looked at her fondly. She was still as beautiful as ever, though her hair was now silver.

"You are as lovely as ever, Jane. If your daughter follows in your steps I am doubly blessed."

"Flattery, Martin. You never change!"

"Nor do you, Jane, nor do you." Taking her arm, he walked her through the French windows into the still-sunlit garden. As they walked, Jane confided her worry about Charles. "Martin, he is so busy at the Admiralty he does not eat properly and gets no exercise. I can see him getting unhealthier day by day. I do not want to lose him. I do wish he would retire and leave it to others to get things done."

Martin agreed with her, but he understood his adoptive-father's reasons for remaining at his post. The war with France was bad enough, but the war with America was just more worry about over-stretched resources.

They walked in silence for a few minutes then Jane brightened up. "Giles and Isabella are here with us, also Lieutenant Brooks will be here with his fiancée, Dorothea Winton, I believe. Do I understand that she is the daughter of the Rector of Wareham?"

"That is correct. He spotted her in passing and could not, nay would not, rest until he had discovered who she was. A meeting was arranged, and as a result they found they shared the same feelings, and that day they became engaged, with the Rector's blessing."

The successful dinner party was the last event before the departure of HMS Vixen. Martin's title of Commodore was withdrawn because the ship was now in company only with their old friend, the schooner HMS Hera, still under the command of Lieutenant John Harris, also present at the party, though as yet without a wife or expectation. He had pointed out to his colleagues that marriage was a lottery, especially for a seaman. It was even more difficult for a man as expert as himself, since he was in demand all the time with little chance to socialise.

At this point his friends would either sit on him, or throw him into water if it was available. Needless to say, apart from being an excellent officer, he was a good friend and popular with his colleagues and crew.

***

The two ships had been at sea for just three days; for the majority of those aboard any initial queasiness was now past, with sea-legs once more well and truly regained.

Martin felt a little odd sailing without his friend, Commodore Antonio Ramos of the Portuguese Navy. Other Portuguese ships had arrived, and Antonio had found himself as senior officer, in command of his own flotilla. He had consequently been sent, with his ships, to the Island of Madeira to ensure there was no attempt by the French to seize the island. This excursion was scheduled to be followed by a visit to the Brazilian seaboard for the same reason. He was due back from his expedition two months hence.

Martin's original task had been to gather information. Since the event of Britain's former colony America actually declaring war, he was now tasked to make a nuisance of himself and create as much turmoil as possible.

But things, however well planned, tend to be altered by circumstances. When the two naval ships were approaching Cap de la Hague, at the end of the Cherbourg peninsular, they encountered the French corvette, Oiseau, which happened to be attempting to apprehend two smugglers escaping through the Channel Islands.

The yawl leading the escape was followed by a former naval cutter, which was just setting her sails fully, to allow her to head-reach on the pursuing ship. The unfortunate Corvette racing under full sail from the channel between Alderney and the Cap de la Hague had no chance to run from the naval ships, her guns were not run out and she was on a converging course with HMS Hera.

HMS Vixen was bringing up the rear, and whilst, at the sighting both British ships had cleared for action, the French ship was just not prepared for conflict.

The Oiseau was a survivor of the French Royal Navy. Her 24 guns were sufficient for her size, and her graceful lines promised a speedy ship in the right hands. Her current captain, Camille Berthold, had been a fisherman. His previous boat had normally carried smuggled goods. His successful efforts as a smuggler had made his reputation in the area, particularly when war had made things simpler, with a blind eye shown to his activities.

The Corvette, under her original name, Garonne, had been part of the rebellion and, as things went in the time of terror, old scores were paid off simply by accusing old enemies of crimes against the people. Feuds were only too often settled with the help of the guillotine.

Camille Berthold had never been prominent in these matters. But he was always prepared to give consideration when a question was put to him. It would only ever be after a sober, initial, public display of assessment. Often it would be a private summing up of whether the accused could be of use to his career, or not. He would advise the people of his opinion. Such was his growing reputation for even-handedness, his judgement was respected.

Still a young man at 35, Berthold had been present when the crew of the Garonne mutinied while tied up alongside at his home town, Granville.

The incident was brought to him since the ship was tied alongside the town quay. He listened to the case for the captain with great interest, also the case for the men. He retired to consider a verdict. It was here that he made the first mistake in his short career as a people-appointed arbiter. He condemned the captain and left the court on the shoulders of the crew, who chose him to be their new captain.

To do him justice, Berthold learned to handle the pretty warship, renamed Oiseau, so that the connection with the former French Royal Navy was fogged, if not actually severed. Since he had taken over, he had made several profitable sorties into the Channel waters, pirating stray merchant ships of all nationalities – a practice that met with his recently acquired crew's approval.

Having worked into his role, and found a uniform, the captain also took part in some naval activities, thereby acquiring a certain respectability he did not really deserve.

It all went wrong when two smugglers failed to produce Berthold's portion of their cargo. Believing they were undiscovered, they left Granville harbour in the night and sailed into the cover of the offshore islands.

Watchers informed Berthold, so he set sail to cut them off at the passage past Alderney, sadly arriving just in time to see the pair passing through into the Channel itself.

Deciding to give chase was where it all went wrong. As he sailed past the Cap de la Hague he saw the two British ships bearing down on him.

Always a man to play the odds, Berthold shrugged, ordered one gun fired, and then had the tricolour lowered, signaling his ship's surrender.

The sails of the two smugglers taunted him as they fled across the waters of the Channel.

When seated and questioned by the British, Captain, Berthold adopted his arbiter stance, treating each question with proper gravity. He was quite open about his port of origin, and his purpose in chasing the smugglers, omitting the subject of his portion, of course. "Granville is no longer fortified, though the walls still exist. Since the siege in 1793 there seemed no reason to continue keeping troops in the area. Apart from the small town garrison, currently one company of local militia, there are none. The militia act as guards for British prisoners taken from ships and shipwrecks over the past years. I believe about two hundred in all." He willingly pointed out the location of the prison. "The prisoners were well fed, and looked after. This I know. They are sometimes allowed out in town to take part in preparing for festivals and occasions."

Martin looked the man sitting in front of him. "I am going to send your crew back to France. I will land them on the Grande Isle. I have also decided to collect the prisoners from the jail."

Berthold sat impassively saying nothing, interested in what this man was saying.

"You will assist if you will, by arranging for that release." Martin sat back and watched the realisation cross the face of the man in front of him.

"My English is good, I believe. You are saying that I am to release the British prisoners?"

Martin nodded. "Exactly, in return for the release of your crew from Oiseau. I will then take the prisoners and send them home along with yourself, for your own safety, of course. I may not have you sent to prison, but I think instead to someone who will be happy to use your talents, to everyone's benefit, I believe."

"I may consider this?" Berthold was puzzled.

"I will be sailing to Granville in your ship one way or the other, as soon as I have completed our discussion." He took out his watch, "You have five minutes." Martin rose to leave.

For once Berthold did not hesitate. "I have decided to accept your intriguing offer, sir. I am at your disposal."

"Capital. Now, how will you obtain the prisoners?" Martin sat down once more.

"I will send a message to the captain in charge." Berthold said.

Martin considered for a moment. "How would it be if we, you and I, with a group of my men of course, walked up to the prison and spoke to the captain personally. Inform him that the prisoners are to be transferred to Cherbourg on your ship. You would need ten guards only, your own men would help if needed. How does that sound?"

A smile spread across Berthold's face. He had not realised that the British could be so devious. "I think it would work, sir. Yes, indeed. a good plan!"

Chapter two

Risks

The Corvette sailed into Granville, with Berthold prominent on deck next to an officer in captain's uniform, the Tricolour prominently wrapped about his waist. The ship was crewed by men from both British ships, many of them royalist Frenchmen.

She came alongside her usual place on the quay. The gangway was placed and Berthold, the captain and six men armed with muskets at their shoulders, came ashore and strode off to the old barrack building which had been constructed next to the port buildings.

The captain of the militia, Armande Artois, leapt to his feet at the sight of the naval officer standing before him. He turned to Berthold. "What is this? What do you want?"

Berthold held out a paper to the militia officer. "Armande, Captain Lature is here to transfer all the British prisoners to Cherbourg. They will use my ship for the short voyage. Be a good fellow and assemble them to travel. I am sure you will be pleased to see them gone. Now, come on. Let us move. I do have the tide to worry about."

Captain Artois took the paper and glanced at the writing. He could not read but saw no reason to divulge that fact, nor reason to question these orders. He rose and called out, "Sergeant, we are moving the prisoners. Get them up and in line. Bring the sick in the wagon."

"Yes, sir!" The sergeant started calling orders. There were seven sick, all placed in the wagon. The column of 170 men led the wagon down to the quay. They were accompanied by twelve guards. All were loaded on board and made to sit on deck, leaving passages between them for the crew to move about. The militia captain returned to the shore calling, "Return my men when the prisoners have been delivered."

The gangway was lifted and the Corvette left the quay side. They departed, passing Grande Isle, where the crew of the Oiseau had already been dropped. There they dropped off the disarmed guards, before sailing up the Alderney passage to rejoin the two British ships off Cap de la Hague.

The prisoners, an assortment of both naval and merchant seamen, realising they had been released were more than happy to volunteer to crew the prize to Falmouth.

Acting Lieutenant Athol Gibbs commanded the prize for the voyage to Falmouth where she would be left for disposal as a prize of war. HMS Hera would accompany her and collect Gibbs, after he had handed Berthold over to the agent for the current 'plain Mr. Smith'. In a note to Alouette, Comtesse de Chartres, Martin had suggested Berthold might be useful in the shadowy world of espionage.

HMS Hera would rendezvous with Vixen at Funchal, Madeira, which was scheduled to be the first official port of call.

***

The voyage to the island was without incident, and the crew were well shaken down in the process.

It was in Funchal that Martin had news of Antonio Ramos and his flotilla. While visiting the Governor in Government House he was informed that Commodore Ramos was presently on his way to Brazil, having called just two weeks ago for a formal visit to the colony.

Martin was well received and he accepted an invitation to dine with his host for himself and his officers.

His Excellency, Carlos Eusavio, said that in Funchal it was de-rigueur to bring the young men from visiting ships, as the young ladies on the island had no other chance to meet people of their own age from elsewhere. The hospitality was lavish and the younger members of the Vixen's gunroom were pestered with invitations from the young ladies of the island.

Happily, HMS Hera rescued them from very serious complications as her arrival, two days after Vixen, signalled their departure from this delightful spot.

Lieutenant Harris brought news of the war with the American State, and the report that American ships were at sea seeking British merchant shipping. The first clashes had occurred between naval ships. Only rumours were circulating. No real news was yet available.

Regardless, Martin was convinced that gunnery was the most important part of any battle and exercises were conducted daily. Target practice with powder and shot was held twice weekly. Sail handling also got extra attention. Martin made clear to Patrick Brooks, 'every advantage we can have over the ships we may face must be taken.' HMS Vixen had been pierced for 40 guns on the gun-deck, a broadside of 20x18 lb guns. To this carronades had been added initially 24 lbs, but at her last refit 32 lbs carronades were fitted on her upper deck, four on each beam. The two stern and two fore-chasers, brought her actual complement of guns to 52 guns in all. All were regularly exercised.

For HMS Hera the broadside was 14x12lb guns, which classified her as 28 gun ship, but she also had two bow and two stern chasers, and four carronades, 24 lbs two each side of the upper deck, 36 guns in all. As did the Vixen, the Hera practiced gunnery on the same basis.

They encountered a mail packet en-route to England three days out from Madeira, the captain reported that merchant shipping from the West Indies was travelling in convoy, under escort of Royal Navy ships, after cruising American ships had been reported in the Bermuda area, apparently searching for British merchantmen.

The mail packet departed, all sails set, anxious to make up the time lost speaking to ships in passing.

***

The American squadron, led by the frigate Augusta 44 guns, included the frigate Bisset 36, and the sloops Wilmington and Dearborn, both 24 guns. The orders, received by Commodore John T Baines, were to seek out and destroy British warships and seize, wherever possible, cargo from enemy merchant ships.

The port of Boston had been busy when the squadron left to sail down the eastern seaboard of the American continent. The first days of the cruise were lucrative, catching merchantmen unaware of the declaration of war between America and Britain. Ten days into the cruise the Augusta encountered a British frigate, exchanging fire while out of range of the other ships of the squadron. Damage occurred to both ships but HMS Bedford, the British ship, decided that facing five warships was not sensible. She presented her stern and managed to out-sail the squadron, eluding them during the night by changing course.

Frustrated, Commodore Baines was persuaded to try his luck alone. His ship was newly furnished with two gun decks, and armament comprised 4x30pounders and 26x30 pounder carronades, on the upper deck and 28x30 pounders on the gun deck. Built like a 74 gun ship but without the upper decks, she was a formidable opponent. Her crew was made up of experienced sailors, most of whom were former Royal Naval seamen. If she met a ship of the line, she could either refuse combat, or fight, with a fair chance of success.

Augusta encountered HMS Vixen, and HMS Hera at 35 degrees North 70 degrees west, about 200 miles east of Cape Hatteras.

***

On Vixen, Midshipman James Woods called down from his place in the foretop, "Sail in sight, starboard bow." Using the telescope he managed to steady it for an instant. "She is closing, sir." He was standing braced alongside his sea daddy, Jacob Godden, one of Martin's poachers, who shared the position with the new Midshipman. Godden grinned as the lad made his report. Looking out for the boy they had rescued from Key West, was a responsibility he had not asked for, but he liked the lad. He was a quick learner. Godden had no doubt he would soon be giving the orders with all the confidence of his fellow officers.

He retrieved the telescope, and took a look himself. Then he nodded slowly. Handing the telescope back he said, "Well done. I fancy we've found one of them big frigates they been talkin about."

Martin received the report of the sighting calmly, and after verification that it was probably the Augusta, he decided it was time to test the American for himself. The weather was looking as if change was not far off. The strange sail showed no signs of altering course. Over the next two hours the ships closed the range, all doubts about the identity of the ship were resolved. Ordering the Hera to stand off, he had the Vixen prepared for action. The wind was rising and the sea becoming more active, but in war a battle occurred when it did, not at the convenience of the protagonists.

They were at a disadvantage as the enemy ship was to windward of Vixen. But Vixen was without doubt the more agile of the two. The first surprise was the range and accuracy of the American guns. The higher gun deck and the bigger guns gave the ranging shot nearly two miles before it dropped to the water.

Martin had realised that he was in for a battle. He called to the master gunner. "Can we reach her?"

The gunner thought about it looking at the approaching ship, "With full elevation and a double charge, I think I might, sir."

Martin smiled. "Then let us upset him. All guns load. Gunner, one shot to remind her we are the Royal Navy."

"Aye, aye, sir."

While the gunner worked over his selected gun, the other guns were loaded, but not run-out as yet.

"Gun ready! Sir."

"Fire at will."

A last look at the ship and the gun, and the gunner touched the match. The double charge sounded incredibly loud, and the gun rebounded almost off its trunnions. The ball tore a hole in the other ship's flying jib.

A lucky shot, Martin thought

"Again, sir?" The gunner asked with a wicked grin on his face.

"As you will, gunner, as you will." Martin smiled. "Well done, that was impressive shooting."

Mr. Brooks, let us see whether we can cross the stern as he comes up to bring us near,"

Brooks called to the Bo'sun, "Haul in the sheets. I want us as close to the wind as you can fetch her." He turned to the Master. "Mr. Watson, suggestions?"

Martin listened to his officers. Brooks was as good an officer as any he had served with, but he was prepared to look to the very experienced Sailing Master and call on his vast experience for advice.

Satisfied, he concentrated on the approaching frigate. There was no doubt she was a formidable opponent, and she made a fine sight as she bore down on the British ship.

***

On the Augusta, Commodore Baines gazed across the water at the British frigate. The schooner was lying off out of the danger area. He nodded slowly, he approved of his opponent's forethought. They had identified the ship. She was HMS Vixen, and that meant Captain Sir Martin Forest-Bowers. It should be an interesting contest. Baines was not worried; his ship would crush the other. Vixen's weight of shot and her lighter timbers were no match for Augusta.

He ordered his first lieutenant, "Load and run-out the port side guns, Mr. Jacobson.

"Port broadside, load and run out." Jacobson used his speaking trumpet. His eyes were on the gunners beside the long line of their charges.

Jacobson had been shocked when the shot from Vixen had ripped through the jib-sail.

That was fancy shooting by any standards and, for the first time since he had been aboard, Robert Jacobson felt a twinge of doubt about the outcome of today's encounter.

The dramatic crash of the Vixen's starboard broadside as the two ships closed, followed almost immediately by the delayed thunder of the four carronades, woke any who had managed to sleep to the fact that a battle had commenced.

***

On Augusta, two of the broadside guns, halfway run out, smashed back off their trunnions, the forward gun swiping a scarlet smear of blood where the crew had been standing. The second ball shattered the embrasure and sheared off the left hand iron peg supporting the gun in position on the carriage. The gun was now useless. Elsewhere along the deck, grape had distributed death with an even hand. Lieutenant O'Leary, commanding the starboard guns, took an unbelieving look to where his left arm fallen from the terrible wound where his shoulder used to be. He had been spun round by the missile, but had kept his feet despite spinning in a complete circle. He looked at Jacobson appealingly, before dropping to the deck, dead before he reached it.

Baines called calmly through the smoke and racket, "Fire as you bear." The reduced broadside fired one by one, as the guns bore. The British ship still close to the wind passed astern of the Augusta and her reloaded broadside took on the stern chasers, and 16 of her guns managed to deliver their fire into the stern of the American ship.

The problem for Martin was that his ship had been hurt. He had felt the impact of the American guns and knew his own ship could not take too much punishment of that calibre.

***

On Hera, Lieutenant Harris was getting worried, the sea was rising and the wind was beginning to box the compass. With the gathering clouds he guessed it was a major storm and, from the looks and sound of things, neither of the two fighting ships was making any preparations, or showing signs that they were aware of what was going on around them.

***

Vixen was a sad sight, her damaged sides still spitting gunfire, her opponent not looking much better having lost her forward top-mast and showing signs of the shattered bulwarks and empty gun ports. Neither side was giving anything away.

Vixen hauled off, and with filled sail, came about to use her other broadside guns.

It was then that Harris realised that she at least had observed the approaching storm. A signal appeared with Hera's number. "Storm coming, rendezvous Cat Island."

***

Then Vixen fired her last broadside and slammed shut the surviving gun ports. Martin let her head fall off with the wind, and felt the storm gusts drive his ship away downwind carrying far too much sail in the circumstances. Brooks called all hands to shorten sail. As the men ran to their positions the last shots from the enemy ship hit the stern of the ship. Martin's elegant cabinets were reduced to kindling. The ball lodged firmly in the mizzen mast and stayed there without snapping it. The other ball took the stern rail. Apart from the shower of splinters, it passed over the deck, missing all the men there and disappeared over the port side of the ship.

***

"Give chase, sir?" Lieutenant Jacobson asked.

"Commodore Baines looked at him. "Are you mad?" He waved his hand at the sky. "Get the canvas off her, man. Lash down for bad weather. This could be bloody dangerous."

Baines was serious. He had allowed himself to be carried away with the action against the British frigate, and consequently not noticed the gathering storm. As soon as he realised what weather they were facing, he knew they were in trouble. This was not just any storm. This was a hurricane.

"Let her head fall off." Like the Vixen the Augusta fled downwind, praying they would pass out of the hurricane's influence.

Jacobson stood, saturated, beside his equally saturated Commodore, as the ship flew before the wind with just a rag of sail to keep her straight.

"Well, we made her run!" He said.

Commodore Baines looked at his young inexperienced lieutenant incredulously. "What did you say?"

Jacobson was startled. "W..e..we made her run, sir." He said hesitantly.

Baines looked at him. He had not chosen him for his position. Lieutenant Jacobson was related to somebody with influence. His so-called experience had been gained in the customs service. With restraint, choosing his words to carry against the background of the wind, he said. "She broke off the action because, unlike us, she realised that this storm was no place to fight a battle, unless we both wished to lose, that is. He didn't run. Thank the lord he made me look at the weather and possibly saved all our lives."

Jacobson was silent at that. He did not know what to say. He was scared of his Commodore. He was just realising that he should have mentioned the worsening weather. It was his job to assist and support this man.

***

As the chastened Jacobson realised his responsibilities and determined to do better in future, Lieutenant Brooks on Vixen was facing a different problem. His captain had been hurt during the final seconds of the action, by the violent movement of the ship. Doctor Mills had forced him to stay in his bed, concerned that the blow Martin had taken may have paralysed him. He had been tossed against the fife rail around the mainmast and collapsed in agony after the impact.

Midshipman Woods had been detailed to attend his captain while he was kept to his bed.

For Martin, with his ship in hazard the situation was desperate, but he was unable to do anything about it. So, as the ship tossed and turned and lashed firmly in place, he had James Woods anchored beside his bed and tutored him in reading and arithmetic.

Brooks made sure that he was kept informed of the conditions and their progress through the storm. In his cabin Martin was also made aware of the cannon ball stuck in the mizzen mast in front of him. James had been curious about it when he first saw it. He had been unaware of its existence. Neither had Martin until his forced detainment commenced. He did notice that the cabinets had gone. They had been regarded as Jennifer's folly, though not publicly.

***

Three days later Martin was allowed up once more. His back was still painfully stiff but no longer regarded as liable to cause paralysis.

The tail of the storm was still affecting the sea, which was rough and creating problems for the carpenter repairing the damage from the battle with the Augusta. The ship was anchored in the bay at Cat Island in the Bahamas.

In Martin's cabin Brooks and Harris were seated, discussing matters with their Captain. Brooks commented, "At least we know now that these new frigates are vulnerable. Their very length makes them clumsy in stays, and the weight of their hull may well be difficult to dent. Their extended sail plan, which does give them speed, also affects their agility, their ability to react swiftly, despite the huge crew they carry. In the case of the Augusta, my guess would be her effectiveness is due to the number of skilled ex-naval seamen on board, and the cool head of the captain."

Martin smiled. Brooks was living up to expectation. "That sums things up pretty well, Patrick. Have you anything to add, John?"

Lieutenant Harris commanded HMS Hera and had been ordered to stay back out of the engagement between Vixen and Augusta. From his viewpoint it had occurred to him that either the American captain had been overeager to subdue the British ship or his officers had served him badly. Had Vixen not broken off the action, both ships would have been in danger of foundering or losing masts in the approaching storm. Both had far too much sail spread for survival in those conditions.

"Sir, I think the American had a skilled crew and captain. I question the skill of the officers. If you had not broken off the action when you did, both ships would have been in hazard. It did mean alerting your opponent to the conditions. Something I believe his officers should have pointed out earlier in the engagement. I'm aware of the efficiency of your ship, sir and allow for the fact that both Mr. Brooks and yourself knew pretty well how far you could go in the circumstances, but I do not think the American was so well served."

"Gentlemen, my ship is in need of care that our carpenter cannot, on his own, provide. We proceed to English Harbour, therefore, to repair and prepare for the next encounter in the game of marine chess!"

He stood, indicating the meeting was at an end, "We will dine together in the calm waters of Antigua."

Chapter three

Find the lady

The harbour at Antigua was calm and the schooner HMS Hera sat on her reflection under the blue sky. In the dockyard HMS Vixen was undergoing a thorough inspection by the surveyors. Carpenters were already working to remove the mizzen mast, anxious that the embedded cannon ball would weaken it to the point where it would break under stress of battle or weather.

On HMS Hera, Martin joined Lieutenant Harris on the quarterdeck and admired the speed and efficiency of the crew in their setting sail. The anchor was a-weigh and the ship was moving already under jib and foresail as the anchor reached the stops. The big main and mizzen were fully hoisted into place and the staysails were already aloft waiting the setting. The ship was gliding across the harbour as if by magic. Martin smiled; no wonder she always seemed to be so agile in battle.

He had decided to make contact with the West Indies squadron at Kingston, Jamaica. HMS Vixen would rendezvous with them south of Hispaniola after he had conferred with the Admiral. It would take four days, maybe less, maybe more, to reach Jamaica, and the dockyard estimated eight days to return Vixen to the water. Brooks would bring her to the rendezvous.

The schooner heeled to the wind and flew. John Harris drove her, showing off her ability for the benefit of his guests.

Peters commented to Martin, "Nice little boat, ain't she. Sails like yacht. Fast too, I'll be bound."

Amused, Martin said, "They just checked the log, creeping up to thirteen knots and still climbing."

Peters nodded his head sagely. "Just as long as he keeps the sticks in her," he strolled along the deck to have a word with the bo'sun.

They sighted the ship in the afternoon of the second day. They had passed a lot traffic passing to and from the islands. The stranger turned as soon as they spotted the ensign at the masthead. Harris altered course and swiftly caught up with the fleeing merchantman, and called for her to stop. Under the guns of the Hera a boarding party swiftly established that the ship Jacob Harper was American. Harris formally seized it as a prize of war, removed the crew and put a prize crew aboard, with orders to take the ship to Kingston for the cargo and ship to be passed over to the Prize court.

The schooner proceeded on to Jamaica leaving the prize well behind.

***

In Kingston they found Commodore Wallace in office. The Admiral was off the American coast with his squadron, involved with troop movements and a series of frustrating operations. The Commodore was interested in Martin's report of his encounter with Augusta. "So, you believe that these heavy frigates can be overcome. But gunnery must be excellent, and sail handling immaculate."

"Basically, we survived because of our well-practiced gunnery and our better sailing qualities. To stand and slug it out is a waste of time, ammunition and men. The gun power of the big frigates and the strength of its timbers give it an advantage that we have no answer for, unless a ship of the line is available."

Martin liked the Commodore. He had a no nonsense attitude that was reassuring. His acceptance of the presence of another officer in his region with a similar set of orders was typical. "Need everyone we can get hold of. I've currently got a problem that you could help with, though."

Martin was curious though cautious, "What have you in mind, sir?"

"When you and your ship are reunited, I presume you will be sailing north along with everyone else?"

Martin nodded. "I had that in mind."

"Are you acquainted with, or have you heard of, a person named 'plain Mr. Smith'?"

"May I enquire why you ask?" Martin asked warily.

The Commodore hesitated, "I have a note here that came in the last despatch package from London." He looked closely at Martin, and then continued, "There are persons who should be in the Florida Keys in the next 30 days, who will require collection and repatriation. It is not made clear who they are, or how they got there. Since the matter is of urgency as the people concerned are being hunted by American authorities, they need to be collected and transported to Canada as soon as is possible.

"At present I have no ships to spare for such a task. In the light of your orders I cannot order you to carry out this task. I am, therefore, asking if you could fit this task in with your plans?"

Martin rubbed his chin. *I should really have shaved a little closer this morning,* he thought. "I believe it would fit reasonably well. If you can provide a cutter to meet with my ship, Vixen, with instructions, I will take the HMS Hera for the pick-up."

He rose to his feet. "Sir, if I may, can I see the instruction from Mr. Smith?"

"I see no reason why not, though I am curious to know why?" He passed the folded note over to Martin, who opened it out and studied the content. He nodded slowly, then turned to the Commodore. Have you ever had a note like this before, sir?"

"No, I am sure I have never had contact with the man."

"I see it is addressed to you, sir, direct. Do you not think that odd in a package from the Admiralty, otherwise addressed to the Admiral himself?"

"Are the orders false, do you think, sir?"

"Not at all. All seem normal with expected replies."

"So they have been stolen and now redelivered, with this extra letter included."

Commodore Wallace thought for a moment only, "Damn it, Forest. I did not think of that. Is it then a forgery? But it came in the official package by naval ship."

"Is the ship long gone? There was no ship in harbour when we arrived."

"It was a sloop. The Lieutenant left the package with my Flag Lieutenant. I was absent at the time. Porter said the man was in a rush to rejoin the squadron north of the islands."

He rang a bell on his desk impatiently.

The Flag Lieutenant came in hurriedly and stood at attention beside the desk.

The Commodore lifted the package of orders. "Who brought these orders. James?"

"It was a Lieutenant Parker, sir, HMS Antelope.

"Did you see the ship?"

"Yes, sir. The sloop came into the harbour, but did not moor as she was tasked to rejoin the squadron going north. He was unable to wait to see you personally, for that reason."

Martin intervened, "Did you yourself personally recognise Lieutenant Parker?"

James Arnold looked uncomfortable for a moment. "Actually, I did. I was surprised to see him, as I thought he had left the service, sir."

"Thank you, Lieutenant." Martin said, and turned to the Commodore once more.

"Will that be all, sir?" Arnold asked.

The Commodore nodded and, when he had closed the door behind him, turned to Martin. "Renegade?"

Martin nodded. "The American ships are mainly crewed by former Royal Navy sailors. There have to be some officers as well. Parker could well be."

"I will write a note to my senior Lieutenant about the rendezvous, if I may, and then I must be on my way."

"You will surely not attend this request now. It will be a trap."

"It is a trap, of that I am sure. The note was written by an agent of Mr. Smith. I recognised the code. It warned that he may be exposed. If I can I will retrieve him. He must be important, or have important information, for the enemy to go to such lengths."

"What do you mean? I thought you said it was a trap for our ships?"

"I think you will agree, Commodore, a ship makes a much bigger target than a man. If they are permitted to get together, they can collect them both in one operation. Two birds with one stone!"

He turned and wrote. He read what he had written and signed it. Passing it to the Commodore still open, he said, "Please could this be taken to my ship. She should be en-route to Jamaica already, so the sooner the better?"

"Of course. Thank you, Captain, and good hunting!"

Martin shook hands with the Commodore, collected his hat and left.

***

The Hera sailed, heading north-east for the channel between Cuba and Hispaniola. Martin decided that the passage past the Bahamas made sense in the circumstances. Taking into account the date on the letter it appeared that the agent would be appearing within the next fourteen days. Martin intended to collect the agent and escape the trap. He was not quite sure how, but he was determined to accomplish both ends.

For Lieutenant Harris, life was good. The task ahead looked daunting but with luck, and luck seemed to favour people like his captain, they would win." He smiled as he considered his fortunes since becoming involved with Martin Forest-Bowers. In his bank was an ample sum which would enable him to support a wife, if he ever encountered the right woman. His mind drifted to Julia Savage, the intrepid captain of the Mohawk, involved in his last excursion to America, in 1811 He had seen her last in 1812, on the return voyage to England when they had battled the French 74 in the fog.

His reminiscences were rudely interrupted by a call from the masthead. "Sail, Ho. Port bow, ship rig, sir, closing."

Martin appeared on deck. He gazed up at the sails and sniffed the air appreciatively.

"You must be pleased to get rid of the stink of Kingston, sir." Harris ventured.

"I certainly am. Who is this approaching fellow. Do we know yet?"

"Not as yet, sir," He called aloft to the lookout, "Anything yet, Meadows."

Meadows had the big telescope. He lowered it slowly. "I believe her to be a sloop, sir. What should not be here."

"What was that he said?" Martin asked.

"Who is she then?" Harris shouted.

"I would swear she is the old Pinguin, but she was lost in 97 during the troubles."

Martin looked at Harris. "He is referring to the 'Nore'. I remember several ships went private at the time. I do remember the captain, Peterson, I believe, was washed up on the beach on the Isle de Lion. He had apparently not suffered any wounds at that time. It appeared the Pinguin was lost in the storm recently past. If she has gone private she may have increased her gun power, though at that time she would have had twenty guns."

Harris nodded thoughtfully "I'm inclined to get a little closer, sir. We could establish her credentials at that time," He smiled at the prospect of an encounter.

Martin nodded agreement. "Indeed, I think we must. If she is actually the Pinguin, it is our duty to apprehend her, or sink her, though we do need to make our rendezvous. So, a little caution, Mr. Harris!"

Martin strolled forward leaving John Harris to work out his approach to the distant ship.

***

Neither ship changed course. And at a converging rate in excess of more than twenty knots, the sloop rapidly grew close enough for Mathews to confirm that she was either the Pinguin or he was a Dutchman. When it was possible to make out her name, her colours had been run up. No longer Pinguin she now professed to be Pelican, a name that struck no chord with either Lieutenant Harris or Martin.

"She is still only pierced for twenty guns, sir." Meadows volunteered.

"Is there anything else in sight, Meadows?" Harris called.

Meadows swept his glass around the horizon in measured sections. He finally called back. "The horizon is clear, nothing in sight apart from the sloop."

"Good. Clear for action! All guns, load!" The cry went out on Harris's order.

The hammock nets were spread, the packed hammocks wedged in, as the guns were loaded, ready to run out.

There was similar activity on the other ship, which Martin thought was sailing under false colours. He used his own telescope to examine the officers on the quarterdeck of the other vessel. As he suspected there was no uniform as such. So the ship was a pirate, not aware that Hera was a naval vessel. He looked aloft and realised that the ensign he expected to see was in fact, aloft but bound, ready to be broken out at the right moment.

There was a house-flag that looked familiar, flying at the sloop's mast head. He was puzzling over it when it dawned on him it was the flag Julia Savage flew on Mohawk.

He had a wry smile as the two ships started to manoeuver for position, following a shot from the other ship, obviously intended as a warning.

"Starboard guns, run out." "Colours, Mr. Welland, if you please!"

The Midshipman yanked at the halyard, the Union colours were clearly displayed. Harris brought his ship even closer to the wind. As the enemy ship tried to counter the move, the schooner's starboard guns began firing as they bore. The sloop tried to match the move of the schooner, but Harris's confidence was vindicated, and the sloop's head dropped off the wind, swinging her round away from the schooner as her own broadside guns fired.

Two of her guns managed to hit Hera at the stern quarter, the other eight missed completely. The damage cost Harris his helmsman, who was struck by a section of the taffrail, shattered by one of the balls. The other ball managed to gouge a trail of destruction across the quarterdeck, without hitting anything vital. It did take two more men killed and three injured by splinters.

The middy, Welland, grabbed the wheel, stopping the ship going into stays. He was replaced by the Bo'sun who brought her about. The First Lieutenant, Max Carter, almost screaming with excitement, called the crew to adjust the sails as she came around into the wind and lined up with the port broadside presented to the enemy, who had also come about, ready to renew the action. Martin observed the damage showing on the port side of the sloop. It had been possible to make out the original name of the sloop as she passed. It had been painted over and the new name superimposed, but the end of the new name did not cover the remaining n from its original title. Also Meadows, the topman, had been confident that she was the ship once called the Pinguin.

The two ships converged once more, though now Hera had the wind advantage. She swung across the bow of the Pelican scoring heavily on the sloop, bringing down the foremast in a clatter of spars and sails. The sloop's bow chasers scored on Hera, causing the number three gun to burst from its trunnions and career across the deck smashing two men in its path. The gun crew was killed by the impact of the ball. The gun itself finished up the other side of the deck and was swiftly secured to the foremast with ropes.

Harris stood off, watching the sloop as it tried to clear up the wreckage of the foremast. Then, with a cool, calculated move, he drove his ship past the stern of the sloop with his starboard broadside ready and started to approach, intending to rake the enemy ship with his guns one by one as he passed.

The flag of the sloop dropped from its place to the deck as she surrendered.

Martin touched the sleeve of Lieutenant Harris. "I don't trust this sudden surrender. It seems to have a small crew for a pirate. Before boarding, let us make sure we know what we face."

Harris looked at Martin searchingly. "Do you really think they would sacrifice their ship?"

Martin nodded.

For what? How would he gain anything by doing that?" Harris was impatient.

Martin pointed to the battered ship. "Look at her condition. See the worn timbers. Listen to the pumps. She has been lost since '94. 18 years without the benefit of serious overhaul. Now look at your own ship, fresh from a shipyard overhaul. Well kept, no expense spared in ropes or canvas. Guns modern and well kept. A clean hull clearly demonstrated by her speed and agility."

Harris looked at his men, poised ready to board the other ship. Realisation of what his eagerness could have caused came over him.

He turned back to Martin. "What would you suggest, sir?"

Martin said, "Looking at the ship, would she be worth saving, d'ye think?"

Harris looked, listened to the clank of the pumps, then turned to the helmsman, "Run us close across her stern."

With all guns loaded and run out as they passed close to the Pelican, Harris called the men at the stern of the ship to gather their boats, and abandon ship.

The Hera stood off and watched as the pirate ship settled in the water, despite the frantic increase in the rate of the clanking pumps, at the commencement of the action, both ships had launched their small boats to keep them out of the way. There were two major reasons for this. One was to keep the boats from damage in case they were needed to abandon ship. The other was, that stacked on deck as the boats usually were, if they were to be hit by cannon fire, the effect of the splintering of such light timbers could be devastating, cutting a swathe through all the men on deck, wiping out large numbers, injuring others, with terrible wounds, difficult to treat, and often resulting in infection and death.

As the British ship stood off, the men on the deck of the Pelican shouted and waved fists at the other ship, and, Harris noticed, they increased in number. Using a small dinghy brought up from below, the boats were recovered. The pumps had ceased working and the ship was settling in the water at an increasing rate. The exodus of the crew was observed to be savage business, entailing the abandonment of the sick and wounded. The men able to gain a place were those fit and well enough to push others out of the way. The boats pulled away one by one leaving at least forty men on a deck that was now nearly awash. Some of the survivors cast themselves off on hatch covers and clinging to spars. Those left just stood, helplessly waiting for death. Harris sent his own boats for them and brought them aboard his ship.

Whilst this was being done the ship was hove-to.

A pirate longboat approached the far side of the ship, to be met with grape shot from two small cannon, placed with just that situation in mind. It suffered badly, with several of its occupants flung into the sea, dead or dying. The bow of the boat survived for just seconds after the impact of the shot. The timbers sprang apart, with the remaining occupants cast into the water.

The blood of the wounded soon finished things up. Sharks appeared, attracted by the blood. No rescue attempt from the ship was made. It would have been wasted effort.

The boats returned from the sinking ship. The wounded brought aboard were in poor shape, and the surgeon shook his head at the state of most of them.

The sinking ship settled for a while with the sea washing over her decks. Quietly she sank on an even keel, the mainmast finally disappearing at increasing speed to the depths of the ocean. Only the scatter of odd flotsam remained, to show the passing of a once proud ship.

***

Martin questioned one of the survivors and discovered that he had been a boy on the Pinguin when she had been taken by the mutineers. He had had no chance to escape at that time. The captain had not been hurt, but he had been forced to leap into the sea off the Isle de Leon. Others, foolish enough to resist, were killed out of hand and their bodies thrown off the ship.

The flag they had been flying had been recovered from a trader on the East coast of America. They had found her cast aground at Isle au Haut off Maine. There had been little left in the way of loot but the flag had been intact and the captain had taken it, to use as a distraction. He said the ship was called Sweetwater. She had grounded after attack by pirates, according to the story he had been told in early 1812.

The pirate career of the mutineers had been mostly stealing small traders, going ashore at obscure ports and drinking and whoring. He had fallen into the way of the others. His story ended before any retribution by the vengeful authorities. He died from infection as the Hera continued north. The sad fact was that all the survivors passed away before the ship reached Key West. Four committed suicide rather than face the rope.

Chapter four

Secrets

HMS Vixen sailed west to meet with HMS Hera on the way to Jamaica. The encounter with the cutter from Jamaica caused Patrick Brooks to alter course north-east to pass through the passage between Cuba and Hispaniola. Ten days later she reached the Florida Keys. As she passed the entrance to Key West, the lookout called down to the deck. "Ship in sight, sir. HMS Hera, she is anchored in the roads."

Patrick Brooks heaved a sigh of relief at the news. He had been worried that he would be too late, or even miss the rendezvous completely. He had driven the Vixen as hard as he could. The men had caught his sense of urgency and there had been times when the ship had seemed to fly through the water.

He had made it in time, which was the main thing. The waters in the channel were smooth and when the anchor dropped, as he walked over to welcome his captain aboard, he felt the weight lift from his shoulders.

Martin greeted Brooks with a smile. "How did it feel?" he asked. "Are you ready to keep command?" They went below to the great cabin.

Brooks smiled back. "Sir, I was terrified I might break it. I think the pressure would be different were she my command in reality."

"Well said, Patrick. I thoroughly agree with you and I will recommend a command when we return. As you say, you will know the difference." He indicated the letter he had received from Commodore Wallace in Kingston.

"How will you know where to find them, sir?" Brooks sounded concerned.

"The wording of the note I was shown was genuine. It had been written by the agent. It is fortuitous that I am aware of certain matters involved in communications with secret agents of Mr. Smith's department.

"The code word included in the text tells me this is real. The mark beside the signature tells me to seek beside the Channel, where the waters meet. And finally, it is Key West all right. Here!" He showed the paper on which he had copied all the marks from the original letter. The signature was Corow.

"What am I looking at? I do not understand."

"Hopefully, neither does our enemy. The agents always use a name ending in o. If they wish to convey a message or give warning, they vary the ending, In this case clearly he, or she, has indicated location. C stands for Key. the Spanish spell it Cay; the W for west.

The shadow of the Hera passed over the window of the stern cabin, as she made sail to the entrance of the channel.

Martin explained, "Harris is covering the meeting of the waters and keeping a lookout for problems, in the form of the American navy."

He sent for the Commanding Officer of Marines.

Major Bristow appeared. "You sent for me, sir?"

Martin looked up at the smartly dressed soldier in front of him. "Relax, Mr. Bristow. He thought for a moment. "Have you still got the equipment Major Jackman left with us?"

"I have, sir; and as you know. we practice daily with the rifles. We do not have much chance to use the clothing as we see little of the land in the right circumstances."

"Your men are up to it, though?" He pressed.

Alan Bristow straightened and his face hardened. "My men are well practiced except for the actual ground training, and they are tutored by McLeod and Godden, as often as I can arrange it."

Martin smiled, "I was not challenging your efficiency. I have a job for your men ashore requiring secrecy and anonymity. A party armed and prepared to comb the woods for an agent we are to meet here. I would like your men to slip ashore unseen in your woodsman clothes, watch the western end of the Key. We are expecting contact from agents here and we know that they are being hunted by the Americans. Keep someone in sight of the ship for signals. They may arrive from another direction, and of course watch for signs of a trap. We are aware that the enemy knows we are connecting with the agents. Hopefully they are not aware where or when."

Martin looked at Bristow. "Take McLeod or Godden, both if you'd rather."

"Thank you, sir. I'll get the men organized. We'll be away as soon as we can manage. Do we have any contact with the shore, sir?"

"Not immediately, though I contemplate visiting the local mayor this evening."

Bristow left the cabin and the clatter of boots signalled a parade of Marines on deck. The twenty-four men were smart on parade and Bristow made a performance of inspecting them one by one. To selected men he whispered, "Woodsman clothes and moccasins. Rifle, flask and cartridges, by 6.30, embark on the blind side of the ship."

Each man selected nodded in understanding. They had trained for this duty ever since they left North Carolina last year.

***

As Martin left for the town on Key West, the Marines departed silently from the other side of the ship.

With Martin went Midshipman James Woods, who would re-establish contact with friends from his past, and a squad of Marines under the command of Major Bristow's new second in command, Ensign Barnaby Crockett.

Honore Verlain was still the Mayor of Key West. He had recovered his self-confidence to a large extent and he greeted Martin cautiously but with some respect. There was no doubt that he had been grateful for Martin's intervention and removal of the pirates who had based themselves in the island. This did not, of course, mean that he welcomed him as a representative of his own nation's enemy.

Martin said, after the courtesies had been observed, "We have not come to impose on you or your people. We are here for a purpose that should not concern you at all. I called this evening to reassure you of that fact."

Mr. Verlaine, whilst still a little wary, replied, "I am pleased that you will not be visiting fire and thunder upon our town. I know that we all here were grateful for our release from the clutches of Captain Newton's pirates. For that reason, if for no other, I would be pleased to entertain both you and your crew, were it possible in the circumstances. Since that would not be proper, I would like to raise a glass with you, sir, calling damnation to all pirates, and my thanks for the part you played in ridding us of them."

Both men drank, and afterwards Verlain mentioned the regularisation of local matters since normal life had returned to the town.

It was at this point that Martin and his party left and returned to the ship. The landing of the marines had occurred without observable mishap and the boat had returned to the ship safely.

***

The period of waiting seemed endless but was actually only three days. The Marines returned in canoes, escorting another, with a giant warrior and a slim woman on board.

Martin was not altogether surprised to see that the woman was Julia Savage. The Iroquois warrior was called David, which did cause surprise, until it was pointed out that he was a Christian.

Julia had been working for the enigmatic 'Mr. Smith' when Martin had first met her in 1811. She had moved from her Boston home to Canada taking her business with her. Trade with the native communities had been the basis of the family business. It also explained the presence of David, as her escort through the length of the American nation.

She greeted Martin with a kiss and a hug as an old friend and the man who had been there when her grandfather had been killed and she had been kidnapped, and rescued.

Though she had made it to HMS Vixen, there was still the journey to Canada to accomplish, where a British fleet were currently based.

HMS Hera returned to join Vixen and John Harris came aboard to report. Martin was amused to see his reaction to the sight of Julia Savage already seated in Martin's cabin. "You have met Miss Julia Savage, I believe." Martin said drily.

John Harris bent over Julia's hand. He kissed it. "We made too brief an acquaintance." He said gallantly.

Julia blushed, despite her tanned face. "Why, Mr. Harris, I truly thought your attention was elsewhere when we met before."

"You were surrounded by others, I recall. I was just one of many of your admirers."

Martin coughed. "Since Miss Savage is the reason for our diversion to Key West on this occasion, we can now consider our voyage from here to Halifax."

Harris said, "Sir, I have to tell you that traders up along the coast are saying that Commodore Baines is searching for you. He believes that you were lucky to escape the last time you met."

Martin looked at Harris. "Well, you were there?"

Harris answered immediately. "I would not have put things quite like that, though I did think the match was more even that the weight of metal might have implied. The other factor is that he has been seen along the coast. The rest of his squadron appears to have been detached and nobody is aware of where they have got to. What is obvious is that the trap is sprung already. They chose the wrong point to intercept Miss Savage, but the advantage is still with them, as we have to make it right up the coast to Halifax, Nova Scotia. However we approach it, there is a long way to go."

"Quite. Well, I do not intend hanging about here, so let us make sail and find out if Mr. Baines is as good as he sounds. There is one thing I must make clear. If we meet Commodore Baines, I will transfer Miss Savage to Hera. It will be your job to take her on to her destination. Avoid conflict if it is possible. She is a precious package and must be delivered intact."

Julia's giggle at these words reduced all three to laughter, Martin realising how pompous his orders sounded.

When they had recovered from the hilarity, the serious business of reaching Halifax, or at least contacting the British fleet was discussed. Julia was left to write her report of her discoveries during the two month journey she had made through the former colonies. In the brief resume she had given Martin she merely confirmed the opinion he had already formed. The infant country of America was alive and kicking and looking to take its independent place in the world.

In the circumstances, Martin wished to be anywhere else in the world at this time. From what he had seen and heard, confirmed by Julia, his sympathy was with the people who had taken the chance to stand alone. He would do his duty, but, as he privately thought, he did not have to like it.

Thus HMS Vixen and HMS Hera nosed northward allowing themselves sea-room, to permit evasion rather than contact, if they encountered American Naval ships.

Chapter five

Playing the odds

At 27 degrees north, they encountered a sinking ship. The masthead lookout on Hera reported the rag of sail from a ship appearing to be in distress. Harris investigated and found that she was a brig out of North Carolina, with a sorry crew and, apparently, a group of bond slaves on board.

It was when the Vixen came close that the crew of the Pharos gave themselves up. They allowed the so-called bond slaves on deck because of the perilous situation with the leaking ship.

Julia Savage joined Martin on deck. "I've come to see what all the excitement is about...Oh my, what is that?" She was appalled at the condition of the people crowded onto the deck of the sinking ship.

The sight of Major Aaron Jackman, being carried on deck on a stretcher by two of his woodsmen, caused Martin to order the Marines to board the American ship and search it. The captain was brought aboard the Vixen, along with the Major who was immediately sent below in the care of the Doctor.

Captain Abbot was not a man of distinction. Ugly and brutish would be a good description to Martin's eye.

His gratitude for saving his life was restrained to the point of a bullying aggressive attitude which Martin was swift to counter.

"Captain Abbot your ship is sinking 170 miles from shore. You have two boats for one hundred and forty souls. If you wish I will relieve you of the responsibility of the so-called bond slaves, and return you and your men to your sinking ship. I understand that the boats are nearly as decrepit as your ship, so you chances of survival are based on the appearance of another ship. And, since you inform me you are not here to meet another ship, survival appears to be extremely unlikely."

Captain Abbot's truculence diminished at this suggestion and he began to co-operate.

"I was chartered to carry the slaves to a plantation on Cuba. We ran into bad weather, which is why you found us here at this time."

Martin said, "Where on the island was this plantation? You are very far north in the circumstances anyway. Who owns the plantation and who chartered your ship?"

Abbot clenched his jaw and Martin turned to Major Bristow. "Send him back to his ship." He turned to his desk and picked up his pen to write.

Abbot shrugged off Bristow's hand. "You said I would be saved if I talked."

"I was referring to the truth, not a pack of lies."

Abbot looked at Martin and his implacable look. He decided that perhaps the truth was the only way out of his situation.

"Colonel Ross Harding arranged everything. He sent his men out. The people in my ship were brought to the beach and rowed out to my ship. I was ready to carry anything at the time. I had found little to do after the declaration of war and I needed the money. Now I've lost my ship and the pay I received."

"Who is Colonel Ross Harding? I wonder why I have never heard of him." Martin said grimly.

"He does not make himself known generally. He has been creating his own private country for the last thirty years. With the war he is able to take advantage of the privateering trade. It seems the Colonel thinks he can increase his wealth by impressing the people from the ships his craft capture, sending them to his plantations on the mainland and also to his island holdings. Any who fall by the wayside or refuse to work, he kills. My orders were to dump all the people into the sea."

The callous words horrified Martin. He had no doubt the man before him would have done just that

"So that was what you were really ordered to do with the prisoners." Martin's voice was dangerously quiet.

"I was ordered to dump them at sea. But I would not, nay I could not in all conscience do that. I call on you gentlemen to note that, despite the condition of my ship, I did not abandon the prisoners to the sea."

Martin nodded gravely. "I have taken note, and it will count for you at your trial."

"Trial! I have done nothing illegal."

"On your own admission, you took people you knew to be innocent into your ship, with the intention of taking them against their will elsewhere. That, sir, is kidnap!" He turned to Major Bristow. "Take him below!"

Bristow took the protesting captain below.

Julia said, "I have heard rumours of Colonel Ross Harding. There are some who regard him as the saviour of the country. Others vilify him. I did not have the time to take my enquiries further because of the agents pursuing me. It seems I should have continued regardless." She touched Martin's sleeve. "My news for delivery to Halifax is confirmation only. There is no real need for a mad rush north. This is serious and needs action. Do not delay on my account.

Martin went to see Doctor Mills. He was working on Aaron Jackman. "How is he, Doctor?"

Roger Mills who had been crouched down over his patient straightened his back with a sigh. He nodded and said, "He will be fine in a few days, now he is out of the hold of that ship.

Aaron spoke to Martin waving the doctor aside. "We were on the Margaret Mary heading back to Charlestown when the privateer caught us. Privateer? Bloody pirate, more like. That was what he really was. Took no notice of our Boston registry, stripped out the cargo and chained us all. We could not resist. We had the women, you see. We were put ashore and brought to the plantation and told we should work or die. We broke out twice, but he was employing Cherokee trackers and we had no chance. His place was well inland, away from the sea, and surrounded by unoccupied land.

"There were beatings of course. But we were deceived by a new prisoner, who was put in to seek out any would-be escapee.

"All the people you rescued are either likely to run, or too weak for the type of work he wants done."

Aaron lay back against the pillows, frustrated at his weakness and at the fate that had made him prisoner of the British.

Martin was thoughtful as he sat in his cabin. He had no intention of keeping the Major prisoner, whatever the rules stated. He owed the woodsmen too much to consider that. Nor would he keep the other survivors. They would all be placed ashore in Carolina somehow or other. The other matter was the privateers who had been issued letters of marque since the declaration of war. His duty, apart from rescuing Julia, was protecting British shipping. The privateers were a definite part of his orders. His re-interrogating of Captain Abbot had established that the Colonel had at least three privateers at sea. They were definitely of interest, as far as the Major was concerned. As soon as he was fit enough he would be placed ashore. After he had been able to scout the Colonel's American base, he would be happy to join forces and raid it. The island plantations could be dealt with, when their whereabouts were revealed.

The Doctor was convinced that the patients would recover quicker at sea than they would on the land, so, as Martin knew of at least one of the plantations, he decided to take a look, and if necessary, close it down. There could be no excuse for the owners of these places, or managers, if in fact they did belong to the Colonel. He reasoned since he is American anyway, it would still be within his orders to interrupt the merchant trade of the American nation. On making his decision he ordered the ships to reverse course south to the Bahamas, There was an estate on Little Albacore that had been mentioned.

***

Little Albacore was one of the most northerly of the Bahamas. The plantation owned by Colonel Harding was on the southern coast and Martin decided that the approach should be overland. He and his party landed from the ships' boats. The Marines came in what they called bush order and carried rifles.

Their approach to the estate was in skirmish order. They scattered through the sugar cane and managed to appear like shadows through the greenery as Martin approached with the Major and Julia Savage, who had insisted that she needed to come, by way of the road. They had managed to obtain horses, which was as well since, though the Major had recovered his health, he had not recovered his strength. Ensign Crockett left Major Bristow and six Marines with the captain, taking the others to find the slave quarters and the staff accommodation, and quietly take them into their control.

Martin and Aaron rode up to the front porch and dismounted. The tall, coloured servant who appeared called a boy to take the horses, and invited the visitors onto the veranda, seated them and provided cool lemonade. He then left them to summon his master to meet the visitors.

It took fifteen minutes for the master to appear. Though dressed, he was obviously put out by the appearance of visitors unannounced.

Martin was in full uniform and had been joined by Major Bristow, who like his men was dressed in his backwoods garb. Julia was dressed a she put it, in comfortable clothes giving her the appearance of a colonial woman.

Ignoring her presence, the man addressed Martin. "Who, sirs, are you to call unannounced? It is not the custom on this island."

"I am Captain Sir Martin Forest-Bowers of His Majesty's Ship, Vixen. This is a British Island, is it not?" Martin answered, not a little upset at the man's rude manner.

"So it is, sir. So it is. Though, what that has to do with anything, I am at a loss to understand."

Martin rose to his feet, and looked the man in the eye. "Who might you be, sir?"

"I am the owner of this estate and the house where you stand. I am Sir Gordon Reece."

"If that is actually the case, can you tell me why you have on your estate citizens of the American nation, in bondage illegally? Also, how is it that you claim ownership of this estate which is registered in the name of Colonel Ross Harding?"

Sir Gordon fell back red-faced, "Damn you. Sir, how dare you? Parker, call my guards and have these men thrown off the property."

The tall, coloured man, Parker, coughed and said, "I am afraid not, sir. There are no guards available." It was evident to Martin that Parker was having difficulty in keeping the smile from his face.

"Impudent swine." Sir Gordon raised his hand to strike Parker, only to find himself unable to move it, being held in the grip of the man beside him. Bristow had stepped up behind the man and intervened, before he could strike his servant.

By this time the slave quarters had been emptied by Bristow's men. A young woman appeared from the house at this point. She saw the group of slaves standing in front of the house and cried out, "Father!" Disregarding her clean white shift dress she ran off the veranda and flung herself into the arms of a middle-aged man in the group. His hair straggled on his head, his clothes filthy and fresh weal's showed through the gaps in his torn clothing, where he had been lashed recently.

The girl turned on Sir Gordon. She screamed, "You promised to treat my father gently." She ran back onto the veranda and flung herself at him, nails raking his face, as he tried to throw her off.

Bristow pried her away, managing to elbow Reece in the belly in so doing. Sir Gordon doubled up, gasping for breath, before collapsing into one of the chairs strewn about the veranda.

Martin addressed the man the girl had called father. "May I know your name, sir?"

The man straightened and answered, "I am Mathew Singer, of Savannah, Georgia, sir. Like these others here, I was taken by a so-called American privateer, off the coast of Florida, from where I was transported here and forced to work at the threat to my daughter's life." Martin looked at Aaron and Julia.

He turned to the others in the crowd. "Are there any others of you on this estate?"

Parker turned round and said, "Sir, if I may, the record books of the estate are in the office through here. The location of all the workers on the estate can be found there."

Sir Gordon rose from his chair and flung himself at the slave. He was angry and slow. Parker stepped to one side and nudged him as he blundered past. Reece, off balance, tripped over his own feet and crashed to the board of the veranda, with enough force to make the structure shudder. He lay there unable to move, stunned. The assembled men looked on astonished. Never had they seen a coloured man lift his hand to a white man before. Though Parker had not technically done that, what he had done amounted to the same thing.

Martin broke the impasse. "Aaron, take Parker and check the books. We need to find all the people on this estate who do not belong here." He turned to the assembled men and women before him. "I think you would like to clean yourselves properly. Is there such a place here?"

The girl, in the now bedraggled dress, spoke up. "Around the back of the house is the bath house. If the women use it first, the men can then use it. I will search the closets of the house for clothing. Though there should be all the clothes in our baggage which came with us. Parker will know where it is. If not, I will beat it out of him," pointing to the stirring figure on the veranda.

The women started to move off around the house to the bath house. Julia said "I will speak with the women." She moved off to join the women on their way round to the rear of the house.

Parker and Aaron came out onto the veranda, "We found the list here," Aaron said. "I guess we need to send some of the boys, with a guide, to collect them. Is there a wagon here?" He asked Parker.

"Sure is, sir. Just over in the barn, horses in the stables behind the barn. I'll get them harnessed, one of the house boys will manage. Meanwhile, I heard the lady ask about the baggage that came with them. It is in the barn loft and should still be in some shape."

Martin turned to Mathew Singer. "Can I ask you to fetch the cases down from the barn? I am sure the ladies will need clothing."

Singer turned to the group of men standing with him. "Well, hell, fellows, what are we standing here for. There's work to be done and we are the ones to do it."

Slowly the first men started to move, then the fact of their freedom penetrated and a lift came into their step. The men began to move toward the barn with a will they had been lacking when Martin first arrived.

"Parker, is there a ship that calls here regularly?" Martin had a thought at the back of his mind. He felt it worth following up.

Parker looked at Martin curiously. He said, "The master keeps a cutter in the creek. I guess it will still be there."

Martin turned to Midshipman Woods, "James take instruction from Mr. Parker and seek out this cutter. Report to me her state and condition." He called out, "McLean!"

The figure of the former poacher appeared from the group waiting orders. "Fetch two other men and that reprobate, Godden, and escort Mr. Wood to the cutter. Parker will give directions."

"Very good, sir." He turned to the group of men behind him. "Archer, Williams, Godden, you lazy bastard. Let's get going."

Parker led the small party through the trees, pointed to a path behind the house and they disappeared from sight.

In the meantime there were several things that Martin had in mind to ask Sir Gordon Reece.

He seated himself on one of the wicker chairs on the veranda and signed for the owner to be seated.

When Reece was seated he asked him, "How did you come into contact with the Colonel?"

Reece was thoroughly cowed by now and his answer reflected this. "He contacted me. The estate was losing money. My fault, I suppose. I had been gambling too much and it was eating into the operation costs of the estate. I had to sell slaves to make up the losses. He bought my debts and the deeds of the estate were transferred to him, as long as I continued to run it.

He arranged to supply slaves, provided I allowed him the use of the estate to store goods and weapons to resupply his ships. So far, I have received two separate consignments of slaves, though I have not had to re-supply any of his ships."

"Did you realise that the man was an American? What you are doing is treason!"

"I was not aware at first. He seemed a normal British Army Colonel."

"When did you realise that he was not British?"

"This month. The latest group of slaves were adamant that he was American. I spoke to the ship's captain whom I entertained. He recommended the girl who...," he coughed. "The young woman you met earlier.

"He was quite clear on the subject and equally clear that I had been trading with the enemy. Therefore, I could not afford to cause trouble."

He sat back looking drawn and worried. "I suppose there is no way...." His voice trailed off as he noticed Martin's expression.

"It is not up to me, and, if it were, I would have to take into account the conditions I found here." From Martin's words Reece realised there would be no easy way out of this situation. He resigned himself to the worst, and hoped for the best.

Midshipman Woods returned with the news that the cutter was in fact there, and in good shape, 68 feet long and seaworthy. That was a relief for Martin. It gave him a way of disposing of the Americans without actually needing to touch land, if it was needed.

Dismissing Reece to the custody of the Marines, he sat contemplating the other problem he faced. "Mr. Parker. What would you suggest I do about you?"

The tall dignified slave looked at Martin surprised at the question. He was after all a slave. Normal white men did not ask such things of a slave. He was rapidly re-assessing his opinion of Martin, taking into account that he was not a normal white man. Speaking slowly as he tried to get his thoughts in order he said, "If you mean what I think you mean, the best I could hope for would be, sold to a good master. There is nowhere this side of the Atlantic I can live as a free man. You have asked a question I cannot answer."

"In that case, I shall send you to the Governor in Nassau, with my recommendation." Martin decided. "The alternative would be for you to join my crew, but that would not suit most people."

"The Governor sound like my best option sir." Parker smiled, "And thank you sir, for your consideration."

Chapter six

The East Coast Patrol

The progress of HMS Vixen was hampered by having to keep a weather eye out for privateers. HMS Hera had been sent to Nassau, with a report to the Governor of the situation with Colonel Harding's estates in the Caribbean, and to deliver Mr. Reece for justice.

The cutter was making reasonable time, but that could not compensate for the delays caused by the route they were taking to achieve the safe return of the Americans. Martin was well aware that the majority of his compatriots would have said that in releasing them, he had already done them a favour. There was no need for anything else.

That would never do for Martin. He could not leave the job half done, if there was a way of completing it.

Using his glass, Martin swept the horizon, noticing as the glass passed along the cutter, the figure of Parker. The slave's decision to go to work for the Singer family in Savannah, Georgia, had been a surprise, but Martin accepted the fact that Parker had settled for a life and people that he knew.

So, making for the Carolina coast, meant losing time in heading due north to make contact with Admiral Cochrane and the fleet.

Several ships appeared and disappeared without making actual contact. In other circumstances Martin might have investigated a few. As it was, they had almost reached the Carolina coastline by the time Hera caught up with them.

The released prisoners sailed their cutter past Cape Fear into Wilmington, North Carolina.

With his responsibility discharged, Martin entertained Lieutenant Harris, who reported that the incumbent Governor of the Bahamas had been delighted to imprison Reece with the promise of trial in due course. With the sworn evidence of the captain and the other witnesses being taken into account, there was no doubt of a conviction. In addition, the forfeiture of the estates in the various Caribbean Islands, registered to Colonel Ross Harding, was already being undertaken. The authorities on the other islands in the region had all been warned of the possibility that kidnapped people had been forced to work on the estates. Investigation could lead to prosecutions in addition to the seizures.

They came in contact with elements of the fleet cruising off the coast of Virginia under the command of Commodore Sir Arthur Mason. The ships reported that they were seeing little sign of the enemy, though the frigate Guerriere had been reported taken after a fierce engagement.

***

In the main cabin of the flagship Campbelltown, Martin was being entertained by the Commodore Sir Arthur Mason who was discussing the American frigates. From the initial contacts in 1812 between HMS Bedford and Commodore Baines in the US frigate Augusta, and the similar incident between HMS Belvidera 36 and the US ships President and United States, both 44's plus the Congress 36 and two sloops, where the Belvidera engaged with President while maintaining her course away from the American squadron. Both ships scored hits and Belvidera managed to keep the President off with her stern chasers and escape during the night.

The unfortunate HMS Guerriere 48 had been taken after she had been reduced to a sinking hulk, in battle with the Constitution 44. The British ship's 18 pounders, with her crew of 263 men, were no real match for the American's 24 pounder guns, and her 476 picked seamen.

Martin detailed his own encounter with Augusta, which had been interrupted by the hurricane. "There is no doubt the American ships are formidable opponents. To a large extent the crews have been trained in British ships and the crew numbers are higher than in our own ships. But war at sea still depends on gunnery and seamanship, and the American fleet at sea is few in number, compared to ours.

The Commodore asked Martin about his orders. "I see you are ordered to inhibit the enemy on the Eastern seaboard of America, though I understand you are en-route to Halifax?"

"I was cruising up the coast and anticipating contacting Admiral Cochrane. There is an agent on my ship who should be returned to report to Halifax. If there is some other project where I might be involved, I will send the lady on the Hera."

"Martin, I am ashamed to admit I was not aware there was a lady here."

Martin was apologetic. "It was her choice not to announce herself. As an agent for 'plain Mr. Smith', she prefers to refrain from drawing attention to herself."

Commodore Mason stroked his chin. "Is it polite to enquire how you two met?"

Martin grinned. "In my earlier career, I was engaged in several incidents on behalf of 'plain Mr. Smith.' Since then, because of this connection, I have been asked to assist agents in the field, and, on occasion, to collect them. This was one of these occasions. I had encountered this lady in the period before the present war broke out.

"A request had been made to Commodore Wallace in Jamaica to arrange a pick-up in Key West. Since it was on my way I agreed to perform the task and was delighted to recognise Julia Savage, a friend of both my wife and I."

Sir Arthur was keen to attach Vixen to his squadron and use Martin as part of the patrol system for the American coast line.

Back on board his own ship, Martin called for Lieutenant Harris to dine with him. With Julia in attendance for the occasion, he detailed his instructions for the delivery of the lady. To his delight, he observed the reaction that John Harris did his best to conceal. His dignified manner was maintained but both Martin and Julia were aware of his pleasure at being given the task.

The transfer would be made the following morning and, as Martin watched the jollyboat return to the anchored Hera, Julia Savage joined him. After a moment she said, "He is a most suitable young man, I am thinking."

Martin turned and looked at her keenly. "Were you my daughter I would approve of your choice....Yes, a most suitable young man. But what of his lordship?" He referred to the Honourable Dominic Gordon, who had pressed his suit during Martin's last cruise to America.

"He was nice but not for me. I would not feel right at court, and that is where such a union would lead me, I'm afraid."

Julia looked back at him seriously. "Would you give me away at the wedding?"

"You are really serious?"

"It is not a matter I take lightly. My father and grandfather are no more, and you are the person I respect and regard most closely for such a task."

"Then, my dear it, would be an honour for me indeed. Though I believe John has not yet proposed, I look forward to attending your wedding."

***

Julia Savage was transferred to the Hera the following morning. The tall figure of her companion the Iroquois warrior, David, stood beside her in the boat as she waved farewell to Martin and the men of the frigate.

At the Commodore's suggestion Martin set sail for North Carolina to maintain contact with the people there. The disposal of Colonel Ross Harding was still very much in mind.

The cruise south brought little of interest for the first three days. The weather was kind and there was time to repair and renew. The crew took advantage of the time to dry off gear which always seemed to be damp, and Martin had wind sails rigged to blow the wind of passage through the lower decks. Godden was busy frapping the cringle on the tail of a skysail, his partner in crime, McLean, was splicing a rope seated on the deck beside him.

"Ere, Jock. What do you think the old man is up to?"

McLean thought for a moment, and then said, "I think that Colonel fellow should be watching his P's and Q's. I think our Martin has plans for him. He was not pleased to find the

Major in that state, and I thought I heard him say to the Major that we would be giving a hand to put him in his place."

Godden was quick in the forest but not quite so quick on the uptake. "Where might that be then?"

"What are you on about now?" McLean's attention had strayed.

Godden said impatiently, "Where will the captain put the Colonel, then?"

"In a box, I think." The voice of the captain answered him. "That's where I'll put the Colonel."

Godden started to his feet, but Martin said, "Stay as you are. What you are doing is important."

He left the two men and continued his circuit of the main deck stopping to talk to a man here and there.

"We got a good-un there." Godden commented.

McLean nodded in agreement.

Lieutenant Brooks was on watch. The Midshipmen were with the Master puzzling over the intricacies of the sextant. Martin joined Brooks pacing the quarterdeck.

"Well, Patrick. How are you enjoying our sojourn in the Americas?"

"Why, sir. I am finding the experience both diverting, and thus far, rewarding also."

"How is Mr. Hammond shaping up?" Martin was keen to know how his second in command felt about Lieutenant Hammond.

"During this last commission he has grown up considerably. I think he has become a fine officer. The men take heed of him and he listens to them, without forgetting his position. We have good men here, sir, with Lieutenant Harmon as well as young Gibbs. I think we have a future Admiral there." Brooks stopped, embarrassed at talking so much.

Martin looked at him. "Mr. Brooks you continue to amaze me. I think you will do well as captain of your own ship, and I will say so in my reports."

"Th…Thank you, sir," he stuttered, watching Martin walk over to the group of Midshipmen still struggling with their maths.

***

The progress of HMS Vixen southward was uninterrupted by alarms, the most exciting event being the sighting of a pod of large whales, identified by the master as 'Right Whales.' They accompanied the ship for several miles before disappearing.

The third day they ran down the coast of Carolina and encountered two trading schooners running close inshore to avoid capture.

The larger of the two was in fact chasing the other, a matter of interest to Martin, who surprised the two ships by firing a gun across the bows of the chasing ship. Martin had been studying the flag it was flying. It was a house flag that he had never seen before.

Pursuer and pursued both hauled their wind, and hove-to, waiting for the boats of the frigate to board them. Martin himself went to the larger ship, taking Marines and McLean, one of his two scouts, who was quick to spot inconsistencies.

The John Henry claimed to be out of Savannah, Georgia and her papers showed her to be the property of Colonel Harding, licenced to privateer by the Government of America, in Washington.

"And what are you doing here in these waters, Captain Cox?"

"I am trading and privateering, Captain, as it says there. I have the right to do just that.

"Then, Captain, why are you chasing an American ship?"

"I declare, Captain, I did not realise it was an American ship,"

"Despite the large American flag at her masthead."

"That can be a false flag, sir."

"And the flag you fly, Captain? I do believe that is also a false flag. I would like to see your cargo manifest, Captain."

"I'm afraid, I was checking it in the storm the other night and it got spoiled, sir."

"Well, just give me a general description of the goods you carry?"

The captain was looking most uncomfortable. "You seem uncomfortable, Captain. Is there a problem?"

"Major Bristow, have the hold covers lifted. Let us find out for the captain here what cargo he is carrying."

"Captain Forest-Bowers, Sir. Please, this is my ship. You have no right to interfere with a legitimate trading vessel."

"Pardon me, Captain Cox. I think describing this ship as a legitimate trading vessel, when you are carrying a privateer commission, is stretching the truth too far. Also, I presume you are aware a state of war exists between Britain and America."

Martin turned as Major Bristow returned. "Yes, Major. Can you tell the captain what cargo he is carrying?"

"Sir, perhaps we should speak in private?"

"No, we have no secrets from the good captain here. What is it you have to say?"

"Sir, there are twenty-four ladies below, locked in a cage. They are all naked and all claim to have been kidnapped and abused by the people of this ship. Their ship was pirated and their men folk carried off to some place on the mainland. The women think they will be taken to a brothel in the Florida Keys."

"Captain Cox, you will have an explanation for this I am sure. Mr. Gibbs, fetch the captain of the schooner to join us please. Make sure he is escorted!"

"Yes, sir!" Gibbs took the jollyboat alongside, and was taken to the other schooner; its name now clearly visible, Alice, neatly painted on her stern. The jollyboat returned and Gibbs reappeared, escorting a rough looking gentleman. Martin turned again to Major Bristow. "Was there no cargo below apart from the... ah, ladies?"

"There was none, sir. The hold was empty."

"As I thought," Martin commented quietly. He turned to the captain of the Alice. "You, sir. Who are you?"

"I'm Captain Lovelace, sir, a coastal trader."

"Is the Alice your ship, Captain?"

"It is, sir."

"What cargo do you carry?"

"Sir, I have beans and rice and a little cotton."

Martin swung around to Captain Cox. "There, sir. You do see what I mean. Captain Lovelace knows what cargo he carries. It is odd that you do not."

Martin turned to Gibbs. "Was there much damage to the Alice, Mr. Gibbs?"

"I saw none at all, sir."

"Major Bristow, what do you make of that?"

"Sir, I'm of the opinion that the demonstration we observed on spotting these two ships, was just that: a demonstration to cause us to come to the assistance of the ship being attacked."

"Do you really think so, Major? Well, we will just have to arrest these two ships for the offence of bad acting. I believe we will find clothing for the ladies down below. Discuss the restoration of their menfolk with Mr. Cox here. Will that answer, do you think?"

Bristow smiled. "It sounds absolutely perfect, sir, the ideal answer in these circumstances."

"Then do let us proceed. The ladies first, I think?"

Martin saw Captain Cox placed in irons with his crew. Captain Lovelace, having returned accompanied to his ship, suffered a similar fate.

The papers, which contained instructions signed by Colonel Ross Harding, were sufficient for Lieutenant Hammond to take immediate action. The hold of the second ship was empty of cargo also, despite the swift verbal reaction to Martin's question, by Lovelace.

With the two ships in train, HMS Vixen sailed south to Charleston, South Carolina, where she lay offshore. Martin sent a boat in under a white flag, to discuss the recovered ladies, and their missing men.

At a meeting with the Mayor of Charleston, Martin discovered that Colonel Ross Harding was a known man in the region, who had his own quay north of the city over the Georgia border, "There is a whole string of islands there, and the few folk who live there scratch a living from the sea. He built himself a deep-water place on one of the islands and keeps himself to himself."

"Mayor, I know our governments are still haggling over how to make peace without losing face. It does occur to me that it would be in the interest of both governments if we could remove the likes of Colonel Harding and his pirates, and certainly release the people illegally enslaved by him. Would you be acquainted with a soldier by the name of Aaron Jackman, Major Jackman, from Wilmington, North Carolina."

"I am, Captain. Why do you ask?"

Martin considered for a moment. The man before him was a slim man with a hawk-nosed sharp-eyed look about him who looked comfortable in his suit, but also looked as if he would be comfortable in buckskin. "Aaron is a friend of mine. We travelled to Raleigh together, during my last tour in America before war broke out. We have also met when I intercepted a slave ship owned by Colonel Harper, on its way to the Bahamas. I was able to release the Major and many of his friends, fellow Americans who had been captured and enslaved by Harding's pirate ships."

Mayor Parker Jones guessed what was coming, but he responded anyway. "An interesting story, Captain. What had you in mind?"

Martin leaned forward in his chair. "I think this is a time to set aside our political differences and put Colonel Ross Harding, out of business." He sat back and waited for Jones to respond.

The Mayor took his time. "Captain, as Mayor of Charleston and a citizen of the Americas, I am appreciative of your efforts to save the lives of these innocent people. Now I am wondering how the devil we can help in such a damn-fool operation. It is liable to ruin your career, and the careers of anyone else foolish enough to participate."

"The idea that I could contact Major Jackman and ask that he bring his riflemen to co-operate with my militia and your marines, it is frankly ridiculous. We would have to mobilise the river craft, and horses, and wagons, with cannon and a food train. Hell, we would need to recruit our Cherokee friends to come and help to keep the Colonel's renegades busy."

"Yes, Captain, I would be happy to call upon Aaron to co-operate with you, but it will take a little time. Bluntly, Martin. May I call you, Martin?"

Martin grinned, "I guess I can call you, Parker. Why not?"

Jones continued, "Martin, it would be a pleasure. But we cannot move while your ship is sitting offshore. It will take weeks to prepare an expedition like this. You understand? And I have to get the backing of my council."

Martin rose to his feet. "I'll come back quietly in six weeks. If I meet the Major, perhaps at that time, we can finalise our plans and get something done between us."

He put his hand out to the Mayor who had also risen to his feet. They shook hands warmly. "Six weeks, Parker."

"Until we meet again, Martin." Parker answered.

Chapter seven

Making Waves

The way south from Charleston took them past Savannah and down the Florida Peninsular. News of the June battle between HMS Shannon and the American frigate, Chesapeake, came to encourage the idea that the American ships were not all-conquering. The wind started to increase as they encountered increasingly heavy seas. As they neared St Augustine, the wind had worsened to such an extent that they were running under storm foresail and reefed topsails only. The shore was far behind as Martin made for open waters to ride out the storm, away from the threat of stranding. As they beat out to sea the changing direction of the wind brought the comment from the Master to Martin. "I fear, sir, we are in a hurricane. Tis the season, I know. But we are doing the right thing. There is no joy in being near land in these conditions."

For the entire period of daylight, the two ships battled the seas, struggling to stay afloat and keep their head into the seas. Twice, the Hera nearly broached as the flying-jib ripped out in a sudden gust. It had to be replaced. Each time, the outer-jib, kept furled, was spread in time to hold the bow head to the waves. The Vixen did broach at one stage, but managed to claw her head back with the welcome help of a cross sea, which caught her as she rolled and forced her head round. The master, Jared Watson, confided in Acting Lieutenant Gibbs, that he had never seen the like of the seas they encountered during that first day. They entered calmer conditions which Mr. Watson identified as the eye of the storm. He forecast a renewal of the wild weather as they passed through the other edge of the circling winds.

Jared Watson watched the crew busy repairing the rigging, and frapping frayed edges. Then he volunteered.

"There is more, sir. But if we take the correct course it will not be so bad the second time."

"How so?"

"We will take the wind on our best point. It will throw us out of the turmoil, not drag us in as it did earlier."

"Ship ahoy!" The masthead lookout called, pointing at the still visible dark cloud behind them. "It's the Hera, sir. She is signalling.

Martin turned to Gibbs. "Get a man aloft with a glass. We need to know what she says."

Gibbs grabbed the telescope from the signals locker slung it over his shoulder and dashed to the shrouds, making his way aloft at a great pace. He joined the lookout and opened the big telescope. He called, "She has hove to and is signalling: 'Ship in distress, dismasted, help needed."

Martin called, "Bring her about, Mr. Brooks. Hoist more sail. Make for Hera."

As they approached their consort, the ship in trouble appeared out of the swirling cloud and into the quieter waters of the eye.

Martin could hardly recognise the battered hulk which had come into view. The Augusta had lost her fore and mainmasts. The mizzen stood, though the mizzen topmast had gone. The foremast was hanging over the side, supporting the broken mainmast which in turn, was dragging the ship over on her port side. Her pumps were going trying to keep up with the encroaching water.

When Vixen reached her, Martin had the men throw grapnels around the fallen mainmast. Leading the lines through tackles, they hoisted the fallen mast out of the water to the level of the Augusta's deck. By taking the weight off the foremast the men on the American ship, were able to hoist the mast back onto the ship. They lashed the mainmast to the deck and, with the help of Martin's men, hoisted the foremast and fished it to the stump, bracing it with cable in place of the normal shrouds. Leaving a group of topmen to untangle the rigging for the foremast, the other men, with the help of the crew of the Vixen, stripped the rigging from the mainmast, and unhitched the cross-masts, to stow the timbers securely on deck. The broken pieces went over the side.

Martin and the doctor were both aboard the American ship. Martin boarded to speak with the Commodore, the doctor to tend the many injured, helping the ships' surgeon who badly needed the aid. When Martin found Commodore Barnes, he was in the stern cabin trapped in his berth with a broken leg. His Cox'n defended him from all comers, while the second officer coped with the damage and repairs.

When Martin entered, he removed his hat in salute to Commodore Barnes who growled. "Who the devil are you sir, and what are you doing on my ship?"

"I am Captain Martin Forest-Bowers of HMS Vixen, at your service, sir. My people are assisting your men in rescuing the ship, and preparing it to face the renewed storm."

Barnes turned to his Cox'n. "Where is that fool, Jacobson?"

The Cox'n spoke quietly, "When you broke your leg, sir, he panicked and ran down to the orlop. He left the deck to the second mate, Mr. Howlet, sir,"

Barnes face darkened, "He what?"

"I think you heard what I said, sir." The Cox'n was not flustered or apparently put out by his captain's harsh words. "I told you at the beginning that he was made of piss and paper. Whatever his father does will never make a seaman of him, nor put iron in his backbone."

Remembering Martin was there the Commodore turned to him. "What shape are we in, Captain?"

"I guess that with what has now been done, better than fifty-fifty. I understand the pumps are now coping and, between our two carpenters, the leaks are being stoppered. The foremast went and is now being frapped and jury rigged, braced with cables, it will take foresails only until you reach a shipyard, I suspect. The main mast fell but has been salvaged, but there is no time to get it re-erected. The mizzen stands but is having extra bracing fitted. Sir, I trust you understand that this truce is temporary, and is between seamen, not politicians. We will be at odds another time."

Commodore Baines looked at Martin keenly. "If you are saying what I think your saying, I am in your debt, sir. As you say our next meeting may well be our last. But for this occasion I would be proud to shake your hand, sir."

Martin smiled. "Gladly, though I believe we make better friends than enemies."

As he turned to leave, the Second Officer, Mr. Howlet, appeared. I have to report, sir, that Mr. Jacobson has fallen and been drowned when checking the level in the bilges."

"Take over the ship, Mr. Howlet. You will have to command through the balance of the storm, sir. Are you up to it?"

"Thank you, sir. Of course, sir. I will do my best." As he turned to leave he stopped, and turned to Martin. Captain Forest-Bowers, sir, the storm is moving on. Your men are gathering to return to your ship."

"I'll come with you then," Turning to the Commodore, "Good-by, Commodore. Let us hope our next meeting will be less stressful."

With a smile he left the cabin and returned to the deck.

It was just in time. Waiting until the doctor finally crossed, he placed his foot in the sling rigged to Vixens' mainsail yard, and was swung over the widening gap between the two ships. His glimpse of the waters beneath him was not re-assuring, but he landed on his own deck safely and the sling was stripped off and stowed. As the Vixen hauled off, the Augusta could now be seen clearly. She looked truncated with her stumpy foremast and mizzen, both now with scraps of sail set and the ship moving under control once more.

"Make the signal 'Godspeed,' Gibbs. How are we situated, Mr. Brooks?"

"As ready as we can be, sir."

"Carry on, then. I'll be below for just now. Call me when we come to the edge of the eye of the storm, once more."

"Aye, aye, sir, at the edge of the storm." Brooks looked after Martin as he went below.

He was thinking. Perhaps, there were other captains he could be serving, but he doubted there were any better.

The three ships survived the storm. Both Vixen and Hera returned to Antigua for some repairs. The Augusta made it to Boston. It was recorded that Mr. Jacobson had died of injuries received during the great storm, one of the thirty-two men who lost their lives. No mention was made of the actions of the Vixen, though Barnes recorded the events, and his appreciation of the help, in his private journal.

***

The repairs would take time. The docks at Antigua were crowded with damaged ships when Vixen and Hera arrived. Unfortunately, there was nowhere else they could get their repairs carried out. The hurricane had swept the Caribbean, and all the dockyards were in a similar state. Martin was frustrated. Time was passing. The sight of Commodore Ramos and his squadron was welcomed. Having returned from the South American coast, where they had been unaffected by the hurricane which had devastated much of the Caribbean his ships were in need of stores rather than repair.

In view of the losses and damage to the Royal Naval ships which would normally be involved in these activities, the Sao Paulo and her four companions were placed at the disposal of the Admiral, to join with the other allied ships in policing the Caribbean waters.

Having been told that there would be an eight week wait before his ships could be ready despite his impatience, Martin decided that it might be possible to contact Major Jackman and Mayor Parker Jones about Colonel Ross Harding.

Having explained the situation to Antonio Ramos, he requested passage for himself and the Marine contingents from both Vixen and Hera to Charleston.

The weapons and other gear were transferred to the hold in the Sao Paulo and, in company with the Lisboa, a second frigate from the Commodore's command, they departed for the American continent.

As a guest on his friend's ship Martin had time to notice the competence of the crew. The influence of their contact with the British ships had made a difference. "In addition," Antonio said. "All of my officers are seamen. All of the favoured appointees in the squadron who have survived this voyage have demonstrated their competence. Those who did not survive are now cooling their heels in Rio. There were only two men who did not make it. I am happy, and surprised to say, that the others decided that they enjoyed what they were doing, and made the decision to get on with things as they were. I was offered and accepted seven young men to train as midshipmen. As you know it was the one area where in the past we had little success. There are now midshipmen on all my ships, young lads training to become officers. In the same way as they do in the Royal Navy."

Antonio beamed at Martin. "I cannot tell you how pleased I am about this matter."

Martin grinned. "You do not need to. It's written all over your face."

Antonio looked puzzled. "All over my face?"

Martin laughed, "It is an expression. When something obviously pleases someone and causes them to smile, we say 'it's written all over their face'. Like a smile."

Antonio got the message. "In our country up to now, the better families have never been happy to let their youngsters come into the fleet at the right age. I am pleased to say that the war has changed all that."

He turned to Martin, his face serious once more, "This adventure into the American continent. I realise you feel that this man Colonel Harding is a dangerous lunatic, but why are you getting involved? This is surely the business of the American people themselves."

"Unfortunately, he also has been sending slaves to plantations on British held islands. This cannot be allowed to continue. I cannot see any other way I can stop him."

"He has privateers in operation, I understand." Ramos stroked his chin reflectively.

"Once again, I have no idea which ships he controls. He seems to deal with each captain separately. Apart from the personal relationships between the odd captains, no one knows who anyone else is." Martin sounded frustrated.

Antonio Ramos considered his friend's situation. He had never considered not supporting him in this adventure. Though apart from actually taking the party to Charleston there was little else he could do. There was no question of his position regarding privateers. His ships would stop and search any they encountered. If they encountered any sign of slaves or unnecessary killing, he would take action. That was the law of the sea as he saw it.

Chapter eight

The backwoods trail

The port facilities at Charleston welcomed the Portuguese ships when they arrived. Word had gone ahead, with a cutter from the islands which had passed with a brief exchange of signals. It had been several weeks since Martin last sailed these waters. He was worried that it had taken longer than he had anticipated for the assault on the Colonel's holdings west of the Carolina and Georgia territories.

The Mayor, Parker Jones, greeted Martin, who was dressed in plain clothes rather than his uniform, and the woodsman's buckskins feeling soft and flexible after wearing the rather stiffer uniform dress he was so accustomed to.

"Well, Martin to me you look a lot less threatening in that get-up, mind you. I would be worried if it was me you were after. Can you use that rifle?"

Martin laughed, "Parker, I was trained by Aaron himself, as were my men. We are prepared to get on with things the moment Aaron arrives."

"You will be on your way within the week in that case. Already, the smoke signals have passed the message on. They will be here by Friday."

***

The expedition set out without fanfares or fuss.

Aaron Jackman, Martin was pleased to observe, looked lean and hard. He had recovered completely from the trials of his slavery. He looked across at the other boats. With one hundred and fifty men, all good shots, all woodsmen. He was well pleased. The addition of the party of North Carolinian Cherokee Indians was especially welcome, since he knew from Aaron's personal experience that the plantation had Cherokee trackers working for the Colonel. Looking up river, he could see there were still some of their canoes visible, forging ahead on the river. The majority had swiftly disappeared out of sight of the slower more heavily burdened, troop boats which were loaded with small cannon in addition to the Marines and the militia.

It would take three weeks to reach the edge of the claimed lands. The second half of the journey would be on land over vague trails and difficult ground, but thus far, the party had made good time on the river. Martin's boat was moving over to the river bank. He saw the gathering of men waiting to board and take the place of the men presently in the boat. Martin would be going ashore with the men when the exchange took place. It was the best way for the men to keep fit and ready for action. The shore party spent most of their time running and walking, not to keep up with the river boats, but to actually scout both banks of the river ahead in case of ambush. By now the Cherokees would be several miles ahead and hopefully clearing the area for the main force. Aaron had ordered the practice as a precaution in view of the attacks when Martin was last in the country.

***

The party travelled for six days upriver, making good time before it became necessary to abandon the boats and strike across country on foot, dragging the carts with cannon and ammunition and powder along the trail. It was on the tenth night as they sat around their fires waiting to eat, that David appeared, his approach undetected. The big Iroquois Chief spoke directly to Martin, "I am bringing news and Miss Julia." He looked around the group, verifying who they were. He then called out, "Come, Miss Julia."

Though not quite as silent as David, Julia was very much in tune with her surroundings. Dressed in buckskin, just like the men around her, the long rifle was as much part of her as it was of any of the men present. With her hair tied back and plaited into a pigtail she could be a young man, but only from a distance. "Hullo, Martin, Major Jackman. Pleased to meet you again." She held out her hand and shook Aaron's. She then squatted down next to Martin, "Guess we arrived at the right time, then," she commented, looking at the food now being dished up for the party.

"Guess so!" Martin commented with a small smile, mimicking her laconic delivery.

When they had eaten he asked her the question the entire party was interested in. "Why are you here, Julia, delighted as we all are to see you. This is no place for a woman!"

"I did not expect that from you, Martin." Julia said reproachfully. "I am sure you are aware of the situation here. It is the business of us all. In fact the reason I am here now is because I became aware of the presence of the Colonel on my last trip south. I have been receiving information that his people were raiding settlements in the west, seizing and enslaving men women and children. I knew you were involved in stopping him. David and I were scouting his country and came to warn you that he knows you are coming, and he has set a trap for you."

Aaron said, "What sort of trap?"

"There is a river across your path with his lands on the other side. It is an ideal place for an ambush. Crossing the river is where you will be most vulnerable.

"He'll be there with his little army, maybe three hundred men. There is another way to cross and perhaps take him by surprise, but it would mean you alter course soon. I have spoken to your Cherokee people. They have cleared the ground well, but we will still need to leave things until the last minute. That man has scouts and spies throughout the woods, and the only reason we have a real chance of fooling them is the fact that your own scouts are so active the woods. Though there are Cherokee on both sides, the tribe is divided like many of the Native Americans. There is no love lost between them, as there are blood feuds between the leading families."

***

The party made good progress through the woodland and scrub country, though the dry conditions caused dust from the wheels of the carts. On the fifteenth day there was a skirmish. An arrow missed Martin as he jogged through the woodland. The light through the trees was plentiful but, because of the scattered clouds and the movement of the leaves overhead, the light flickered and made shooting difficult. Martin, aware of the arrow, dropped immediately to the ground and brought his rifle forward as he did so. There was no sign at first of the enemy, though a man did appear after several minutes had passed. He was stripped to the waist wearing leggings and moccasins. Not tall, but with his lank hair falling to his shoulders and the single feather drooping from his headband, he looked dangerous enough. His bow was now loose in his hand and his other bore a knife. Martin eased his pistol from his belt and guessed that the sound of cocking it would alert his opponent. He gauged the space between them and made up his mind. A shot would warn the others anyway. Taking a chance, he cocked the pistol, raised it and fired. The ball took the enemy in mid stride, stopping him without killing him. The flash dazzled them both, though Martin recovered first and, leaping up from the ground with his knife in hand, he met the Cherokee chest to chest. Both had knives raised to strike, but Martin was quicker. His first strike was over the shoulder of the shorter man, striking his back but only penetrating about an inch. Drawing blood but no serious injury, his opponent's blade drew blood from Martin's arm. Having little force behind it, it failed to inflict serious injury.

Both men drew back, circling, but Martin could see that the other man was hurt from the bullet wound in his chest. He feinted to the left and leaped right. The other man was quick to react, but stumbled into Martin's extended blade. With a sigh he sank to the ground taking the knife with him.

Martin stood up and breathed deeply, amazed at how tired he felt after such a short fight. He checked the man on the ground. As he knelt he saw the life go out of the man's eyes. Recovering his knife, he cleaned the blade before returning it to its sheath. It was only then that he realised that he was surrounded by others from the expedition.

David appeared from the woods behind Martin. "He was not alone, but the gun warned the others off.

Aaron appeared. "Let's get moving. Our scouts are on the trail of the others in the hunting party. Hopefully they will prevent them taking any information back.

At his urging, the party dispersed. Martin picked up his rifle and loped off into the trees once more, the blood still leaking a little from his arm.

Reminded, he pulled a cloth from his small pack and ripped off a strip to bind the wound and stop the bleeding.

He caught up with his place in the line, men stretched in three rows with the wagons in the centre of the middle row. Their progress was based on the trail where the wagons travelled. The scouts re-established contact with the leading row, and the report came back. The intruders had been caught and dealt with. The problem was as Aaron pointed out. They had come up with a group, but they could not guarantee there were no others who may have been separated from the group earlier.

As the raiders neared the Saluda River, preparations for the diversion and the detour were made. Darkness fell. Aaron and his woodsmen, with the Cherokees, disappeared.

Martin, with Major Bristow and the marines from Vixen and Hera, plus Julia and David, created enough fires to account for the missing men. Bristow had dispersed his men through the surrounding woods to give the impression of a much bigger party encamped there. The following morning they would march with plenty of dust thrown up to simulate the complete column approaching the river crossing.

The night passed slowly for Martin. He lay staring at the stars, blazing against the black sky, wondering if perhaps someone up there was looking down doing just as he was. Eventually he got up and walked over to the fire. The figure beside the fire was Julia.

"Can't you sleep either?" Martin growled.

"I have too many questions without answers. Not a good recipe for sleep." Julia answered.

"There always is," Martin said. "For me, the answer is often a stroll around the deck, but this place is not a good substitute."

"I know what you mean. Every tree can hide an enemy here. At least on a ship there is little chance of that being the case. Peace of mind of a sort anyway, I found that on my own ship."

***

On the other side of the river, just over an hour away, the big house stood outlined against the sky, tonight ablaze with lights and the sound of music. Built by the Colonel as a state capitol and residence, the building was designed to impress. The gathering this evening had been arranged many weeks ago. The reason it was still happening with an attack imminent, was because the Colonel felt that if he cancelled he would lose face.

Colonel Ross Harding stood in his apartments in 'Casa Verde', the mansion he had built for himself on the spot selected for the future capital of his country. Six foot tall in his stockinged feet before the mirror reflecting his trim physique, forty-six years old, and fitter than many of his younger followers. As for wealth? Almost sufficient to maintain the standard he had selected to live at, he was nearing the point where he could consider making a formal declaration of Independence. The resources of the new American state were stretched to the limit. Mexico to the south was corrupt and despoiled by a succession of despotic viceroys and insurgents who between them had bled the country dry. With the growing armoury he was amassing and the increasing population, his land would soon be able to stand on its own feet. He must think of a more suitable name than that which the local inhabitants used prior to his acquisition of the territory.

He finished his dressing with the simple black jacket, with silver buttons produced from his own silver mine. Almost a military tunic, though not quite, it resembled more the dress Argyll Jacket, worn with Highland attire. He slipped on his shoes, and his valet gave a final buff to the silver buckles

His servant brushed off a touch of dust from the shoulders of his master's jacket and stood back, satisfied that the Colonel was ready. His wife, dressed in a blue ball gown, joined him from her own apartments and they descended to the gathering below.

The sound of music as the Colonel and his lady descended the stairs assured him that his current mistress was carrying out his orders. He had decreed that the entertainment start at seven in the evening, and start it must, regardless of the absence of the host. He had been deliberately late. It was one of the ways he employed to stress that he was in sole charge of affairs.

As they entered the ballroom the orchestra stopped playing, and then played the short melody he had selected as his personal anthem. The guests clapped at his appearance and Mariette, his mistress and the organiser of the evening, trotted over to lead them to the centre of the room to receive the greetings of the guests, perhaps sixty people representing the cream of his created society. The ladies were dressed in formal ball gowns and the men mainly in suits ranging from brocade to broadcloth. All appeared clean and tidy, and, as the Colonel himself had observed, in this place, at this time, it was a reflection of the civilisation he had brought to this uncouth, backwoods area.

His wife stayed to greet guests while the Colonel led the assembly into a dance, matching the grace and elegance of his partner, Mariette. He then led her through to the drawing room, tonight laid with a buffet supper for the guests. Once more re-assured by the beautifully arrayed display of food on this occasion, he excused himself and took a place on the veranda with the men gathered there where he accepted an offered cigar from the visiting politician from Georgia. Out in the open air he paused for a moment, listening. He heard nothing out of the way, no shots and no other sounds that did not belong.

On the veranda there were visitors from other states, though none would allow their presence to be linked in any way with official business. Harrison Benson was one of many politicians living in the shadows around the seats of power in politics. He was a fixer, a lobbyist and the person who normally knew where the bodies were buried. He was here on behalf of those in Georgian politics who wanted to be prepared for any upheavals in the borderlands of the state.

To the Colonel, Harrison was something else. Recognising the possibilities in the new country, Harrison was ready for the proposal put to him by the Colonel and able to offer other services to make the Colonel's life somewhat easier. The acquisition of lands on the coast of Georgia had been achieved without publicity. The Colonel had reciprocated with a grant of lands in the new country, which Mr. Benson would be able to take up when the establishment of the nation was finalised.

The Colonel's rank had been gained in the war of independence against the British. The rank was a return on the provision of a battalion of infantry for Washington's army. It did not mean that Harding was a good soldier, merely a rich one. In fact, he had also been lucky.

His own opinion of himself was rather higher than he probably deserved. It was a reflection of the achievements of his later life, rather than anything else, that his present situation had come about. He had seized a large area of comparatively unsettled land using that battalion of infantry. The allocation of land to the survivors who had joined him after the war had, it seemed, been enough to secure their loyalty thereafter.

The sight of Major Strauss, immaculate as ever in his dress uniform, created a twinge of disquiet for the Colonel. Though always invited, the Major was not an habitué of the Colonel's get-togethers.

The fact that he was here prepared the Colonel for bad news. The Major did not disappoint.

"May I have a moment of your time please, sir?" The Major's English was as immaculate as his uniform, though the accent still betrayed his German origins.

The Colonel placed his cigar carefully in an ashtray and stepped off the veranda accompanied by the Major.

"What is the problem, Eric?" The Colonel and the Major had been associates for many years now. Though the formal distance was maintained between them, there was a trust that was shared by no others.

"The raiding party are at the river and it seems they anticipate the ambush. They have set up camp and their scouts are very active, possibly on both banks."

With raised brow, Harding said, "Recommendations?"

"Wait. They must cross at some point. We are still not sure of the numbers involved. Whether they planned it that way or not, the continual ebb and flow of their woodsmen and native tribesmen has made it difficult to assess the number of troops involved. My hunch is that we outnumber them."

"Hunch?" The Colonel smiled, shaking his head.

His face, flushing slightly in embarrassment, the Major corrected himself. "My instincts tell me that our men outnumber the enemy substantially."

Harding considered for a few moments. "Very good! I accept your 'hunch'." The smile re-appeared. "So let us return to the party and enjoy the evening." He led the way back on to the veranda, collected his cigar from the ashtray and brought it back to life with a series of short puffs. When it was drawing to his satisfaction he commented, "You may take the Savage woman if she survives the action."

Strauss looked at the Colonel as he puffed away. He shook his head. He had never accepted any woman as a gift from the Colonel. Nor would he ever, except, he thought wryly, the Colonel's wife!

***

Across the river, Martin was receiving the reports of the scouts who had returned under cover of the night. Between Martin, David and Julia they had worked out that the opposing forces numbered about two hundred. It also appeared that they were camped along the river with a stockade erected, commanding the ford. But there seemed to be little effort turned to their rear, which they apparently regarded as secure.

Contact had been established with Aaron and his men who were now encamped a half ile to the rear of the enemy army. The messenger had produced a note suggesting that they set up the guns, to keep heads down on the other side of the river, with just the gun crews and a section of Marines with Cherokee back-up for protection. Then bring the other Marines across downriver with the messenger. The combined force could then take the enemy from the rear against the river.

Chapter Nine

Payback

Meanwhile, at the mansion the major drew himself up and clicked his heels together with a sharp nod of his head. "You are most generous, Colonel. I appreciate your generosity." Dismissed, he left his Colonel and joined the throng at the food tables, seeking out the only woman he desired and was really close to. Alicia Harding, the Colonel's wife, was thirty-five years old, and lovely. She had survived the arranged marriage, and produced two handsome children. Both were in attendance this evening.

Edward, her son, now seventeen years old, looked like his father, and, in the opinion of his mother, had the morals of a goat, and the manners of a pig. On show, on an occasion such as tonight's gathering, unless he got drunk, he would behave impeccably while under the eye of his father. His sister, Emma, by contrast at the age of sixteen was beautiful, well-mannered and intelligent. Her academic talent ranged from mathematics to literature and from science to politics. Alicia had schooled her well to maintain her tact when in company, and she never allowed any suggestion of her education to become apparent beyond the expectations of a normal young person of her age.

The Colonel had plans for both son and daughter. Alicia had alternative plans which did not include those of her husband.

As she worked the room, ensuring that the guests were enjoying the occasion, she was aware that Eric was present and following her progress. It was a comfort that she had allowed herself to enjoy over the past seven years. The completion of this house had permitted separate apartments for her husband and herself, making it convenient for him to indulge in a series of mistresses over the past years.

Their marriage had never been a love match, though she had admired him in those early days. With motherhood, she had become aware that Ross had found alternative outlets for his sexual appetites, so it had been in many ways a relief to find that after the birth of Emma, she would no longer be able to bear children. This released her from the need to submit to the attentions of her husband on the basis of begetting, as the bible put it. The mutual withdrawal of sex from their marriage had suited both partners, releasing Ross to find activity where he, as a man, may? And for Alicia also, provided that any of her liaisons, unlike her husbands, were kept secret.

The relationship between Alicia and Eric had been kept between themselves until Emma had walked innocently into the situation. At the age of fourteen, when, frightened by a severe thunderstorm, she ran to her mother's room for comfort, she encountered the Major closing the bedroom door on his way out.

Eric put his finger to his lips, indicating silence, and then quietly left.

Emma, shocked, went back to her own room, deciding it was something she would need to think about. Since she loved her mother the secret remained with her.

***

The crossing was not as easy in the dark, as it would have been in daylight. It was possible only one mile downstream. Though not a natural ford, a bank had appeared created by the effect of a storm just ten days ago. Two trees had fallen, nearly damming the river. Debris had built up behind the tree trunks, and, although there was a gap between them allowing the water to race through, the gap was easily bridged, thus permitting the men to cross.

The party managed though, as Martin observed, they may not find it in place if they decided to return this way. They linked up with Aaron Jackman and his men, after an hour of careful progress through the woods.

"The big house has a party going on with what looks like most of the society of the country present.

"We have contacted the slaves in their quarters. They are keeping quiet until they hear gunfire. Then they will break out. My scouts have identified the Colonel, as well as Major Strauss, and among others, at least one Georgia politician. My suggestion is to surround the house and move in, nice and quietly."

"I agree. If we keep it quiet we can then work on the problem of the army afterwards. Otherwise we could find ourselves barricaded in the house going nowhere.

The combined force of Marines and woodsmen moved out to surround the house which was lighting up the night with lights and music. Aaron retrieved his uniform from his bag and climbed into it. Martin did not realise until Aaron pointed it out, that the uniform was an army uniform, rather than the more familiar militia garb Aaron had once worn.

The flag produced was a National Flag, the stars and stripes. Martin raised an eyebrow but said nothing. Aaron said, "I was inducted into the US army, after I returned to Wilmington, North Carolina. The Governor wrote to the President about Harding. He has approved this action and even turned a blind eye to your presence. He expects the war will end by December this year, and he accepts the fact that it is in the interest of both nations to stop this man."

Martin suggested that he command the attack from the rear while Aaron went into the front. When the men were deployed, Aaron walked up the steps onto the front veranda. Several people looked at him curiously as he stepped through the front door and stopped, facing the interior. He turned back to the people on the veranda. He spoke quietly, but all heard what he said.

"I am Major Aaron Jackman of the United States Army. This house, and you, are all under arrest." He nodded at the surrounding area. At his signal, armed men appeared from the darkness.

He turned and walked into the house toward the sound of music and dancing.

He appeared at the doors of the ballroom, wearing his hat, with sword and pistol at his side and his rifle in his arms. While he stood there people noticed him and silence descended on the room in stages. A burst of laughter from the group of men beside the garden doors was suddenly cut off as the Major's presence made itself felt.

The music stopped at a signal from the Colonel who stepped forward to face the Major. "How dare you interrupt my guests in this rude manner."

The Major smiled at this, which did not endear him to the man before him. The Colonel opened his mouth to say more, but he was checked by the raised hand of the Major.

"Sir, the last time I was here I was a slave, having been kidnapped, along with the rest of the passengers on the ship bringing me to my home in Wilmington, North Carolina. One of your privateers pirated the American ship I was on and delivered all the passengers and crew here to this illegal haven on United States soil. I am placing you under arrest for the offences of piracy, murder, and kidnap.

The Colonel's face paled. "How dare you! Major Strauss, remove this impudent upstart."

Eric Strauss stepped forward. Behind him stood a rifleman accompanied by Martin and several other riflemen who gathered the guests together, herding them into the centre of the ballroom.

Two men came forward and seized the Colonel each taking an arm and swiftly lashing his wrists together behind his back.

Aaron spoke to the German soldier. "Major, if you call your men to stack their weapons and come forward, it will save unnecessary bloodshed. The slaves have already been released and people have already departed to retrieve the slaves at the mines."

The German soldier shrugged. "Very well." He turned and made his way out of the doors to the garden followed by Major Bristow and four men.

Harrison Benson stepped out of the gathering of people. "I am Harrison Benson."

"I know!" Aaron said. "Your reputation precedes you, Councillor. Since you are not on a diplomatic mission, I presume you are here on some private matter."

"Sir, I must formally protest at you cavalier manner in dealing with the Colonel."

"Mr. Benson, I do not give a damn what you have to say in this matter. I represent the President of the United States of America. In my book what he says goes. Do you understand, sir?" He skewered Benson with a look that would have stripped paint.

Benson decided that this could turn nasty and beat a hasty retreat, back into the anonymity of the crowd.

Major Strauss had been keeping his eye on the situation for the past months. His reaction was to cooperate with the raiding troops and see the Colonel hanged. It was however Alicia who concerned him more at the moment. Her safety was paramount. Having ordered the remaining troops to stack their arms, and remain in their quarters, he returned to the house with Bristow to speak with Aaron.

"You see the lady was sold to the Colonel by her guardian. She has taken no part in his activities.

"Captain Forest-Bowers, I understand you are in command of this expedition, and I am making no plea on my own behalf. But on behalf of Alicia Harding and her children, I do wish to point out that she has never had anything to do with her husband's activities. In fact her situation has been one of estrangement for the past fourteen years. Her appearances have been demanded on this sort of occasion. Since the birth of her daughter, it seems that Ross Harding only had use for her as a mother to his children. Since the doctor declared that she could no longer give birth, the Colonel ignored her as a woman and concentrated on his own stable of mistresses."

Martin looked at the German soldier. "And what is /was your position here?"

"I trained troops, and in the fifteen years I have been here, that is all I have ever done. Where I have been asked for advice on tactics I have always been forthcoming, but I was employed as a training officer and that is the function I have performed."

"Where are the balance of the troops and how many are there?"

Strauss smiled grimly. "Will you be punishing them?"

"Depends on if they resist, or not. If they resist, what happens, happens. If they do as they are told they can return to their homes, and accept the fact that they are settlers of the United States, rather than the Colonel's ill-fated kingdom."

Strauss thought about what Martin had said. He looked Martin in the eye and made his decision. "Let us go down to the river. I'll see what can be done. There are one or two who don't like me much, but I think the others will agree."

Martin called Bristow, "Get six men, riders and bring extra horses for the Major and me."

The small party rode down to the river, where Major Strauss called out to the men grouped behind the stockade along the river bank. "Captain Williams."

A tall man detached himself from the group and walked over.

"Don't you trust us, Major? This is your.......Who the hell is that?"

Major Strauss spoke quietly, "Captain, the Colonel had been arrested by United States soldiers. He is no longer in command of the force here or, apparently, the dream of an independent country here in the wilderness. The Representatives of the Government have stated that any people who have established settlement here will be permitted to register their lands as a part of the nation. This land, apparently, is part of the land purchased from France by the American Government, and therefore was not open to annexation as the Colonel has stated. I mention this because US soldiers are already established at the house.

"One more thing, Captain. The released prisoners, used as slaves, are not happy. If your men were considering dispersing, I suggest the sooner the better. If any have unwilling slaves on their homesteads, in their own interests they should return them here promptly."

Captain Williams was looking thoughtful. "I guess I need to have a word with my men. Mostly they are landowners, but I need to ask them."

The Major nodded his head. "I understand, Captain. We will be at the house, on the veranda, when you have discussed the matter. I do advise you to come unarmed or with a white flag. Any alternate might be misunderstood."

***

There was a sober group meeting in the house later that night. Martin took a back seat as the issues were decidedly local. The table was big enough to seat the number of people around it. The meeting was chaired by Aaron Jackman, with the Carolina politician seated beside him. This was a pragmatic decision and added a grain of authenticity to the group.

The Colonel's lady was present, seated beside Major Strauss. The group was brought to order with the appearance of Captain Williams.

He stood just inside the door waiting.

It was Major Strauss who asked the question. "Well, Captain. What do you have to say?"

The captain smiled grimly. "Well, sir, most of the boys agreed with your suggestion right off. The others have decided to head for Texas. That would be about fifty of the unmarried men. They are being supervised by my Lieutenants and Sergeants at present. Provided the arrangement you suggested is a serious offer, my men will supervise the departure of the westbound party.

There was silence as the group began to realise the enormity of the task before them.

Chapter ten

The Race

News of Napoleon's removal and banishment to Elba had led to a strange situation. Though, now an established situation, there was still conflict with rogue elements of the French navy. Many of the ships had dropped out of sight.

With the last days of the conflict with America over, the two British ships were once more returning to Britain. To Martin's surprise he had the pleasure of Julia Savage's company for the voyage, a situation which had the wholehearted approval of Lieutenant Harris, on HMS Hera.

David, her Cherokee companion, had returned to Halifax with the schooner, plus a negotiated cargo of cotton which it was now legal to acquire.

Julia accepted the offer to travel with HMS Vixen and made a hurried tour of the Charleston shops to collect a suitable wardrobe of clothing to replace her buckskins.

For the crews of both ships the journey ahead of them was welcome. The coast of America seemed far distant. Fighting a country that shared a common heritage and language had never seemed right somehow. McLean observed to Godden, "I saw three of our people in Charleston. I said naught because they were dressed better than I had ever seen them in Plymouth."

"Wuz they deserters then?" Godden asked belligerently. Godden did not like deserters.

"I didn't ask, you great lummox. All I know is that they wuz there." McLean threw his hands up at his friend's pugnacious attitude. "Why, Lemuel, my lad, how the devil would I know. I didn't ask, nor did I want to know. I see no sense in rattling cages, because, my son, like you, I've got a few skeletons in my cupboard that I would rather not disturb."

"That business of the Colonel was odd, d'ye think?" Godden changed the subject. A small shiver ran up his spine when he recalled the reason he was here and alive. "What does yew reckon, McLean?" He referred to the fact that the Colonel had escaped on the journey back to Charleston.

McLean paused from frapping the bitter end of the sheet he was tidying. "I think the Colonel realised he would hang, and decided to commit suicide." He turned back and resumed his work on the rope-end.

"But he didn't kill hisself! Like he tied himself to a tree, then used himself as target practice? You call that suicide?"

McLean shrugged. "Short of eating dirt how else could he do it? Bang his head against a tree? He could not run, not with everyone on edge knowing there were savages trailing us near the whole way back. I think he knew what them savages would do. He decided he couldn't face being topped in front of his own kind. Nobody expected him to just walk out into certain death. We was all watching for them coming in, not the other way round. By the time we knew he was gone it was already too late. You found him remember?"

Godden shrugged. "They made sure of it I must say." He recalled the sight of the naked man, disfigured, his torso punctured by dozens of cuts and stab wounds, his breath a faint hiss, still alive but begging for release. Godden had not hesitated, his knife mercifully closing the account for the Colonel. He had said nothing, allowing the others to believe he had found the man already dead. McLean knew though. He was the second person there. He had touched the still warm body as they cut him down. He had looked at Godden and nodded his head in approval. It was another secret shared between them.

As Godden turned to leave McLean at his work, he thought that was something he had not shared with his friend. As McLean had pointed out, there were things in his past he would rather not bring out in public. He was only now beginning to get accustomed to being treated with trust and respect. It was an odd feeling for someone like him, but somehow comforting to know that, in a fight, the entire crew was on his side. He and his mate, McLean were here in the ship because the alternative had been rotting in jail, or transportation. During his early years, before he fell in with McLean, life had been sustainable only by his careful poaching of the landowner's birds and deer. He felt no guilt for that part of his past. He had quickly come to the opinion that wild animals belonged to everyone, and putting 'Sir' in front of your name did not make you into a divine person. On the estate lands that he had roamed, the owner tended to shoot poachers and claim it was an accident. In private it was his boast that he was culling the herd.

Godden smiled grimly to himself. He didn't boast any more. Godden had seen to that himself. Sir Peregrine had a habit of looking over the 'fillies' in the stables. That was the way he described it to his chums. Lining up all the young women on the estate at the harvest party he threw to celebrate the gathering in of the crops, he insisted all the people of the estate attended. There was always a parade of the young men and young women, who would dance in a circle, girls in the inner and men in the outer. Sir Peregrine would join in and select, at that time, the best of the bunch, to come and work at the castle.

When he entertained his friends, he would indicate his own preference and allow his friend to make free with the others. There was nothing said of this practice. If a girl came home pregnant, they were blessed with noble blood in the family and perhaps a small purse to sooth her parents protests.

Unfortunately for Sir Peregrine, he chose Godden's fancy, and her subsequent degradation led to her taking her own life.

Within a week of her burial, Sir Peregrine had a riding accident leaving him paralyzed from the neck down, when his horse shied at a difficult fence. The horse survived.

Sir Peregrine had enough time to realise that he had been hurt. His last memory was of Godden's face and voice. "Just to let you know, sir, my name is Godden. You murdered my intended bride, Alice, after you and your friends had raped and abused her. I arranged this little accident. I'm happy to let you know, by doing what you did, you killed yourself." The face looked up at the sound of voices and horses. "That will be your friends coming to rescue you and care for you. Your death will be a shock, until they decided how best they can steal your possessions.

"I see you are thinking, 'I am not dead and I will tell all to my friends. They will hunt Godden down'. They won't, because you'll tell them nothing, because you are dead. Go sleep in hell." Godden had then lifted Sir Peregrine's head sharply, saying, "Look!" The neck broke and Peregrine was dead.

Godden had let it drop with a thud to the grass, and stood up to greet the riders approaching.

"Who rattled your cage?" McLean's voice brought him back to earth, or rather the deck of the man of war, as he moved off.

"What do you mean?" Godden retorted. "I am perfectly well and just studying how to get my revenge for being hosed down this morning, while they were skylarking with the hosepipes."

"I already planned how we could do that."

"I thought I could find a better way. But maybe not, we'll go with your way this time."

As Godden walked off, McLean shook his head. As a partner, Godden was second to none, but he sometimes thought......?" Shaking his head, he continued tidying up the rats tails in the lower rigging wherever he found them.

***

The call for Julia had been contained in a message received upon their return to Charleston. The news of the end of the war with America arrived too late to prevent the final battle. New Orleans had been won and lost, while Martin collected his repaired ships preparatory to his return to England. The event actually took place after the war was officially over. Neither of the combatants had been aware of this as the news took time to arrive from Europe, where the peace documents had been signed. The message for Julia had followed the news of the end of the war. It had found her in Charleston, rather than Halifax through the good offices of her own staff in Canada. The schooner carrying the message was still in Charleston when the British party arrived.

Martin completed the letter he had written to Jennifer with a flourish. He read what he had said and signed it. 'Forever, Martin'.

***

Two days out from Charleston and the wide Atlantic before them. He stood and stretched, feeling the healing bruises and scratches from the long trek through the forest from the Colonel's land to Charleston. Thinking of it, made him recall the look on the face of Harrison Benson when he had realised that he would be returned to Charleston under guard and on foot. The indignity of it all had, in the beginning, had its effect. But he had to admit, by the time they saw Charleston ahead of them, the politician was slimmer, and fitter, and ready to talk his way out of trouble. By the time Martin was ready to sail, the politician was on the quayside to thank him and wish him farewell. Martin smiled grimly, still astonished at the resourcefulness of the man, and his ability to turn defeat into advantage.

The fact that the war with America was over was a relief. But Martin was still aware that there could be American ships not yet informed of the peace treaty between the two countries. In addition, the broad waters of the Atlantic Ocean could well hide rogue French ships waiting to ambush any unwary travellers. Though hostilities had ceased, there would be no relaxation of the watch that was always kept at sea. He donned his boat cloak and hat before going on deck to smell the wind and walk the deck. He recalled his captain in the early days of his career, 'Always make sure the people see you on a regular basis. It reminds them of their place in the scheme of things, and, under fire, proves that we share the risks of war, regardless of rank.'

Martin was thinking of those words as he walked the deck.

The sun appeared and with it Julia Savage, dressed now properly in bonnet and gown. A chair had been set out for her, but she ignored it and strode over to Martin. "May I join you,

Captain, please tell me if I intrude, though I need to stretch my legs, if that is agreeable to you"

Martin bowed and smiled, "Captain Savage, as a colleague you are welcome, and as a friend, doubly so. Will you take my arm and we can walk in harmony."

Julia laughed out loud. "You are outrageous, Captain. I will report you to Lady Forest-Bowers as soon as we arrive." She took his arm and together they walked the deck in the sunshine.

As they came abreast of the midshipman of the watch, Martin said, "Mr. Woods, signal Hera. Request the presence of Mr. Harris to dine if it is convenient." He glanced around and aloft at the weather signs. "I anticipate the weather will hold this dry spell for a little longer.

Julia did her own inspection of the sky and the sea about them, "I believe you are correct, sir. Though in this season we can encounter mist in morning and evening, an effect of the Gulf Stream I am told."

"As you say, Captain. With your experience of these waters, I am pleased to agree."

A hail from the masthead reminded them both that the ship was still in dangerous waters.

"Sail ho! Approaching on our forward port quarter. Looks like a sloop."

Lieutenant Brooks thrust Midshipman Woods forward with the telescope. "Hop aloft, James, and tell us what you see."

Slinging the strap over his shoulder, James Woods raced up the rigging to the masthead, where he braced himself and lined up the telescope on the approaching sail.

He reported swiftly, "It is the Levant from Commodore Ramos's squadron. She is flying the signal, 'Enemy in sight, sir'."

Brooks looked at the captain, and then called Woods down. Turning to the Master he said, "Let us put on sail, Mr. Watson. It looks as if our friends might be in trouble."

Martin was at the rail when the hands were called and Julia had seated herself in the chair provided, waiting until the sails were set before going below to change. Their consort,

Hera, was crowding on sail also, and moving ahead of the Vixen closing the distance to the Levant.

Turning to speak to Julia, Martin realised she had already gone below, the crew having increased the sail as ordered. She reappeared on deck as Martin spoke with Brooks. She was wearing her buckskins once more and carried her sword belt and scabbard and sword, ready to strap it on.

Martin smiled as she approached. "Ready for action, I see. Though it will be a while yet, I fear. "Faintly, the sound of guns could now be heard, though the ships firing were still out of sight, ahead of the racing ships. The Levant and the Hera were closing fast, the schooner flying under a cloud of sail and now well ahead of the slower frigate. The Vixen was logging between twelve and thirteen knots, but would never catch the schooner on this tack.

The Levant had reversed her course and swiftly, also out-sailed the Vixen, racing to catch the Hera, and return to the battle.

The sound of the guns was more apparent now, a combination of heavy metal and the lighter crack of the smaller guns involved.

There now appeared what, at first they thought to be just clouds, was actually mist and gunsmoke from the many guns firing. The fresh breeze driving Martin's two ships was beginning to rip the choking clouds apart. Ships could be seen as brief shadows appearing and disappearing in the man-made fog. Hera was now closest to the battle.

Once more, James Woods, Midshipman raced up the rigging to read the signals hoisted by the schooner.

"Hera has opened fire!" The excited voice of Midshipman James Woods called from the maintop. She is signalling enemy in sight, numbers four!"

Martin looked at Brooks. "It will be another half hour before we get close enough to make a difference here. Clear for action." He looked at the sea and then the sky. "Mr. Watson! What say you? Will this wind hold?"

The Master was studying the clouds, noting the wisp of 'mare's tails' high above against the blue. "Aye, sir. We are bringing the wind, and I believe it will probably freshen through the day."

Martin nodded. It was what he had decided himself. "Try the royals, Mr. Brooks. We will have time to take them in before we are committed to action."

"Aye, aye. Sir." Brooks turned to the Bo'sun. "Royals aloft."

Chapter eleven

Plunder

They took in sail as they reached the action, the smoke clearing as the breeze freshened. Sao Paulo and Lisboa were engaged with three French ships. There was a merchantman, heavily laden with her foremast in ruins and her men trying to clear the raffle of broken gear on her deck.

A two-deck sixty-four gun ship was making a lot of noise with little effect on the other side of the merchantman. The Porto 38, and Faro 44, were both engaged, standing off, and causing her serious trouble. The other French frigate had turned to engage Hera and the sloop Levant. She was concentrating on the Hera, the popguns of the Levant making little impression on the heavy frigate opposing them.

With guns run out Vixen entered the action. The battle flags, fluttering in the wind of her passage, standing out bravely as she engaged the frigate involved with Hera. The French ship was late turning to meet the new threat. She was only half way round to present her broadside when the Vixen fired her starboard guns in a single salvo, causing the British frigate to roll to port in response.

The effect was devastating for the Frenchman. Her bow received the full impact of the four carronades, from a range that was ideal for the best effect, from the ship-smashing guns. The remainder of the salvo reduced the starboard main deck of the Frenchman to utter confusion, her surviving guns fired, seemingly at random, were late to respond. Though they created some damage to Vixen, it was all superficial. Martin was aware of the cries of the wounded on his own deck. But the damage his ship had suffered was minor compared with the damage to the French ship. As he sailed past the stern of the Frenchman, her mizzen mast toppled, snapping sheets and ripping the shrouds from her shattered side. He noticed her name, Hirondelle, before the sailcloth from the falling mast dropped and obscured it On Vixen the gun crews were reloading and running out their guns, while the dead and wounded were being cared for.

Ahead, the 4th rate ship of the line, her 64 guns ranged along two decks, showing 32 guns in each broadside, was not making much impression on the two Portuguese frigates. Seeing that they were holding their own, he turned his attention to the third frigate engaging Sao Paulo and Lisboa. She was in process of moving to cross the stern of the Lisboa. Martin decided that this could cause problems, as the Portuguese captain seemed unaware of this danger. He realised that there was room for his own ship to intercede and cross the Frenchman's bow. As they approached, the French captain saw Vixen bearing down on him, and guessed what was about to happen. He made the decision which cost him his ship and his life. He called to turn to starboard, presenting his broadside to the British frigate. Martin turned to port, bringing his own broadside into line with the turning French ship. Martin called, "Starboard broadside, Fire!"

For the second time that morning, before the French ship could fire her own guns, Vixen's guns fired a full salvo, into the portside of her opponent, the cannonballs smashing into the French ship, even as the order to fire her own guns was being given. Both the quarterdeck, and after end of the main-deck, took the brunt of the carronades' impact. The swathe of pistol balls, from the grapeshot fired from one of the carronades, cleared the officers and men standing there, and shattered the ship's wheel causing the head of the ship to fall away to windward, sending fire, from those guns which could still fire, astray. One shot severed the anchor chain from the Vixen's starboard anchor, and punched a hole through to the chain locker forward.

Swift action by the Bo'sun could not prevent the lashings securing the anchor from parting, and the anchor was lost.

So far, the Vixen had borne a charmed life, four men lost, killed, eight wounded, mainly by splinters, the hole in the chain locker and one gun dismounted.

Lieutenant Brooks pointed out that the French 64 was still in action and both the Portuguese frigates were beginning to show signs of damage. Their last opponent was still sailing in circles as the crew attempted to repair her steering. The loss of many of the officers was not helping.

Martin nodded to Brooks and ordered him to set course for the battle between the Porto and Faro, and the French 64. The arrival of the Vixen on the scene caused the captain of the Martinique problems. She had been in the West Indies for the past eight years. Though the crew were trained, they were mainly locally recruited, as the original crew had suffered from the heat and disease of the station. Others had been accused of being royalists and had been executed. He himself had been the sailing master, and, as the only professional officer left on board, had inherited the captaincy. A job he had neither aspired to nor wanted. Now here he was battling for his life against ships from finest navy in Europe. All because he had been unfortunate enough to capture pirates who had, in turn, captured a Spanish bullion ship loaded with gold and silver.

It was to go to the Emperor of course, though Spain was technically friendly with France. The treasure, having been recovered from pirates, belonged to the finders. He cursed himself more than any other. He could have hidden the loot and come back for it later. Then he would not have been in this stupid position now. The cabin shuddered as the guns fired. Thank goodness for his first lieutenant.

The American, Michael Foster, had been a genuine asset ever since he had encountered him in St Pierre on the island. He was big and tough and hated the English. He had escaped from a prison in Grenada, where he had been held on a charge of piracy. A former captain of his own warship, turned pirate, he had been ready to serve in a warship again. The captain rose to his feet with a sigh. He could not stay here when a battle was outside to be won. Jean Partout, captain in the French Navy, straightened his hat and stepped out through the lobby and onto the main deck of his ship.

On deck, Jean saw immediately that he had problems. Apart from the fact that he only had men to man the guns on one side of the ship, the pumps had to be manned all the time now, as the ship leaked badly from badly maintained hull timbers. Money that should have been used for the purpose had gone elsewhere. Martinique had never been expected to cross the Atlantic again. This bloody treasure ship had made the Governor send her on this impossible voyage, despite Portet's efforts to make it clear that the ship could not stand up to the weather, let alone enemy gunfire. He shrugged. He was here now. He had to make the best of it.

Twenty-six guns fired, causing him to jump. He had not heard the orders.

Seeing him on deck, Lieutenant Foster approached and saluted. "We are holding them off, sir, but that is always the worst thing we can do in these circumstances. I think we will be forced to surrender if we stay.

"Surrender?" Portet was surprised.

Foster nodded to the two ships off to one side. The Portuguese flag flew above the French, and the guns were silent on that side. Elsewhere the other Portuguese ship had gone to the aid of the Hera and Levant. A boarding party was even now climbing to the deck of cargo ship with the treasure on board. The two frigates in the immediate vicinity were showing no signs of letting up their attack, despite the noble efforts of the gunners. A third had now appeared on the other side of the Martinique. As he watched in horror, it swung across the stern of his ship. The side disappeared in a cloud of smoke as the frigate opened fire. The ship beneath him shivered at the impact of the 32 pounder and 24 pounder guns. He could hear the crashing and shattering noise of the cannon balls destroying the deck below. With a start, he realised that, had he not come on deck, he would probably be dead by now.

Foster reported, "We are keeping them busy. But I'm worried about the water in the bilges. It is rising now, despite the pumps. I think we have some blockages that cause them to be less effective than they should be. The ship shuddered again as they spoke together.

Foster looked at his captain. He had done well to keep the ship afloat so far. But he could feel from the way the ship was sitting in the water that her time was limited.

The captain felt the same way. Making his mind up, he turned to Foster. "We have lost, Mr. Foster. You know that, and I do. I think it is time we saved as many as we can. Drop the colours."

There were tears in his eyes as he gave the order. Foster carefully acknowledged the order and went to haul down the Tricolour personally. Then, raising his voice, he called "All guns, cease fire. Bo'sun, get a new crew to the pumps. Bring the wounded up on deck."

He turned to the Midshipman on duty. "Get a crew and take the sea-boat. Gather the other boats and bring them alongside."

As the Midshipman ran off he hoped that the boats, they had cast adrift at the beginning of the action, had not drifted too far away. He had the feeling that the ship would not remain afloat for too long.

***

Martin had come to the same conclusion. Mr. Brooks, have the boats gathered. I do not like the look of that ship Signal the Hera and the Levant to join us. We may need them to go alongside to save the crew." Looking at the waterline of the 64, he could see she was definitely sinking.

Sao Paulo swept up alongside Vixen. The Flag Lieutenant called across. "Could Captain Forest-Bowers join the Commodore, please?"

Martin looked at Brooks "It seems you will have to manage on your own just now."

"Of course, sir. Captain's gig, Bo'sun."

***

On the Portuguese flagship, Martin was piped aboard with full honours, greeted by smiling faces all round. Well known to the crew of the Sao Paulo from their past mutual association, he had always been made welcome on board the Portuguese vessel.

In the great cabin of the ship, Commodore Antonio Ramos rose to his feet to embrace his friend. "Martin, it has happened again. You appear to be a magnet for treasure."

"Whatever are you talking about, man. What treasure?"

"You did not know? That merchantman, wallowing about without a foremast, is carrying treasure from the colonies."

Martin shook his head sadly. "You do realise, Antonio, the Spanish are the only source of treasure at this time and they are our allies. If that is their treasure, we cannot keep it."

"It is you who does not understand. These Frenchman took the treasure from the Spanish. It is now legitimate spoils of war, and, under the law, the treasure belongs to the people involved in liberating it from the French."

Martin shrugged. "Perhaps you are right. But I caution you, the Government may not agree with you."

"What would we do if the treasure ship sank?" Antonio chuckled at the thought.

Martin grinned and said, "They will take it out of your pay, week by week. It would mean you would have to live for the next 150 years and serve all that time too. So perhaps we would be better taking it home and seeing what they decide to do with it. After all, the Spanish have changed sides more than once already in this war. Perhaps they are enemies already. In which case your wishes may be granted. After all, since they trans-shipped the cargo, they must have taken the ship some time ago. I seriously wonder whether they actually knew if they were at war at the time. My guess would be that it is for that reason they trans-shipped the cargo in the first place, with apparently no Spanish prisoners to embarrass them.

"I recommend your interrogators find out just how the cargo came into their hands. By the way, what form does the cargo take, bullion, silver and gold ingots, or perhaps precious stones?"

The Commodore rose to his feet. "Come. See what we have. Then we will speak to the captain of the merchantman." He led the way through to the sleeping cabin, separated from the day cabin by a removable wooden screen.

On a pair of trestles stood a large trunk. The lid was closed but not locked. Ramos walked over and flung the lid back.

Martin gasped. The light through the stern windows turned the contents of the trunk to a container of vibrant colour. Dancing reflections filled the cabin as the ship rose and fell. The sunlight, now breaking through the earlier clouds, created reflected patterns of light moving up and down the bulkheads with the motion of the ship.

With a casual sweep of his palm, the Commodore pushed the layer of jewels aside to reveal crafted ornaments, and small ingots of gold and silver, scattered randomly through the contents of the trunk. He picked up a silver coin and tossed it to Martin.

He caught it and studied it. "This is Portuguese!" Martin commented.

The Commodore tensed suddenly and pulled a piece out of the trunk. In a suddenly grim voice, he said, "This came from the Church of the little Saints, in Maceio, Brazil." He lifted a short, heavy gold cross crucifix with the ivory figure of Christ. He turned the 30 centimetre tall cross around and showed Martin the writing across the back. 'Fra Francisco Ramos'

Martin and Antonio sat at the Commodore's table, the cross between them.

"My cousin placed that cross on the high altar of the Church of the little Saints, when he became the priest for the region. As far as I know he is still there, but this.".... He took the cross in his hand, gripping it, his knuckles white with the strength of his grip. "This tells me I may never see him again." He sighed. "It also tells me that these Frenchmen have raided Brazil. I shudder to think of the damage they may have created, but this is sacrilege. There are other things there from churches I cannot identify. I fear these people we have captured, have questions to answer."

With a grave face, he called for the captured ship's captain to be brought through for interrogation.

The man in front of them was at ease with a small smile on his face. He glanced at the crucifix on the table. "You have good taste, gentlemen. It is high value gold and ivory, carved by a master, I think. Worth much money, I believe."

Martin put his hand on his friend's arm, feeling the tension at the manner of the man in front of them. "How did you come by this piece?" He said quietly.

The Frenchman smiled and said, "We called in for water at this little town on the Brazilian coast. The men landed with the barrels and a pretty girl appeared. One of the men started to chase her. It was fun, you know? Then suddenly it was serious. This priest appeared and there were words exchanged. You know how it is. Someone had shouted, 'We are at war with Portugal. We can take what we want." He grabbed the girl by the hair and dragged her off to the nearest house. The priest interfered." The man shrugged.

In a controlled voice the Commodore said, "And then?"

"A knife for the priest. they stripped and used the girl. And then went seeking more. Suddenly the place was in flames. People were screaming and dying." The man seemed to get satisfaction out of the words he was saying. His final comment was, "C'est la guerre." The shoulders lifted in a Gallic shrug, apparently explained, and excused all.

In the silence that followed the man's words, Martin thought to himself, *'That comment had excused the actions of followers of Napoleon, since the first declaration of war.'*

Seeing the controlled anger in his friend's face, Martin dismissed the French captain, determined to speak with him again at another time.

Chapter twelve

Discretion

Lieutenant Santos of the Sao Paulo admired Captain Forest-Bowers. When Martin approached him, he was quick to make available the most cooperative of the French prisoners in his charge. On deck, the Commodore was walking out his fury, pacing back and forth on the quarterdeck, simmering down. His anger at the casual description of the rape of his cousin's parish in Brazil was seriously disturbing. This was a man with a cool head, normally, in the most trying of conditions.

Meanwhile, below deck Martin was beginning to make sense of the situation leading up to the action they had just now concluded.

The man, he was interviewing, was happy to speak frankly to someone who would listen. He was a conscript pressed into service from Martinique. When the French squadron had arrived they were escorting the Spanish treasure ship which had rounded the Horn, sustaining damage and in need of repair before completing its voyage to Spain.

The friendly relations enjoyed between the French commander and the Spanish captain were the result of an arrangement they had made, to transfer the treasure to another ship and then witness the loss of the treasure ship for the benefit of witnesses. The treasure would be divided between the two men, who had promised that the crews would be taken care of in the share-out. Charles Monet was not a fool. Having heard the story, he found himself being brought in to supervise the division, his post in Martinique having been chief teller at the central bank. The kidnapping of himself and several other key personnel had been calculated to muddy the waters in the small community. Rumours were circulated that they had emptied the till and run, leaving families and responsibilities behind.

Speaking to Martin, he made it clear that he was grateful that they had been captured by the allies. "I expected to be killed as soon as I was no longer needed. The others from the Island were either working the rigging or swabbing the decks. I think that they had some chance of surviving. But, in my case, I was aware that I knew far too much to be allowed to live." Monet sat back waiting to learn his fate.

Martin thought about the man's story. It was supported by the fact that the treasure had been trans-shipped in the first place. Why else would they go to the trouble? Disguise the origin, and even if caught, it could be declared as plunder taken from pirates.

It was also supported by the fact that the men had destroyed the Brazilian port of Maceio, without any suggestion of punishment, and, judging from the content of the captain's chest, the officers' active participation.

The interview had been conducted in English, a language that Monet spoke well. Martin addressed him in French. "What would you like to happen now?"

Monet looked up in astonishment. It was not usual to find an Englishman who spoke such fluent French. "Pardon me, but what do you mean with your question? I am your prisoner. I must do whatever you decide." He sat back unsure what Martin meant.

Martin smiled, well aware of Monet's bewilderment. "We are sailing across the Atlantic to European waters. I presume your family is in Martinique. Do you wish to return to them?"

"Ah, I understand. No. I have no family in Martinique. My wife, 'God rest her soul'." He crossed himself, "Died of fever just one month after we arrived. Fort-de-France was an unhappy place for me. I did not really enjoy living there."

He hastened to explain. "The bank in Amiens had asked for volunteers to go to the West Indies. My wife and I, we were uncomfortable with the new regime." He shrugged, "Poor Charlotte suffered during the voyage. When the fever came she had not recovered from her sickness on her journey."

"I take it you are not altogether in agreement with the present government in France?"

"I watched the whole affair as a young man. I lived in Paris, and the activities of the Sans-Culottes disgusted me. My parents sent me to stay with my uncle in his shop in Amiens. They did not survive the unrest which followed within just a few weeks. However well the Army fared, when Napoleon took command, it did not improve the lot of the ordinary people of France.

"The answer to your question is 'no'. I am not in agreement. Nor do I think it has bettered the lot of the people of the country." He sat back.

Martin looked at the man in front of him, "Would you be happy to serve the allies? As you have seen, several of your countrymen serve on these ships, either because they are Royalists, or they have been targeted by people they thought were friends. It is a matter of either taking a positive part in the war, or sitting in a prison camp until the war is over."

***

In the great cabin, a less disturbed Commodore Ramos listened to what Martin had to say.

"You believe this man?" He said eventually.

"I think I do. Yes, I do. He has nothing really to gain from lies at this time. Perhaps someone that Alouette, your wife, might find a use for?"

Antonio Ramos considered this comment before making his mind up. "I will transfer him to your ship. I think such matters are best left to those who understand them best." He smiled, "I trust that will be agreeable to you?"

Martin nodded and rose to leave. He was checked by the Commodore.

"In view of what you have discovered, I have decided that the plunder recovered will be regarded as spoils of war. Have you any objection to this?"

"None whatsoever, Commodore." Martin shook his friend's hand, and left the Portuguese flagship accompanied by Monet, the French prisoner.

***

Back on board Vixen, Martin passed Monet over to the purser, to assist him for the present, in the management of the ship's stores. The augmented flotilla, in company with the captured French ships, resumed their voyage to the English Channel and home. The lack of further conflict was welcome to the men who had been away for many months.

***

Because the ships had been reported off Falmouth, the news travelled to Portsmouth and specifically to Eastney. The household stirred at the news. Messages were sent to the Oxfordshire home of HMS Vixen's captain. So that, by the time the ships had moored in Portsmouth Harbour, the word had spread to all the interested parties who descended on London in time to greet Sir Martin and his friend Antonio.

Having posted up from Portsmouth, the two officers were greeted by their respective wives, who were waiting for the coach together. The carriages took them off to the house in Ovington Square, where preparations had been made to receive them. Alouette had just returned from a trip to Europe, an event of concern to Antonio, who had presumed that their marriage had marked the end to the dangerous part of her activities.

The Admiralty was their immediate destination, after they had refreshed their attire and themselves. This greeting was rather the reverse of Martin's first experience. The immediate respectful attention was flattering. When the two officers were ushered into the presence of Admiral Bowers, the tea tray was produced before they had been seated.

Remembering, Martin grinned. When the servant left the room he greeted his adoptive father warmly. The Admiral's appearance reflected Lady Jane's concern for him. Martin thought, for the first time, that he looked old. The sag to the once-square shoulders bore witness to the effort he put into his position in the Admiralty, and the toll it took of his health.

After the greetings had been exchanged, the Admiral spoke of the encounter with the French in the Atlantic, and the prizes and plunder taken. "The action took place while Napoleon was imprisoned in Elba, and this country was no longer at war with France. In the circumstances the attack on the Commodore's ships was an act of piracy, and all the people involved in such an act are subject to the death sentence. If, however, it is accepted that both parties acted in ignorance of the truce between the two countries, the outcome remains the same, except the prisoners and ships are treated as the spoils of war. The prizes and plunder remain a subject for the courts to decide. The prisoners would be returned to their own country."

Commodore Ramos answered immediately. "Sir, I signalled the news of the treaty and Napoleon's abdication, at the beginning of the action. The answer was a broadside from the sixty-four.

"When overcome, we found that the Admiral in command had been murdered, after a mutiny over the distribution of the treasure in the merchantman. If I may say at this point, the approach I made to the French ships had been carefully planned. The initial broadside was ineffective. I was prepared for treachery and able to avoid serious damage as a consequence. My ships were positioned to cover me and the lessons learned from my colleague about the importance of gunnery practice, gave me an advantage. All of my ships practice gunnery every day.

"I dispatched the sloop for assistance knowing that Martin was close behind me. I had been informed of his presence and already decided to wait for his flotilla and make the rest of the journey in company. The encounter with the French in the mist was unexpected.

"After the action I was made aware that some of the plunder we found had been taken from the Brazilian coast where they had called to collect water. From their own mouths, I heard that they murdered the entire population of the town and burned the houses. It was this, that convinced me that the men had become pirates and no longer served France."

The Admiral turned to Martin. "And how do you see things?"

"I have to agree with the Commodore, sir. The men were mostly not in uniform, and, though they fought under the flag of France, there was little about them of disciplined seamen, sir."

The Admiral sat back in his chair. "Gentlemen, enough. I am aware that you came up from Portsmouth overnight. I now suggest you return to your homes and await my call. This matter will be resolved, probably by compromise. Perhaps we will release the men and keep the booty." He smiled at this. "I will look forward to seeing you both this evening, I believe, at the entertainment and party that your ladies have prepared. Good Day to you both."

Martin and Antonio left the Admiralty a little dazed, both with the travelling and the words of the Admiral. "Home it is." Martin said, and called their carriage forward.

***

The celebration of their return was an affair confined to the two families. Antonio Ramos and Alouette, his wife, joined the combined Forest-Bowers in Knightsbridge, now becoming very much a part of fashionable London. Captain Giles Masters and his wife, Lady Isabella, were in attendance, and the Admiral pleased Lady Jane by being there also.

***

The uneasy peace between Britain and France survived until the escape of Napoleon from Elba. His return to France revealed the fragile nature of the interim administration. His progress through the country, gathering forces and influence, made it clear to the allies that a resounding victory was needed to halt the progress of the Little General.

The ships of the Portuguese flotilla were dispatched to the command of an Admiral selected by the interim government of Portugal. For Captain Ramos, a post at the Portuguese Embassy was created as Naval liaison Attaché, once more attached to the British Royal Navy.

Martin went back to sea as part of the blockade of the French ports used for Napoleon once more.

Chapter thirteen

Colonel Cormac O'Mara.

Colonel Cormac O'Mara had been waiting for some time for the return of Napoleon. Now that he was back, he could implement his own plans, to ensure his future in the soon-to-be peaceful, country of France. The Colonel had been employed in the French Service for many years now and he had decided that retirement, suitably rewarded of course, was the only option now. The one thing he was no longer sanguine about was the victory of Napoleon over the gathering European forces.

Cormac's position as officer in Napoleon's army had never been as comfortable as he would have liked. The Irish companies had been gathered from the runaways of the British Army, and the back streets of seaports throughout the conquered countries of Europe, plus troops recruited by agents in Ireland itself. The Colonel's command had been, up to now, a partial fiction to cover his operations as a spy. Despite his men always being counted as auxiliaries, whenever called upon to fight, they had acquitted themselves well. It had been a rude awakening when the Lieutenant General in charge of the auxiliaries ordered him to gather his troops and prepare them for a place in the line of battle.

The only reason Cormac had been in the barracks at that time was that he was broke once more. At least there he got meals and warm clothing. He had always regarded his post as honorary rather than actual. The General had noted that whenever the Irishmen had been called, their Colonel was always there to lead. They never broke under fire and they clearly would follow their Colonel wherever he led. Deciding he had a honed weapon at his disposal, instead of sitting in the reserves, or mingling with the enemy seeking information, the General gave his orders accordingly. Thus the Colonel was jogging along the road on this nag, his equipment jingling, destined with his men, to fight in the line.

He had ridden most of the day in deep thought. As evening approached, the lights of Calais showed up through the faint layer of mist between the road and the sea. A plan started to take shape. He straightened up in the saddle, easing his feet in the stirrups, and immediately felt better. He pulled his horse over to the roadside and allowed the companies of the third battalion to pass, each body of men following their company commander on horseback with the sergeants chivvying them at each flank. Eventually his Adjutant appeared, giving the marching men space, to allow the dust to settle a little before he came along.

Peter Mahon had been a close colleague of the Colonel's for the past twelve years. From different parts of Ireland, the two men had recognised a kinship immediately and they had worked together ever since. In certain places it was said, if you face one beware the other behind you. A warning people ignored at their peril. Both had saved the other's life on more than one occasion. Their empathy on the battlefield had saved the day in more than one battle.

"Peter, this is a dusty trail to follow, is it not?" The Colonel held out a flask to his friend, who took it gratefully.

After a swig of the brandy, Peter handed it back. "You've been cooking something up, I would guess. Something to do with a journey overseas to Cork, I'll be bound." He grinned, his teeth bared. His voice was soft and light for such a well-built man. "I have been watching and waiting, seeing the signs, wondering when you would be ready." He paused, head to one side. "I'm right, am I not?"

Cormac had turned his gaze to the sea. The waves were breaking white in a line along the shore less than a half-kilometre away. The murmur had been with them since they had set out from St Inglevert yesterday. The sounds had increased as they passed Cap Blanc Nez, Now with Coquelles behind them, the port city was here, and time was passing.

"Perhaps tonight!" He said tersely, spurring his horse away, leaving Peter Mahon to follow in his position at the rear of the column. "Attend!" He called to the marching men as he passed. "We are the Irish Rangers. Let the people know we are here." As he passed each of the companies they straightened up and the words of 'The West's Awake' could be heard from the bold singers in the column. It amazed him how the sound of a rebel song could make a column march in step and in tune. By the time he reached the head of the line the chant of the men was carrying them into the city, arms swinging, heads up, their Irish Colours aloft beside the Tricolours of France.

***

Later that evening, the two friends were standing watching the British ships blockading the port, cruising offshore beyond cannon shot, but only just. Every now and again one of the cannon from the fort would try the range. The mild weather made it possible to watch the fall of shot, sometimes close, but never quite close enough.

"It's a game they play!" Cormac sounded cynical.

"It could be lethal." Peter suggested.

"Never, Peter! The men in control don't even get near them. It might get dirt on their pretty uniforms."

Peter looked at the green jacket of his commander. The elbow patches and the frayed cuffs demonstrated the fact that Cormac O'Mara, Colonel or not, was a working soldier. The powder burns had marked his hands and face over the years. Peter had long decided that if he had to face the infantry and cavalry of the allied armies, there was no one he would rather have by his side.

He noticed his friend was watching the activity at sea with particular interest and turned to see what he was looking at.

A sloop with all her sail set had slipped between the blockading ships and was hell bent on reaching the harbour. A Royal Naval cutter was in pursuit but though it was pacing the sloop it was not able to close the gap.

Cormac muttered, "Now what will you do? If you fire a gun, unless the ball strikes the sloop, it will cost you the race. But, short of a mistake by the sloop, you've lost anyway?"

Peter said, "He will take the risk. The cutter ran off the wind slightly, to line up his forward gun. The sloop jinked and a dinghy dropped from her lee side, the sloop recovered and powered onward. The dinghy, with sails up, and heeling to the wind, made for the shallows between the beaches, west of the harbour entrance. Cormac had his small telescope out and trained on the cutter. He swung to see the sloop, but the press of sail obscured sight of the people in her. The dinghy was sailed by a grey-haired man and carried in addition two other figures, a man and a woman.

Back on the cutter the master made a bad decision, wavering between the dinghy and the sloop. The result was he got neither. The dinghy disappeared beyond the wall of the docks to the west. The fort fired a shot at the cutter which had sailed too close to the wind to avoid the risk of coming into range of the guns. She escaped by the skin of her teeth as the sloop sailed into Calais, shedding her sails as she passed the entrance.

"That, Peter, my friend, is how you smuggle agents into France.

"I thought it a little dramatic and rather obvious.

"So, where will you seek the spies?"

"I am guessing the sloop, the dinghy a diversion?" Peter was still unsure.

"The dinghy, I would say, based on that fact that there was a woman in the boat. The British use women sensibly as spies. Their success rate is high, and, in the event of capture, they can sometimes spread their legs and create an opportunity to escape. They are also quick witted and not pre-conditioned by service in the military." Cormac had begun walking toward the beach, "It is probably time for us to make contact.

Mystified, Peter followed Cormac over the dunes to the beach. The dinghy was drawn up with the oarsman seated with what Peter suddenly realised was a rifle in his arms. He looked like nobody, which meant he was dangerous. Peter said quietly, "Cormac, perhaps we should have a few of the lads with us here."

Cormac grinned cynically. "Much good that would do, that bastard at the boat is McLean. I know of him. I was in America when the Carolina business with the renegade Colonel

Harding and the land grab occurred. I learned about McLean. There, you can depend on it, Godden will be here too."

At Peter's mystified look Cormac smiled and stepped forward "I'll explain it to you when we get back to camp. Just keep your hands off your weapons, and we'll be as safe as in our houses. Trust me!"

The two men went down to the shore to meet the lady.

***

On the sloop Captain Antonio Ramos, of the Portuguese Royal Navy strode back and forth nervously, his stride and balance easily countering the lively manoeuvers of the small ship.

"Starboard broadside, standby, on the uproll. Fire!" The gun captains called, pulled and leapt back as the six pounder guns recoiled. The crash of guns, like the smoke, whipped away on the wind of their passage.

The midshipman at the wildly swinging masthead screamed, "A hit, a hit." After a pause he called, "Return fire from the battery." Then. "Falling short, sir. We winged the guard-boat."

Captain Martin Forest-Bowers strolled over to his friend, Antonio, "Alouette has two of the best protectors with her. They will not allow any harm to come to her, you will see. Also, I have known that lady to survive in situations where strong men quail. McLean and Godden are with her.

The sloop reversed course, swinging once more into the shoaling waters lying off the beach. Up aloft, the Midshipman had turned his attention forward and through his glass could see the tiny people on the beach ahead.

"Dinghy in sight, sir. It is putting off now, with two passengers."

The sloop sailed down to the dinghy during the next half hour. As they finally approached, taking far too long in Antonio's estimation, it seemed they were one man short. Alouette and McLean were present, the other passenger was dressed as Colonel of the Irish Brigade of the Napoleonic Army.

Antonio and Martin exchanged glances. Curious, the two
waited until the dinghy had been hooked and the occupants
brought aboard. "Your cabin, please, Captain?"

Lieutenant Pierce who commanded the sloop, led the
way. His man served wine and withdrew. The five stood
looking at each other, while McLean drank his wine in one
swig and said quietly, "I'll be outside, if I'm needed," and left
also.

The Colonel was introduced by Alouette to the others.
"Colonel Cormac O'Mara, of the Irish Brigade. Captain Sir
Martin Forest-Bowers, RN and Captain Antonio Ramos."

Cormac turned to Martin, "Your reputation precedes
you, sir. I was in America recently, and was told that you
carried a rifle and walked with your men; was that true?"

Martin smiled and nodded, "My feet still complain."

Cormac continued, "I contacted your lady here because
the Irish Brigade has been recalled to follow Bony once more.
Now make no mistake. I have no love for the English. But I
think this campaign is bad. Coming through France it was quite
obvious to me that the Emperor is not regarded as he once was.
He is no longer the 'Golden Warrior.' Generally, the people do
not want him back. The Old Guard are fanatic. The others don't
dare refuse. But I will say this. If Nosy doesn't defeat him,
wherever this battle is to be fought, then the people all over
Europe will suffer."

Alouette served more wine, and Martin asked the
question in both Antonio and his own minds, "Why are you
here?"

A slow smile spread over the Irishman's face, "I
wondered when we would get around to that." He was thinking
that these people were not quite the same as some of the
arrogant bastards he had dealt with in the past. The tall
Portugee was impassive. His face gave away nothing, innocent,
perhaps, but he was no fool. The other, Martin, was a different
matter. He was aware, and there was a look about him that said
to Cormac, 'watch your step!' "I came to tell you something
that I think you ought to know, to warn you. I have been
fighting the English most of my life and I make no excuse for
that. When I return to shore I can assure you I will be once

more fighting the English and their allies just as hard as ever. When this last battle is decided, those of my people who survive will be leaving Europe forever. I thought at one time I would remain here under Boney for the rest of my life, but it was not to be. Following him through the country these last weeks has convinced me his day is done. If he wins the next battle, Europe will be torn for the next twenty years."

He paused for a few moments, sad to say what he felt he must.

"I see now that the writing was on the wall when he was driven to abdicate in the first place. Whatever happens, Nosy must not let him win this battle; for the future of France, for Britain, for the world. It must end here. I know the lady you call Alouette." He nodded to her. "I contacted her to tell her myself; not some distant observation made by some dilettante politician but the opinion of a battle-hardened soldier who has lived through too much war to be deceived into betrayal with sweet words."

He turned to Martin. "I came here to tell you myself, at the lady's request. I will now take my leave, if you will be good enough to recall the dinghy."

Martin bowed, "Of course, sir. If you will permit me?" He drew forward a bottle of Irish whiskey and passed it over to the Colonel. "I believe there is a chill in the air."

He escorted the Colonel back to the ship side where the dinghy bobbed waiting. McLean took the oars.

Chapter fourteen

Skirmishes

As the two men on the beach watched the dinghy disappear back to the sloop once more, Cormac turned to Peter Mahon. He lifted the bottle of whiskey, "'Spoils of war'" He said with a grin. "Let's go and kill it between us." Both men turned back to the dunes behind them and made their way back to the camp.

The French spy who had watched the pair, rose to leave and report to his master in Calais.

The prick of the knife in his neck caused him to freeze. A soft Irish voice whispered in his ear, "You would not be impolite and leave without talking wit' the Colonel personally, now, would ya."

***

Inside the headquarters tent, the Colonel was seated at his desk. Peter Mahon stood to one side easily relaxed, and the Commander of the Dragoons stood in front making a request for extra feed for his horses.

The captain stood aside when he saw the miserable looking Frenchman tiptoeing into the tent, held just off the floor by Sergeant Flynn, in charge of HQ security.

The Colonel looked up. "What is this, Flynn? Have you been emptying your boots again?"

"I have to report, sir, that I have been saving the neck of this unfortunate man."

"Explain, Sergeant?"

"While Your Honour was visiting with his lady friend, this man was a watching from the dunes. Now, I would like to say that I spotted him, but it was that man left with Mr. Mahon, sir. He looked quietly, and started to move. I saw him though most would not have, as he just sort of drifted into the dunes. I then saw this man." He shook his captive causing him to squirm. "I was in time to save his miserable life, but only because I thought you might like a wee chat with him." He stood the man on his own feet. "He will no doubt be some sort of spy." The Sergeant stopped and waited for his orders.

Cormac looked at Mahon, eyebrow raised. Mahon shrugged, "I was busy with my own thoughts, sir. I hardly noticed the man, Godden, disappear. He was like a ghost, so he was. I never even saw this one. He would have got away, left to me."

Flynn broke in, "Oh no, sir. That man with you was like a snake. He would have killed him before he would have gone ten yards, sir."

"Did you know the man? Godden, did you say, Sergeant?"

"I knew the look of him, sir. I have one in my company like him. A shadow that's what he is. None of my others can lay a finger on him, unless he allows them to." He smiled and waited.

"Right, Sergeant, feed him and keep him safe for me to speak with later. We'll see if he is a patriot or not?"

The Sergeant marched out with the unfortunate Frenchman no longer dangling, leaving the officers to continue their discussion.

***

The sloop beat out to sea and joined the ships of deeper draught patrolling offshore. As the Vixen hove-to, Alouette was slung across in a chair from one ship to the other. The two captains were carried across with their two-man escort in the dinghy they had used earlier. Hooked to a sling from the main-yard of the frigate, the boat was controlled by ropes for the short journey to the safety of the deck.

In the captain's main cabin, the three – Alouette, Antonio and Martin – now seated in comfort, looked at each other.

"Tell me what that was all about?" Antonio spoke, looking really puzzled.

Martin raised an eyebrow and, at the slight nod from Alouette, he elected to answer his friend. "That was confirmation of information that has been coming in from different sources over the past days since Napoleon escaped Elba. The initial euphoria of the beloved leader's dashing return has come up against harsh reality. The trail of reprisal and conscription that has, as always, followed armies, has brought people to their senses. After years of turmoil and upset, they have been enjoying a time of peace, and a return to the settled prosperity everybody spoke about but never had. Now the return of the great man has on one hand raised emotions, but on the other, also shown the price they will have to pay, for at best, an uncertain future."

Antonio listened carefully to what Martin said, then, "But he is the hero of France!"

"Yes!" Martin said.

Antonio looked at them both. "So tell me, why was that meeting so important?"

Alouette, Comtesse de Chartres, leaned toward her husband. She held out her hands to him, and he took them tenderly in his. "Darling Antonio, if I tell you that I have the confidence of the very highest in the land behind me, you will believe me?"

"Of course, my love. You know I do, as does Martin here."

"In the halls of the highest, there were those who did not approve of a woman assuming the cloak of 'Plain Mr. Smith', and on certain matters, it is essential that a point be driven home. This forthcoming battle is a case in point. There must be no doubts of the outcome. My unsupported word may be doubted. As my husband, yours also. But nobody will doubt the word of Captain Sir Martin Forest-Bowers RN. Nor will they put aside the fact that the word came from a famous soldier in the Emperor's Army, Colonel Cormac O'Mara."

***

The Admiral passed Martin's report to Horse Guards, with his own endorsements, and was given assurance that the message had been passed in turn to Lord Wellesley. Though it is not recorded, the comments from the Lord General on the matter were probably fairly picturesque, on the lines of "I am not in the habit of losing battles that can be won. Why ever should you think I might change my ways at this point in my life."

***

Peter Mahon had his Colonel carried from the field at Waterloo. Cormac had been stunned by a sideswipe from a sabre from a charging Scot's Grey cavalryman.

Peter had decided that the time had come to leave the field, when he saw Napoleon turn his horse and canter away from the sight of his Old Guard being cut down in swathes by Wellington's artillery, and the relentless volleys of Picton's Infantry division, followed by the bayonet charge, which stopped the elite French soldiers in their tracks.

The remnants of the Irish Rangers withdrew in good order before turning, and setting out for the coast, and the ship that would take them to their new home, wherever it may be. That would be decided by their Colonel, Cormac O'Hara, who was beginning to stir as the sound of the guns grew fainter.

***

Admiral Lord Charles Bowers sat with hands laced over his expanding waistline. "I have a ship for your man, Brooks, if you can spare him. Only thirty guns, but a well built and found ship, captured as so many from the French. Named HMS Alderney since it was where she was captured." He stopped reading realising what he was seeing. "Of course you will know her. You captured her. She was named Oiseau in the first place. Well, well, it is a small world indeed. Now, can your man take over command while she is in Portsmouth Docks? He will need her ready to sail under orders of Sir Edward Pellew. Lord Exmouth, I suppose we must now call him. He is charged with clearing up the Barbary Coast. I expect he'll be needed to keep an eye on things until Pellew can get his other ships together. You know how it is."

Martin smiled. Young Brooks will need to arrange his wedding a little sooner than anticipated. But I am sure the ladies will get that sorted out before he gets the sawdust off his boots."

"What are you talking about, Martin?"

"Brooks is engaged to the daughter of the Rector at Wareham, sir. I know Lady Jane and Jennifer take a personal interest in the young couple and will undoubtedly wish to arrange and host the ceremony."

The Admiral stood and smiled. "I believe the time has finally arrived for me to step down from this position, and take a more active interest in my grandchildren, and the estate. Be a good fellow and call my clerk."

As the mystified Martin did just that, the Admiral opened his desk drawer and removed a folder of papers and a bag of small things that jingled and clacked metallically together. As the clerk entered the Admiral called over, "Departure bag, Bates, please."

"Of course, sir." He disappeared and returned with a carpetbag already packed to some extent. He came to the desk and placed the contents of the drawer into the bag with the other things. He clipped the top of the bag closing it and went to the clothes rack for the Admiral's cloak and hat. By now Martin had his own cloak and hat ready.

"The letter, Bates?"

Bates produced an unsealed letter. The admiral took it, opened the envelope, signed and dated the letter, then gave it back to the man. Seal and deliver this to the First Lord, 09.00 tomorrow, Bates, without fail!"

"Gladly, sir! Goodbye and my best wishes, sir."

From his pocket the Admiral drew another bag that clinked, and passed it to the other man.

"Come, Martin. I have no doubt the ladies await us even now."

In the carriage Martin could contain his curiosity no more. "Tell me, sir! I feel that that moment had been planned for some time, between you and the clerk."

"Certainly, Bates and I had discussed matters before now. Jane has been worried for some time about the state of my health. She recruited the services of Bates.

"Bates and I concocted a scheme where, when the time came, I would walk out leaving no loose ends. Finding the captain for Alderney was the moment. Even now, new things are pouring in, new matters to be dealt with. But, at that moment, when I called for the departure bag, there was no task on my desk."

Martin looked at his watch. "I believe, sir, that if we leave now, we can post to Eastney. But it occurs to me that one or two matters can be dealt with, before a more leisurely departure tomorrow. Mr. Brooks is presently at Knightsbridge awaiting my return. If we send him direct to Mr. Bates, will he be delivered his orders?"

"He certainly should be, especially carrying a note from me." The Admiral smiled.

"So we will repair to the house and send Brooks in the carriage to the Admiralty. We will dine out, I think, possibly with my friends, the Commodore and the Comtesse. How does that sound? Otherwise we will dine alone at home and have a restful evening. Tomorrow we set out early to Eastney."

The Admiral was already nodding off as the carriage arrived at Ovington Gardens.

***

Patrick Brooks wondered what was happening when the carriage arrived back after such a short period of time. Martin had given no indication of his intentions when he left, so it was a surprise to find that the returning carriage contained the Admiral, as well his captain.

When they stepped down from the vehicle, the driver went immediately to change the horses. Patrick, who came out to meet the carriage, followed the two senior officers into the house. The Admiral wrote a note and handed it to Patrick. "This must be delivered by hand to Barnes, my clerk, at the Admiralty. You should dress in your best for the visit; my colleague is not keen on casual wear."

Patrick glanced down at his working tunic and hastily went to his room to dress in his best uniform.

Martin and Charles, his adoptive father, looked at each other as the carriage drove off. Both burst out laughing, delighted, as they anticipated Patrick Brooks reaction to being given his own command.

Both were relaxed and refreshed by the time the carriage returned. The still-shocked man was ushered, in his hat and cape removed.

When he was seated with a glass of wine in his hand, Martin spoke. "Well, Patrick. Did you collect your orders from the Admiralty?"

Patrick took a sip of wine, placed the glass down on the table and sat back. With a grave face he said. "I accepted my orders as I must, though I anticipated receiving them from you, sir." He nodded to the Admiral. "I had no idea what you gentlemen had in mind, so I brought them unopened, so that you may be present at their opening."

Both Martin and Charles sat forward in their chairs at this comment.

In front of them both, Patrick opened the stiff envelope and removed the orders within. The smile that crossed his face told it all. "I am to command Alderney, the Frenchie we captured on our voyage out to America. She is uprated to 30guns, and is in Portsmouth fitting out." He sat listening to the congratulations of the other two, hardly taking things in. He had not anticipated this, typically performing his duties under a captain who trusted him had been enough. Now the future opened up for him in a way he had hoped for without real expectation.

The voices of the others now started to penetrate the euphoria.

Martin said, "Time is of the essence. We must get you to the dockyard to read yourself in and take over your command."

He started forward, only to be checked by his Admiral's hand, "Hasten slowly, I think! First, what about your wedding? It will need to be organised before you depart. Do you not think?"

"Dorothea! Of course. I must give her the news and set things in motion, if she will allow." Suddenly animated, Patrick started to his feet once more, before being checked a second time by a restraining hand.

"We leave for Eastney tomorrow early. Accompany us and we will recruit the ladies to assist and organize the wedding. They know your fiancée and are practiced now at organising these matters. As you know the Hera is in the dockyard. It occurs to me that Lieutenant Harris and Major Bristow of the Marines will wish to be included."

Once more Patrick sat back into his chair, while a list was made of his movements for the next few days at least.

Chapter fifteen

The Barbary Coast

With the other ships in the group spread out across the heading, it was a sight to lift the heart of both poet and peasant, or so Martin thought, as he paced the deck. The flag of command flew at the masthead. This squadron of ships formed the vanguard of the British Naval effort to stop the Barbary pirates for good. The Admiral would follow in his flagship. He would join with them after calling at Gibraltar to collect the latest intelligence on the region. Meanwhile Martin would take his ships through the straits at night, hoping not to arouse interest in his task force.

Here, in the sunshine off the coast of Portugal, he compared the comparative calm to the hectic activity during the past weeks. The arrangements for Patrick Brooks' wedding, had begun calmly, until Lieutenant John Harris of HMS Hera announced that he and Julia Savage also wished to marry.

The ladies exploded into even more activity at this announcement, and when Julia had arrived at Eastney to claim Martin to give her away at her wedding, everything became much busier, excluding the men completely. The Rector at Wareham, prepared to perform the ceremony for his daughter and her fiancé, was confronted with a double ceremony. With the cooperation of the naval Chaplain and necessary permission of the Bishop to deal with the legal matters, the resulting double ceremony was held with the cooperation of the local Rector, in the church at Eastney, in the presence of all four clerics. This permitted Dorothea's father to give her away, alongside Martin, who performed his part for Julia Savage.

The following breakfast, attended by many of the crews from both ships, lasted until long after the two couples departed for the few days that remained for them to be together before the departure of the squadron for the Mediterranean.

Martin sighed. His eye caught the glint of activity on HMS Alderney sailing to windward under her new captain Patrick Brooks. He shrugged and smiled at Lieutenant Neil Harmon, acting as first Lieutenant, and looking comfortable in the role. Realising that Harman had been the midshipman who had escorted his friend Antonio's ward, Maria, on more than one occasion he wondered?

"Mr. Harmon! Are you satisfied with the trim?"

Neil Harmon looked aloft briefly, then back to his captain. "I am sir. She rides easy on this course."

Martin smiled. "I believe I agree with you. Keep her so." He continued his even pacing until his Peters, his servant, called him for lunch.

Lieutenant Hammond, who had stepped up into Patrick Brooks shoes, was already in the Mediterranean. He had taken the cutter, Rosemary, ahead of the squadron with instruction to survey the port of Tunis, their first destination. There was report of disaffection in the area between the desert tribes and the Prince who ruled under the Ottoman Emperor.

As darkness fell, the ships turned to thread their way through the straits. The loom of the Rock to the north was outlined by starlight. The lights of the seaport of Tangier slipped astern to the south, as the lights of Gibraltar harbour came into view to the north side of the strait. HMS Vixen, bringing up the rear of the squadron, followed the shaded light at the stern of HMS Alderney.

They had been joined by HMS Carfax, a bomb vessel. She was commanded by an older man, Commander Murdo Dunbar. He had been at Copenhagen with Nelson, and had earned a reputation for deadly accuracy with the monster mortar dominating the foredeck of the brig he commanded.

He had joined the Squadron off Cape Trafalgar, having sailed from Lisbon to the rendezvous on orders of the Admiral, who had called there on his way to Gibraltar. He had brought the orders for Martin to proceed to Tunis. The cutter, now commanded by Hammond, had accompanied HMS Carfax.

Rosemary was expendable. She had lost her commander to fever, and her crew members were to be taken into other ships. But her size and rig made her a suitable spy ship for the

North African coast. Hammond had been briefed and, with the addition of McLean and Godden, he had taken over the cutter and disappeared into the Mediterranean bound for Tunis.

Martin was ordered to contact the Prince and inform him that all Christians captured and enslaved were to be released. He had permission to enforce these instructions with any or all of the resources available.

Their rendezvous with Rosemary was, according to Hammond, just in time. One of the reasons for the disposal of Rosemary had been a persistent leak, which had defied all efforts to repair. The fast passage to Tunis had not improved matters. They had beached her while they spied out the situation in Tunis.

Having re-floated the cutter to rejoin the squadron, Hammond had requested that the entire crew be transferred to Vixen, before the unfortunate cutter finally gave up and sank.

Lieutenant Harman joined Hammond watching the final moments of the cutter. "She was a pretty boat!" He commented.

Hammond responded with a nod. It was not easy to see your first command sink in front of you. Though he had known her days were numbered from the beginning, it still hurt.

The two small ships being reported from the lead ship Alderney seemed innocent enough. They both passed the two lead ships with little show, but, at their approach to the Vixen and Carfax, activity on the ships became more obvious. Almost by signal, the two British ships split apart and made off, leaving the two strangers to explode alone, causing only minor damage to their intended targets. The unfortunate crew members stood no chance as the two ships erupted. Martin turned to the Master as the patter of debris stopped. "What makes them do it, Mr. Watson?"

"Why sir. They believe that death in these circumstances ensures a stay in paradise with unlimited virgins, food and drink, at least something like that. Meanwhile, with permission, I will call the hands to action stations, we should see the follow-up any moment now."

Martin called to Lieutenant Hammond, "Signal action stations to the squadron."

The Midshipman on duty leapt to the flag cabinet and produced flags, clipping the signal together on to the halyard. Then a swift haul to get the signal aloft, and a jerk releasing the flags allowing the signal to be read. The other ships responded with the single 'A' to acknowledge the signal. The rumble of the guns being run out prepared for action could be heard across the water.

Martin nodded to himself, well-pleased at the speed of response, none too soon he noticed, as the first of the warships appeared from the wings of the harbour entrance.

The galley was fast, the row of oars driving her without the wind to assist. She headed for the first ship that came into her view. HMS Alderney was not unprepared. Her own sweeps had swung her to cover the harbour entrance, and Hera was closing her to assist, if needed.

The bow gun on the Barbary ship fired, the ball skipping and sinking without reaching Brook's command.

The broadside in return was not wasted. The crowd of men on deck disintegrated into a bloody smear as the canister from the 12 nine pounders and the balls from the two carronades impacted the unfortunate pirate. The galley stopped. The holes created by the carronades allowed water to flood into the stern, causing the ship to list. The oars began to flog at the water once more, but were only catching the water at the stern of the ship. The screaming increased as it started to sink by the stern. The sea was suddenly covered in struggling humanity. The slaves chained to the oars were left to drown where they sat.

Brooks ignored the men in the water, to concentrate on getting out of the way of the two-decker ship approaching the harbour entrance. The crescent-flagged ship was towed by two galleys to the point where the wind would allow her to use her sails, already set to catch whatever wind there was.

Hera and Alderney both managed a broadside into the two towing galleys, without much obvious effect, before they hauled off to take station on Vixen and Carfax.

Having been warned that the ship was in the harbour, it was no surprise to Martin that it was coming out to threaten the British ships. McLean had checked the ship while they were surveying the harbour. His report to Lieutenant Hammond was succinct. "I stuck my knife into her timbers. They were rotten. Her guns are a mix of sizes and also in bad condition. One broadside from Vixen and she'll fall apart."

With his words in mind, Martin swung Vixen round to expose her broadside and gave the nearer of the two galleys the full benefit of her heavier guns. The effect on the near galley was hidden briefly by the smoke created. As it cleared it was easy to see the smashed oars and the wrecked side of the ship. The towline, broken, had caused the head of the towed ship to fall off and it was currently headed for the far wing of the harbour entrance.

There was damage on the other towing vessel where the grape and ball shot had passed over or through the main target. They had now cast off their lines to the tow. The two-decker had regained some control and was lining up with the harbour entrance under the light winds off-shore.

The crash of the mortar from the gun ship took all by surprise. The explosion that followed was even more ear shattering. The shore battery had not yet managed to get into action, and certainly the arrival of the monster shell in its midst did not help. When Martin looked, he saw a fan of flying bodies and gun parts rising from the centre of the quay where the battery had been located. Of the guns there, seven were definitely no longer in place. From the size of the explosion it seemed possible that the powder store had been involved, which suggested that the battery would be inoperative for some time.

As the big ship started to clear the harbour mouth, the Master muttered, "It's the Chappel. She was reported lost with all hands at the Nile."

"You know her, Mr. Watson?" Martin asked.

"She was part of the French fleet at the Nile when Nelson caught them. Sixty guns, not young then, but she gave a good account of herself at the time. Last seen I recall, drifting to the west, dismasted. I had the impression that she was afire, but it was long ago and I cannot be sure. It was assumed at the time that she had been lost."

"So, apparently not as lost as suspected. Still a formidable opponent, d'ye think?"

"From the state of her rigging and the look of her woodwork, I would suspect she will shatter at the first sharp knock. I would hesitate to fire her guns in a broadside. I think the recoil would rip out the stopping ropes, and possibly most of the bulwarks at the same time."

Martin was watching the progress of the ex-French ship, noticing her patchwork of repair, the way the rigging was braced and the sad-looking canvas. He was inclined to agree with the Master. But?

"Let them know we are here, Mr. Hammond. Put a shot across her bows."

"Aye, aye sir. Starboard-bow chaser, waken them up, please."

The activity at the forward gun was brief, the aim adjusted and the gunner satisfied. "Gun clear!" He reached forward, and jumped back. The sound of the gun made Martin start, despite being prepared for it.

The ball rose in the air and flew in a long arc to plunge into the water beyond the bow of the enemy ship.

There was no response apart from waving and cheering from the deck of the big ship, though it began to turn to expose its port broadside guns, with the gun-ports being opened to allow the guns to run out.

Lieutenant Hammond had his telescope on the other ship. "As McLean reported, she seems to have as assortment of guns in her broadside. From 9 pounder to what looks like a 32 pounder carronade."

"Thank you, Mr. Hammond!" Martin considered a moment. "Starboard broadside stand-by! Bring her head round, Mr. Watson."

As the Vixen turned, he called, "As you bear, Mr. Gibbs."

Lieutenant Gibbs smiled grimly. His guns were not normally allowed to tackle a ship of this size and armament. "As you bear, fire!" He called. The first two guns of the broadside fired.

As Jared Watson suspected and McLean had reported, the former French ship of the line had not been properly maintained and her dried out timbers were fragile. Judging from the damage caused by the first two guns, she would not last long afloat.

Her guns opened fire in a ragged volley. The water between the ships was ripped and roiled with the erratic aim from the enemy ship. Two missiles reached Vixen. A 12 pound ball smashed the rail between number six and number seven gun. Though there were injuries to both gun crews, both guns fired.

The second hit was to the mainmast and the 9 lb shot impacted the mast. To the watcher's amazement it dropped and rolled into the scuppers, leaving a small dent in the massive timber.

The cry of the lookout snapped attention back to the enemy ship. The effect of the disciplined broadside from Vixen had been difficult to assess, until the four carronades had done their work. Mr. Watson's prediction was not quite fulfilled. A collection of small boats swarmed around the enemy ship. Her port-side was shattered and if her masts had not tilted to starboard she would have been inundated by the waters of the Mediterranean. The list created by the weight of her masts was all that was allowing her to remain afloat. The people swarming down to the boats around her were unaware of the effect they were having on the stricken ship.

Hammond shouted, pointing, "The fools, their weight will overbalance the ship." Even as he spoke the inevitable happened, the added weight on the port side, allowed the water to surge through the torn planking and the balance of the hulk was lost. The main mast teetered and swung over to port. The ship rolled over, swamping the entire scene, smashing the small boats and the ships company under as it capsized, exposing the scarred, weedy bottom timbers, disintegrating as they watched in horror.

The bubbling waters around the sinking ship were soon littered with the debris of what was once a fine ship. Bodies of the unfortunates came to the surface, no signs of life amongst them. Of the ship there was now no shape or form to identify its passing. The planks floating among the bodies were just that, planks, shape and form gone. The mast shot out of the water, released from the rigging that had held it, and smacked down, rolling among the wreckage.

Martin sighed. Whatever he had imagined this day would bring had been eclipsed by what had actually happened. Judging from what they had observed, the casualties on the big ship alone must amount to nearly 1000 people. He turned to Lieutenant Hammond. "Signal the squadron to form on Vixen and prepare for action! Mr. Weston, we will enter the harbour now."

He turned and found a tray in front of him with a cup of coffee, filled and hot. His servant, Peters, said, "Something hot, before we go into action, sir?"

Martin smiled. There seemed to be a logic followed by his servant which did not allow him to deviate from the routine he had established. With a shrug he collected his cup. "Thank you, Peters, I'll just take it here on deck."

Peters said, "I will fetch your sword belt, sir." He left Martin with the coffee and went below, returning a few moments later with the sword-belt and a pistol, and proceeded to arrange them around Martin's waist.

Martin sipped his coffee and smiled. He had told Peters on several occasions that he did not require a nanny. It made little difference. He settled the belt more comfortably around his waist and finished his coffee. The cup disappeared and Peters returned, armed and ready, for whatever the day would bring.

The ships passed through the harbour entrance one by one, guns run out ready, but on instruction from Martin they would not fire unless fired upon.

There were several ships within the harbour, none of them very big, and most oar-driven with just a single large lateen sail carried on one or two masts. The long spars carrying the sails were secured while the ships were idle, in harbour.

Lieutenant Hammond observed drily. "All the galleys seem to be armed with cannon and swivel guns."

"Noted, Mr. Hammond," Martin replied quietly.

"And all appear to carry crews on their oar benches," Jared Weston observed.

"Is that the Palace of the Prince?" Martin asked, indicating the big building fronting the harbour with an assembly of outbuildings all around, and several small ornate boats moored at the quay in front of the grand entrance to the building.

Jared Watson answered, "It has grown since I saw it last. But, yes, I would say it is still the palace of the Prince. Hammond confirmed the fact. "The buildings to the left of the quay are the slave quarters.

"Is there water for the ship beside the quay?" Martin asked thoughtfully.

Mr. Watson replied swiftly and positively. "The waters at this point are scoured by the incoming tide flow. No great thing in these waters but enough to keep the channel swept. As you may observe, the empty berth alongside is big enough for the Chappel. I believe that was where she was moored."

"Take her alongside, Mr. Hammond! Major Bristow, Marines to form a guard of honour! I intend calling upon the Prince, or whatever he calls himself."

***

"Mr. Hammond, keep the guns loaded covering the quay. If the ship is threatened, open fire!"

"Yes, Sir. Open fire."

The other ships anchored offshore, their guns covering the city. Martin called Lieutenant Harmon to accompany him when he made his call on the Prince.

So far no-one had appeared. The Marines in their red coats and white pipe-clay made a blaze of colour on the sand-strewn stonework of the ancient quay.

Martin descended the gangway and stepped ashore. Lieutenant Harmon followed with Peters close behind. Finally, Jared Watson, in his broad-brimmed hat against the sunlight, completed the party. The group flanked by the Marines approached the main doors of the Palace.

Wondering whether they would have to knock to gain entrance, Martin was relieved to see the great doors swing open.

A turbaned man was revealed, standing with a European man in eastern garb beside him.

The turbaned man spoke and bowed. The European translated. "His nibs is saying you are welcome to enter his home. Please treat all within as your own."

Martin looked at Watson, eyebrow raised. "More or less, sir," Watson agreed.

The European looked at the still-bowing man with him, he whispered "Do not let them know you speak their lingo."

"Rise, Karim Pasha," the European said in Arabic. He looked as if he would prefer to kick the Pasha.

Martin said, "I have come to see the Prince."

The Pasha received the translation unhappily and broke into a spate of Arabic.

The European smiled and said, "He is saying the Prince cannot be disturbed as he is sleeping at present. He will receive you this evening when the air is cooler."

"What is your name?" Martin asked the European.

"They call me Abu. My real name is Carlo Valdez."

"Tell the Pasha that, having received the invitation sent by the Prince, I am not prepared to wait until tonight. I expect to see him now!"

Abu spoke to the Pasha at length, causing him to wail and clench his fists, but nonetheless to turn and lead the way into the Palace.

Abu whispered, "The Prince will be annoyed at being disturbed. You are not supposed to be here. He thought the big ship would have driven you off!"

"Do you mean the ship that sank in the harbour mouth?"

Abu stopped, and then hurriedly caught up. "Sank?" He said, unbelievingly.

"Yes, she was lost, along with most of its crew sadly," Martin confirmed. "How did you not know?"

"Here in the Palace it is quiet. People do not disturb the Prince when he is resting. I presume nobody dared to disturb him with bad news. Especially, since his brother was captain of the big ship."

"I presume he will be upset." Martin said quietly.

"About the ship, yes! His brother, perhaps?" Abu replied with a shrug which spoke volumes.

The Pasha stopped suddenly, realising he was hearing voices in foreign language and not receiving the translation.

He turned on Abu and fired a stream of Arabic at him.

Abu bowed and fired words back. Jared Watson relayed to Martin what the man was saying.

One look at the Pasha was enough to see that he was hearing things he would rather not have been told. He dropped to his knees, covering his face with his hands rocking back and forth in despair.

"Unhappy?" Martin said.

"He thinks this will be the death of him, and his daughters will be sold into slavery."

"That bad?"

"Probably!" Said Abu unfeelingly. "Quite fancy his daughter myself," he mused.

Martin looked sharply at the man. Abu straightened up realising that was probably not a reaction that the visitor found acceptable.

He said in his own defence, "I have been here for twelve years. During that time I have been beaten, spat upon, rowed a galley, survived two battles and watched the Prince and this old fart take what they wanted, from whoever they chose, at will. My reaction does not reflect my love of this place, only my instincts for survival."

Martin looked keenly at the man, realising that he might have misjudged him. "Have you tried to escape?" He asked.

"That was my first session in the galleys," was the simple answer.

Martin nodded briefly. "Pick him up. Let us go now and see this Prince!"

The Prince's chamber was behind more great doors, thrown open with gusto by Abu.

The ante room was tenanted by six women dressed in flimsy robes hiding nothing of the bodies beneath.

Ignoring them, Abu said, "He will be in the bedchamber, and proceeded to fling open the door to the inner room.

The Pasha was on his knees where he had been dropped by the two marines who had carried him there. He was muttering prayers into his beard.

The bedchamber contained a large bed at least twelve foot across. There was a figure rising from the bedclothes with a pistol in hand. Martin's sword tip caught the trigger-guard and the pistol fell out of the reach of the man who had lifted it.

"How dare you break into my room like this!" The man spoke in French.

Martin replied in the same language. "How dare you send a ship to fire upon my flag! You have cost the lives of many people and lost your big ship."

The man stood and slipped on a robe. Ignoring the woman still in the bed, he strode to the door. "What do you mean. I have lost my big ship?"

"Your ship fired upon mine and I fired back. Your ship broke apart and sank with all hands."

A look of shock passed briefly over the otherwise impassive face. "Sank with all hands?" He said. "How can this be?"

Martin shrugged. "The ship was old and had not been maintained properly. With rotten timbers and an untrained crew, she was all show and no strength. Perhaps, she may have scared off ignorant people, but to me it was obvious. Had she fired her main guns all at the same time, she would have fallen apart. As it was, she fired several of her guns at my ship. I fired one broadside and that was enough."

"Survivors? None you say?"

"My boats are searching, but none so far. Perhaps some made it to the harbour wall." Martin shrugged.

The Prince sat on one of the ottomans scattered around the large room. His arrogance, seemingly for the moment, subdued.

Martin presumed the story about the Prince's brother being in command of the lost ship was the reason.

The Prince stood and clapped his hands together. "You will of course be taken and placed in the dungeons, until I have decided upon a suitable punishment for your actions.

A dejected-looking man entered and bowed to the Prince.

"Have these people placed in the dungeon." The Prince said dismissively.

The servant coughed and made no move.

"Well? What is it?" The Prince suddenly realised that things were not as he had thought.

He looked at the party with Martin, the armed Marines, Martin's sword and pistol.

"Ah, it seems I have misunderstood the situation. I am your prisoner?"

Martin said, "If you get dressed, perhaps we can sit down and discuss the situation. Any further action can be taken at that time."

Chapter sixteen

The Contract

The room where the discussion took place was airy and the atmosphere civilised. The Prince made great play of the fact that, as a part of the Ottoman Empire, he was not in a position to make agreements for the Turkish Government.

Martin smiled and allowed him to speak at length on the subject. When the Prince ran down, Martin spoke.

"Having listened carefully to your comments, I find it necessary to remind you that I am not here to negotiate with the Government of the Empire. I am here to arrange the repatriation of all Christian captives, and the end of the piracy carried out by ships from this city."

The Prince looked at him with astonishment. "But this cannot happen. We need the slaves we have. The country cannot carry-on without the trade brought by our ships.

Martin rose to his feet. "In that case I will have you placed in your own dungeons and find someone to take your place, who will agree to these terms." He signalled Major Bristow, who called two of his Marines to take the Prince below.

The next few minutes were interesting to Martin, as he saw how the advisors to the Prince reacted. Half of them rose to his defence, but several of the others were looking pleased with the suggestion.

Order was restored and Martin faced the Prince once more eyebrow raised in question?

The Prince sat down and shook his head in despair. "So, what is it I must do?"

"The Christians and the piracy!" Martin reminded him.

"They will probably replace me," the Prince said miserably.

Abu whispered something in his ear. The Prince brightened immediately. "Very well, sir. I agree. Produce this contract and I will sign."

The contract was produced, signed and witnessed.

Throughout the entire proceedings the Prince cooperated, always with a small smile.

Martin was intrigued and finally cornered Abu. "What did you say to the Prince?"

Abu looked innocent, but Martin would have none of it. "What exactly did you tell the Prince to make him agree to cooperate?"

"Ah! That is what you would like to know. First, I told him that his brother had survived the sinking of his ship. I did not tell him that the little rat was hiding out with his friend, when he should have been on board ship."

"Why did that make the Prince happy?"

"Because the Prince is the younger brother. He can abdicate and leave his brother to sort out the whole matter. He knows his brother cannot refuse. His brother's friend, by the way, is a man. As ruler here he will be forced to bed women, if he wishes to survive. The Prince has a home on the Red Sea shore and has always wanted to retire there. So my message was the one thing that made the whole thing possible for him. Did I do wrong?"

Martin smiled and shrugged. "There is a place in my ship, if you wish to join us."

Abu looked surprised. He said nothing at the time, but went his way thoughtfully.

Martin had just decided that, with the contract signed and the point of the foray achieved, he could enjoy the moment. He and Patrick Brooks proceeded to dine on the food prepared for them by the Palace kitchen.

Abu had reappeared and was informing them of the various items placed before them. He tasted everything before the two officers did, thus ensuring that nothing lethal was being offered the guests.

A servant entered and spoke quietly to Abu, his eyes darting uneasily at the two British officers.

Abu waved him away and said quietly. "Sirs, a problem has occurred!"

Martin shrugged. It had all been too simple. He should have realised that nothing was simple in the world of the diplomat. "Well, Abu. What now?"

"The Prince's brother has taken his new role seriously and has called the people to rise and drive out the infidels." He paused and nodded at Martin. "That is you and your men. He has currently gathered the Berber tribesmen from the southern area where the desert caravans camp. It might be an idea to return to your ships and prepare to leave."

"How many men can he call upon to help him?"

Abu thought for a moment. "Now, maybe two-three hundred. Later, one thousand perhaps."

"Where are the released prisoners?" Martin asked, now on his feet, the meal ignored.

"They have been assembled in the warehouses on the Palace quay."

Brooks asked, "The Palace armoury?"

Abu, also on his feet, turned and indicated the door behind him. "Here!"

Martin turned to Peters. "Get Major Bristow to bring the released slaves here now!"

As Peters ran off, Brooks snapped the lock on the door to the armoury. The room was lined with racks of French muskets. Barrels of cast balls and gunpowder stood between the racks. The centre of the room was occupied by two wheeled guns, Martin guessed nine pounders. They were field artillery weapons to be pulled by horses.

He turned to Abu. "What the devil is all this?"

Abu shrugged. "The Prince had an agreement with the French. When they delivered the equipment, he changed his mind and dismissed the troops."

"Dismissed?"

"He gave them a feast, the officers, that is. For the men there was a party, the survivors are part of the slaves you released today."

Major Bristow appeared with two marines and a group of raggedly dressed men. The Palace was astir at the unease created by the hurried departure of the Prince, and the release of the Christian slaves.

Major Bristow reported, "We seem to have several trained soldiers among the slaves, sir. I took the liberty of bringing the surviving senior officer, a Major Dubois."

Martin turned to the short man he brought forward. "Major, you are aware that Britain and France are no longer at war?"

"I am, sir, and I am grateful for your efforts in releasing us from slavery."

"Yes, yes, of course, I understand. It now seems that your release comes at a price. The new Prince has decided to renege on the agreement we have just made and has aroused a mob to drive us out. Will your men fight beside us for your freedom?"

"Proudly, sir!" The Major drew himself up and saluted. "At your service, Captain."

Martin looked at Bristow, "Bring them forward, trained men first!" He turned to Brooks, "Off you go to the quay. Land the Marines and the Cox'n with his extra riflemen. Warp the ship offshore. Inform Commander Dunbar that his mortar will have some work to do. Land the remainder of the squadron's Marines under the command of the Ensign Crockett, to join the command of Major Bristow."

To Bristow he said, "I will send re-enforcements to you. Meanwhile clear the houses and warehouse on the quay. Barricade the alleys and I will join you as soon as possible."

Bristow left, as the first of the newly armed French troops formed up in the long hall of the Palace. The flow of men in and out of the armoury was interrupted by the movement of the two artillery pieces. They were manhandled out through the door one at a time, the caissons containing ready-use ammunition and powder, dragged out and linked to the gun trails ready for deployment. Major Dubois ordered that a barrel of musket balls be brought with the guns, and ripped down the gauze curtains draped around the room to be torn up to make bags for the musket balls to be fired from the cannon.

Martin said, "To the quay!"

The self-appointed gunners leapt to drag the heavy pieces down the steps to the main doors, opening onto the quay.

The French Major turned to Martin, "With your permission, sir, I noticed your Marines have rifles?"

Martin nodded, "Yes, Major, trained riflemen."

"I suggest, sir, that my men go to the quay with their muskets. Your Marines man the windows of the Palace with their rifles."

"Liaise with Major Bristow on the quay. Leave your Sergeant here, in charge meanwhile."

Peters reappeared. "Sir, what shall I do with about the other freed slaves?"

"Bring them here. The women can prepare to look after the wounded. Use the entrance hall, but keep the doorway clear."

He suddenly became aware of the sound of drums from the desert edge of town.

A clatter of boots heralded the arrival of the first of the Marines. The sergeant in charge, shouted to the French, "Allez, allez," and pointed to the open door to the quay.

The French sergeant, at the nod from Martin, shouted at the armed men who turned right and marched off through the door down the steps to the quay, muskets shouldered and in step.

Ensign Crockett saluted Martin. "Reporting as ordered, sir."

Martin smiled. "Take positions at the windows." He pointed toward the desert and the noise of the drums. "That side, I think. Man all the windows, Keep your heads down, and shoot to kill."

With another salute the Ensign was gone, calling to his men, "All the windows, men. Kill the bastards."

More Marines arrived and then the Cox'n appeared with his dozen riflemen. They took the windows on the ground floor. McLean and Godden stayed back with Peters, reminding Martin that he had bodyguards, whether he liked it or not.

He went up the stairs to the upper floor. The Prince's private apartment had been ransacked by his own servants when he left. There were still several of the women in the Palace, and, in two of the rooms, they were serving the Marines with food and drink.

Martin ignored it and looked out of the upper windows.

The drums and the torches were progressing through the crowded buildings most of them on the main artery from the waterfront to the desert to the south.

The crowd was close enough for the front ranks to be visible in the flickering light of the torches.

On the quay, there was a loud cough, repeated. Martin realised the two field guns had been fired. The front ranks of the Arabs disintegrated under the terrible hail of musket balls fired from the guns. The mob tried to draw back from the terrible slaughter of the leaders, but the pressure forced them to stumble forward through the bloody mess of body parts. They were thrust, screaming, into the path of the next two shots from the cannon, now backed up with volley fire from the muskets.

The relentless fire of the cannon and the disciplined volleys in support broke the mob, who found escape in the various alleys and over the heads of the people behind them. The retreat up the road back to the desert was not a rout, but it was a retreat, giving breathing space for the defenders.

Martin made a round of the positions. From the quay he noticed that the bomb vessel had been warped round to cover the town.

The noise from the crowd under the control of the new Prince increased. Accompanied by the rumble of wheels a large cannon appeared, being dragged by a team of camels. The gun was lined up with the street, pointing at the palace.

As Martin watched, another group of men dragged wagons in the way, to protect the men working to load the great weapon, which Martin guessed was at least a 32 pound shot. Rifles cracked and men fell, but the cannon was loaded anyway and the sound of the gun echoed around the town. The shot hit the wall of the Palace, and brought down a section of the outer wall.

A cheer went up from the enemy and the reloading commenced.

Martin looked at the damage, deciding that the Palace was not built to withstand that sort of battering.

The roar of the mortar on the gunboat was a sound that shocked those near. The missile was visible as it climbed high into the night sky. It described a fine arc and descended upon the desert edge of town to explode with a satisfying crash among the packed mob behind the gun.

The screaming and wailing of the wounded was lost in the noise of the second discharge of the gun, aimed at the same point but, due to the barrel now being heated, it struck the wall at a higher point, bringing further sections of the outer wall down. Martin ordered his men away from the increasing breach, though they were still in a place to cover access to the Palace.

The mortar fired once more. The shell fell to the other side of the mob, creating more casualties, mainly from the casing of the mortar bomb, which exploded sending the shrapnel of the shattered casing in all directions, causing terrible wounds and death to all within three metres of the impact.

The gun fired once more and the wall was breached, a great section of it crumbling and tumbling into the street below. From the Vixen, a shell from her carronade hit the street in front of the great cannon. The canister shell bounced and exploded. Its contents stripped the area of living beings, and damaged the wagons forming the barricade in front of the gun.

Martin became aware of the shadowy movement in amongst the houses opposite the Palace. McLean appeared beside him. "Sir, it is time to join the Major on the quay. This place is about to warm up."

"I can see that for myself, and I believe Mr. Hammond has noticed as well."

The crash of the carronade once more produced results, shattering three of the small houses opposite the Palace. The screaming and wailing underlined the effect on the gathering mob infiltrating for a mass assault on the Palace from one side of the main street. The two field guns fired together aiming at the houses on the other corner, and, while not having the same impact of the carronade, the resultant mayhem indicated that they were still massing. The two field guns poured fire into the houses until they were reduced to rubble.

The great cannon fired once more. The Palace wall was breached again making a 10 foot gap in the wall.

Anticipating this, Martin had called for the rest of the powder and shot in the armoury to be brought out and stacked behind the broken wall. The men stacked the barrels and piled the broken rocks from the wall on top. The riflemen continued choosing targets until it was apparent that the gun was going to fire again.

Martin guessed that the shot would pass through the gap and smash the wall on the quayside of the Palace, but he withdrew the men anyway. The defenders streamed out of the Palace as the latest shot impacted the rear wall of the Palace, starting the wrecking of that section of the building. Following the last shot, the gathering mob poured out of the ruins in the street and through the broken down wall of the Palace. Godden lit the fuse and ran through the Palace and out of the front door. None of the bullets that followed him caught him.

It was with a satisfied grin that he heard the powder barrels explode,

The Palace was wrecked, as the entire, shattered town-facing wall was flung into the air. The smashed rock swept up the street like grapeshot, clearing the attacking mob. The gun crew suffered too, under the rain of falling stones.

The roar of the French contingent, bayonets fixed, followed the fleeing survivors up the road. The former slaves were not interested in anything but revenge for the treatment they had received.

The great gun was stoppered by the Marines supporting their allies.

They found the new Prince, spread-eagled and castrated in the ruin of a tent. The desert Berbers were gone, taking their people with them.

With resistance over, Martin had the people of the town assembled and selected six of the major traders who had survived the uprising. They were told to clear up the mess created, gather the dead and burn the bodies.

With his captains, he discussed the options for the future of Tunis.

The major, Dubois, made a suggestion. "Sir, my people have been here for several years. They feel they have lost contact with their families, who believe them dead. They would be happy to stay here as free men. I also have no one to return to and, like many of my men, have interests here. If the traders will agree, we would be happy to stay here and act, perhaps, as police. We could train others to take over the duties. It would allow us to see that the piracy ended. I believe many of the other former slaves would join us."

Martin looked at the Major speculatively. Commander Dunbar was nodding, "It would make sense. They already know how things work here, and, with the defences properly maintained, pirates would find it difficult to operate, and traders would find a secure port."

The others around the table were all nodding in agreement.

Martin decided that they were right. "We will meet the traders and see what they have to say. Meanwhile, I will have another contract drawn up for the Freeport of Tunis."

Chapter seventeen

The Pirate

Back at sea once more, Lieutenant Hammond confided to Major Bristow, "Thank goodness we have got away from that cesspit of a place. I still have not got rid of the stench though we have been clear near a week."

The Major smiled grimly. "William, you may think that such places are pest ridden havens for disease and squalor, but, to my knowledge, such places are the reason you can eat the exotic foods, spiced with herbs and simples, you would never otherwise know. The wealth of the world also passes through such places. Perhaps you should think of the stench as the smell of wealth, rather than reek of poverty."

Will Hammond looked at his friend with surprise.

The Major smiled. "At the wedding of our friend, Patrick Brooks, did you not notice the clothes of the ladies?"

He strolled off along the deck, leaving a rather puzzled William Hammond behind him.

*****

Captain Robert Shaw was a happy man. He made a point of letting his crew know that. His crew was under control because he was happy. He had a fine ship, a former, French-built frigate won from the Swedish navy. He had acquired her while cruising the Baltic during the multiple disputes between the various countries bordering the inland sea.

His own ship at the time was sailing under British colours. They had found the Torqual near sinking from an encounter with another ship which had been ended by a gale saving her from further damage. In her battered state she was in no condition to withstand the insistence of Captain Shaw, who knew just the place to get the Torqual refitted. The crew of the stricken ship were in no state to resist, and the villagers in the Russian port were always in the market for slaves.

With the Torqual repaired and refitted and her new name, Asterid, clear on the transom, Captain Robert Shaw was a happy man. His old ship was handed over to the Russians in payment for the work undertaken, and a profit from the sale of the slaves made the entire transaction mutually satisfactory.

The transit to the Mediterranean had been made with just a few diversions. Calling on a village with a well-armed frigate meant that provisions were easy to obtain. In two cases other ships, traders, meant a welcome addition to the coffers, and the recruitment of additional crew on one occasion. Sailing mainly during the darker hours made it easier to avoid contact with the increased number of warships in the area. The final dash into the Mediterranean during the night was made without problems.

The weather was generally better than the Baltic, and the pickings much richer. Though there had been distant sightings of warships they had managed to elude them so far. Collecting the odd trading ships off the North African coast had been easy, and the collection of slaves was increasing nicely. In fact Captain Shaw was well pleased with the change of scenery and climate, regarding the voyage so far as, financially, a success.

A negotiated visit to Algiers disposed of the slaves and a healthy proportion of the cargo accumulated on the voyage so far. Thus provisioned and refreshed the Asterid made course to the Black Sea, where, on advice, they understood many exotic cargoes awaited the bold corsair.

They had done some good business in the Sea of Marmara. Having entered the Black Sea, but finding it too hemmed in for Captain Shaw's peace of mind, they had turned back. The trader they had taken in the Sea of Marmara had provided several acceptable women, and a fine variety of cloth from the Eastern lands which he knew would sell well anywhere along the shore in the Mediterranean, or elsewhere in Europe he suspected.

The lady of his choice had, to his surprise appeared well pleased with her lot. She had settled in his cabin without demur and performed a series of sexual gymnastics which intrigued and satisfied him. Of the others he knew little, having turned them over to the crew.

After negotiating the narrows into the Aegean Sea the following days had been idyllic. Trading with the odd fishermen had assured fresh food, and three trading vessels had yielded oil and wine in quantity to partially fill the hold.

Entering the Mediterranean once more south of the island of Sicily the idyll lost its way.

The appearance of a sail on the horizon had at first cheered him even more, until it was reported that the sail was part of the rigging of a frigate, and that it was accompanied by at least two other ships. So far, his attempt to quietly slip away had not had any effect. One of the ships was now hull up, and he could dissemble no more. Nor, he decided, could he run. The schooner approaching had the legs of him, and the other ships were to windward, and all now clearly British.

Captain Shaw was also British basically, though he had long decided that he was now a citizen of the world. Among the accumulated papers of the past ten years of free-trading, a word he preferred to that of piracy, an encounter with a privateer had allowed him to acquire a letter of marque from the Kingdom of Naples. The holders had not given it to him, but to Captain Shaw that was incidental.

He put men over the stern of the ship on a platform to change the privateer's name on the transom. It was thus the Marco Polo which stopped to converse with the schooner Hera.

The conversation was friendly. Lieutenant John Harris, found nothing remarkable in the appearance of the Italian ship. She had the look of a Frenchman, but then so did three of the ships of Captain Forest-Bowers squadron.

The two ships, having satisfied themselves that they were what they seemed, separated to go their different ways.

As the Marco Polo showed her stern to the Hera, the rear gallery windows opened and a white sheet appeared. Written on the sheet was the word 'pirate'.

The flag that rose to Hera's yardarm just indicated 'alert'.

Martin received the report as he came back on deck. "Bring us close to the Marco Polo. I wish to speak with the captain."

Lieutenant Hammond acknowledged, and called for the helmsman to steer small to bring the Vixen close abeam of the privateer.

The ships neared. As they drew close, Martin called across to Captain Shaw. "With your permission, Captain, could you join me for a discussion and a bite to eat. We have fresh provisions and a passable marsala."

Now there might be occasions when an invitation like that could be refused. With four naval ships around, it was not one of those. The ships hove-to and a boat was sent over to bring Captain Shaw and his First Lieutenant to the Vixen.

As the captain Shaw left his ship, a boat from the Alderney slid under the transom of the Marco Polo. A grapnel hooked over the stern gallery rail and Patrick Brooks climbed the rope ladder to the gallery. The window to the captain's cabin opened. The lady who had waved the pirate notice welcomed him into the cabin. The other men from the boat were on the gallery waiting when Patrick opened the window once more and nodded to the Midshipman waiting there. The signal was a simple red or black flag. The black flag warned the watcher on the Vixen that the Marco Polo was a pirate. On the Marco Polo, the crew became aware that all of the ships around them had run out their guns. When Patrick Brooks appeared on deck accompanied by the captain's lady, the crew lay down their personal weapons and allowed the Marines from the British ships on board.

***

Peters entered the captain's cabin where Captain Shaw was being entertained. He leaned over and whispered the news to Martin.

"Captain Shaw, I have just been informed that the ladies you kidnapped from the ship in the Sea of Marmara have just been released by my men. The men on your ship have been arrested. You and your lieutenant are my prisoners.

Shaw leapt to his feet reaching for the pistol he carried, only to find himself facing Peters, whose own pistol was centered between his eyes. The amenable lady who shared Captain Shaw's cabin was in fact the daughter of a merchant, who had been sold to an old man to make his declining years enjoyable. The pragmatic lady had learned the ways of lovemaking, since it placed her in control of the relationship. Her husband had died and the now extremely rich widow had been on her way to West Europe where she would be in a better position to enjoy her great wealth. Captain Shaw was not the worst option in the circumstances, but she was always happier in control. Shaw being strong minded was his own worse enemy.

After weighing up the options, the lady, Lydia Rostoff, decided that her original destination offered better prospects for her future. Hence the sheet, and the abandonment of the services of Captain Shaw, pirate!

***

Asterid now lay at anchor in Gibraltar harbour, her future uncertain as the war with France was over. The British fleet was being, once more, reduced.

Martin was hopeful, since the ship was a good example of a fully refurbished warship, well-armed and rigged, not really suited for trading.

The Admiral had been and gone from Gibraltar though he had received the report of the situation in Tunis.

Having provisioned once more, Martin took his ships to sea in pursuit of the Admiral.

Chapter eighteen

Privateer

After the excitement of the uprising in Tunis the remainder of the campaign in Barbary had been comparatively peaceful amounting to little more than several skirmishes with pirate galleys attempting to escape before the new policies were enforced. Martin actually felt there was little purpose in the employment of so many ships. Jared Watson, the Master, suggested that there were so many ships available because using extra ships was convenient for the people reducing the active side of the Navy. It allowed them to concentrate on the ships lying idle. They could deal with those in active service as and when they returned to port.

Having returned to Portsmouth by the end of the year, there was another reason for celebration for Martin, Jennifer and the family. The Admiral, having retired from his position in the Admiralty, was now in better health and enjoying life back with the family. He was still called to consult at the Admiralty enough times to feel that his naval career had not been wasted.

The big news upon Martin's return was that his great friend, Captain Antonio Ramos of the Royal Portuguese Navy, had been retired. In his own words "I was too successful for the politicians who have returned with a vengeance to Portugal. It was suggested that I would be better off with my pension and wife here in Britain. My lands in Portugal have been allocated elsewhere, though I have received compensation for their value." Antonio spoke with a smile, but Martin was aware of the sadness and disappointment that Antonio felt at being discarded in such an offhand way. King Peter the third, who had succeeded Maria the First, in 1816, sent a private letter to Antonio following the announcement of his retirement. It expressed his personal gratitude for Antonio being there and acting positively when all the politicians were fleeing for their lives, and defecting to the French. Unfortunately, the King himself was now more and more under the control of his politicians. With Napoleon no longer a threat, their navy had become yet another political pawn. The one compensation he was able to confirm was Antonio's promotion to Admiral at the time of his retirement. This did ensure an addition to his pension, though in Antonio's case money was not a problem. His accumulation of prize monies had ensured that he and his wife would not suffer hardship during their lifetime.

***

It was at a reception in Antonio's London home that Dominic Gordon approached Martin and Jennifer. The Ambassador was looking fitter, and in many ways more assured than he had been in their first encounter. He approached them, accompanied by his wife of two years, Lady Margaret Gordon.

Jennifer, realising there were matters to be discussed, took Lady Margaret to meet Lady Jane and the Admiral, who were chatting with Lieutenant Harmon and Maria Diaz, ward of Antonio Ramos their host.

Martin looked at Dominic, eyebrow raised.

With a grin, Dominic said, "Alright, I was going to approach you officially. But since we are both here, I decided to see how you feel about a slight problem causing a certain amount of agitation in the Foreign Office."

Martin smiled, "How could I be of help, I am like so many of my colleagues, 'on the beach', cast aside by my Lords of the Admiralty."

"That is exactly why I wished to talk to you. The problem upsetting the Foreign Office is an echo from the past."

Martin took Dominic's arm. "Let us stroll in the garden The night is pleasant and there will be less noise to contend with. You were saying, 'an echo from the past'?"

Dominic looked about them checking there was no-one near. "In the 1790's Spain started to gather ships in the Pacific Ocean with the intention of taking Australia. There were some elements in Spain who were worried about the expansion of the

British Empire, suggesting that it might interfere with Spanish influence in the region."

Martin made to comment, but Dominic held his hand up. "The plans came to naught, after all. Napoleon became a more immediate problem. But the plans had only been shelved temporarily. There were still ships in place no longer needed for the invasion. In the turmoil of changing rule and alliances, three of the ships had broken away under command of disillusioned, in effect disaffected, captains. They had turned to piracy in a place where there were few ships capable of standing up to them. All was not well between them either. The division of loot had become an issue; one of the three had gone independent.

The other two hunted their former colleague down and, in the conflict, the runaway was sunk. By mutual agreement the survivors cooperated, dividing the Western South American seaboard between them. This meant effectively that no traffic could sail from the west coast without the threat of one, or both, of these ships."

"Interesting! But why me? Surely if you wish action to be taken, have words with the Admiralty. I have no authority in a matter such as this!" Martin was puzzled and intrigued.

"In the first place the Admiralty wants nothing to do with Spanish ships in what are, essentially, Spanish-controlled waters. Also, Cochrane is on his way or already there, having been given the rank of Admiral in the Navy of the Chilean Republic, the patriotic army attempting to free the country from Spanish rule. They are embarrassed by this. They are aware of, but not willing to admit to, knowing of the reason the ships were there in the first place. If a private venture was to be attacked by either or both of these ships, and then successfully defeated them, they would be happy to turn a blind eye and welcome the re-establishment of communications with the west coast once more."

"Dominic, you are asking us to perform a task during a commercial operation. Dare I ask what compensation you are prepared to offer on completion of the task?"

Dominic looked taken aback, then realised he had been caught out. Having specified a commercial proposition, he could hardy ask them to lay their lives down for nothing.

"I will arrange a payment of two thousand guineas on successful completion of the task. Will that serve?"

Martin thought about the matter, "You would need a well-found ship for a job like that."

"What do you think of the Asterid?"

Martin thought back to the ship he had taken from the late Captain Shaw. She had been a well-built, and well-looked after ship. Under-gunned of course, but that could be corrected. Otherwise a most suitable ship, depending on the size and condition of the Spanish ships.

"What can you tell me of them?"

"The reports state that the two remaining ships are both frigates, built in 1789. They are sister ships using the same design. The lost ship was older and bigger. She had been a two decker, 60 guns, but her age and lack of maintenance in tropical stations had taken toll of her condition. Her loss had been through treachery as a result of disagreement between the three captains. She was mined at her mooring. They say she was lost with all hands." He shrugged, "My source was himself under suspicion and was forced to leave before that could be verified. Though he did see the ship blow-up and the wreck sink in Coquimbo, in Chile before he left." Dominic stopped and looked directly at Martin. "Why not discuss this project with your friends and family. I really do not think there would be a problem with a crew at present. Since this would be a private venture, there could well be private funding in addition to the rewards from two grateful governments."

Martin stopped Dominic at that point. "Leave it with me. I will discuss matters with my family and I will have an answer for you with a week." Dominic smiled. "Thank you, Martin. One week would be very acceptable. This matter has gone no further. I will keep it that way until we meet again."

They returned to the ballroom and the bustle of the guests.

***

Martin stood watching as Dominic moved off, stopping and talking to people here and there as he passed through the crowd. Jennifer spoke from behind his shoulder. "What was Dominic so keen to discuss with you?"

Martin turned with a smile, slipping his arm around her waist and hugging her. "I'll tell you when we all get home." He bent and kissed her lightly on her lips."

"Promise?" Jennifer said.

"Promise!" Martin re-assured her. "Let us re-join the others."

***

In the garden room in Ovington Gardens, the group returning from the reception was relaxing. The late summer evening light was still enough to make the use of extra lighting minimal, and the warm glow was welcomed after the rather harsh lighting of the ballroom at the reception.

The Admiral Lord Charles and Lady Jane were deep in conversation with the Countess Alouette, while Antonio chatted quietly to Maria and her escort Neil Harmon, who was still in uniform, though expecting to be on half pay along with many of the other officers no longer required by the Navy.

Jennifer looked at Martin, eyebrow raised?

Martin nodded, and Jennifer tapped her glass to get the attention of the party.

"Martin has a matter to speak of, something to do with Dominic Gordon." She sat down and looked at her husband expectantly.

Martin cleared his throat and spoke. He explained what Dominic had suggested in detail, and when he finished he sat back and waited for the inevitable questions.

Neil Harmon spoke first, "Sir, should I even be here? Should I leave now?"

Martin was quick to say. "You are our guest, and this matter could affect you. Please remain, and feel free to suggest or comment if the situation arises."

He turned to the others "Well, ladies and gentlemen, what do you think of this proposal?"

Lord Charles grunted, "How much credence do you put in the word of this man, Dominic?"

Martin considered the question seriously. "Before the American venture I would have found the entire matter suspect. By the time the American venture was over, I saw that boy become a man. I am now inclined to believe him, and I would say that he believes what he has told me."

Antonio commented, "With the state of the Navy at the moment, there is little likelihood of employment, even for you, Martin. But if there is a venture in trade involved, I would be happy to join you." He looked at Alouette as he spoke, but she merely smiled enigmatically.

She added, "I can confirm that Dominic spoke the truth. The situation is as he described. In addition, there is a substantial amount of trade goods accruing on the western shore which someone could well take advantage of. If such a venture was undertaken, I would be inclined to include a cargo ship in the expedition."

Lord Charles said, "This ship he suggested, do you know her?"

"Indeed, I captured her in the Mediterranean. She is a well-kept working frigate, now lying in Portsmouth, though as yet not purchased by the Navy." Martin was thoughtful. "I think the prize court might be happy to have a private buyer for her. I know the Vixen's crew would be happy to see a return from her."

"Then let us visit the yard tomorrow and see what will be involved if you decide to go along with Dominic Gordon's suggestion." Lord Charles rose to his feet, holding his hand out to Lady Jane, politely bid the company good night, and they left for their own home next door in the Gardens.

To Lieutenant Harmon, Martin said, "If this venture goes forward, would you be available to sail with us?"

Harmon flushed with pleasure. "I would be happy to, sir," he said.

Antonio rose to his feet. "In that case we will expect your company tomorrow at the shipyard, Lieutenant."

Alouette smiled. "Since the Lieutenant is occupying the garden room while staying here in London, you can discuss tomorrow's visit over breakfast. Now come, my dear, I feel it is time for us to leave our host and hostess to their private affairs." Turning to Harmon and Maria, she said, "I presume you would rather walk on such a lovely evening." We will see you at the house."

The guests all departed. Jennifer dismissed the housekeeper who had served the party. Then, turning, she stood on the staircase and flirted her skirt, looked sideways at Martin and said, "What's your fancy, Guv?" With a giggle she ran up the stairs with Martin in hot pursuit.

Chapter nineteen

Another World

By the time the ships were ready, it was obvious that there would be no lack of volunteers to crew them. The slimming down of the fleet had created a huge surplus of trained seamen. Despite the talent and skills of the pool of beached officers on half pay, regretfully, there was still sufficient influence wielded for many of the places in the standing fleet to be taken by favour, rather than talent.

For Martin, the selection of people for the flagship of the venture, Asterid, was more difficult that he had at first thought. There were two other ships to man, in addition, since it was decided that a merchantman should accompany them. The Alderney was due to be laid up by the Admiralty and her crew beached. Permission to purchase the ship had been obtained, and along with the Crown Agent's sale of Asterid; the newly formed company became the proud owner of two effective fighting ships and an East Indiaman.

The purchase of the Asterid had been funded in part from government monies, albeit not part of the public purse. Since the second ship, Alderney, was a private purchase, the clearance of her tween decks and hold was carried out with care to maximise her commercial potential. It was accepted that the two warships would carry high value, low volume cargoes, leaving the bulkier cargo to the Castletown.

The merchantman purchased was a strictly commercial project funded by public subscription, though the largest shares were in the hands of Antonio Ramos and Sir Martin Forest-Bowers. The Castletown was an East Indiaman, and configured as a naval ship with a full gun deck, requiring a crew to match. Despite her role as a merchantman, she was well able to look after herself in most circumstances, despite being less agile than a true warship.

The crewing was to a large extent from share-holding former crew members of the various ships Martin had commanded. Since most had benefitted from the prize monies serving under Martin's command, they were only too willing to gamble on a venture led by him.

Patrick Brooks became captain of the Castletown and was happy to have his wife Dorothea to accompany him in the generous accommodation provided. His First Mate was Neil Harmon

Both Antonio and Martin were sailing with the expedition, announced as a combination of a surveying and trading mission to the Pacific. Command of the Asterid was given to John Harris, whose wife, Julia, was accompanying Dorothea, Martin's wife, Jennifer, and Maria Diaz, adoptive daughter of Antonio Ramos. All the ladies were travelling in the Castletown. The Indiaman had accommodation for passengers, having been built for the Passenger/Cargo trade to India.

William Hammond now commanded the Alderney with Lieutenant Gibbs as first lieutenant.

Each of the three ships had parties of Marines aboard commanded by Major Bristow, who had resigned his commission to accompany the expedition. The recruitment of his former American-trained Marines was almost farcical; as soon as the announcement was made the entire company, less two, volunteered. All had benefitted from the rewards gained on the past voyages with Captain Forest-Bowers. All offered up their money to purchase shares in the enterprise.

It came as no surprise to Martin that both McLean and Godden had been recruited by the Major to instruct any new marines in the use of the rifle and field-craft. In view of the unofficial nature of the expedition the Marines did not wear their traditional uniforms, Jennifer had obtained a supply of unmarked dark green uniforms as worn by the Irish regiments, with horn buttons and black pouches for cartridge and shot. A much more suitable colour for the men, as McLean pointed out, especially if they deployed in country areas.

The departure of the ships was low key. Each one left without ceremony.

The parting for Antonio and Alouette was painful for both, but Alouette assured her husband that this would be the last time her duties would keep them apart.

***

Three days into the voyage, the Marines' training began. The ships, now in formation, were enjoying a fair wind and steady progress. All had settled into cruise mode and the benefit of experienced men who had worked together before was quickly felt.

The Marines, no longer constricted by the stiff collar, heavy uniform, and without shako, were now expected to climb the rigging, and run and tumble on deck. McLean and Godden were merciless in their determination to take the starch out of them and turn them into all-round fighting men.

While the weather remained good, the Marines suffered. Interestingly, though the sailors mocked them, when minor punishment came their way they were made to join the Marines in their torment. This gave the Marines the chance to get their own back. By the time the small fleet was into the doldrums, the opportunity for inter-ship competition was seized, and the result of the training really made itself apparent.

The Marines rowed the longboat from Castletown. They had practiced when the ships took time to communicate whenever there was good weather. The captains and the ladies normally met on the Castletown. She was roomy and had the accommodation the others were lacking. Thus the boats from Castletown were in regular use.

When the races occurred between the stationary ships in the doldrums, the Marines from the merchantman made a showing that surprised the sailors.

When the wind finally came once more, the Asterid parted company from the other ships. They went to call at the port of Maceio, where Antonio's brother had been murdered. There they found that the town had been rebuilt and the church restored under another priest.

Martin left Antonio to speak with the priest while he accompanied Captain Hammond to purchase fresh water and stores.

For Antonio it was a sad moment. He was taken to his brother's grave, where he said a prayer for him and his congregation. Before leaving, he gave the priest the gold and ivory crucifix to replace in the church where his brother had placed it.

He told Martin what he had done, on the way back to the ship.

***

Through steadily worsening weather they fought their way south to Cape Horn.

Captain Hammond elected to keep the southerly course until the loom of the ice became apparent. Only then did he turn north-west, to claw his way past the mass of small islands on the western side of the great island of Tierra del Fuego, keeping tight to the wind and making way past Punta Arenas and into the Pacific Ocean.

The rendezvous was in Golfo de Penas, north along the coast of Chile. It was there they found the two other ships. Alderney, close alongside Castletown, having her mizzen mast re-stepped. Though Asterid had not lost a mast, the ship did not make the transit unscathed. Having lost several sails, there had been several broken bones and one death during the journey, the unfortunate man being caught by a broken boltrope from the flogging ripped sail. It had ripped his throat. He had lost his grip, and, according to the doctor, been dead before his body reached the deck. His death was recorded and his family would receive his full share from the voyage.

They spent three days at anchor while the re-rigging of the mizzen was carried out. The crews, took the opportunity to socialise with a make-and-mend as soon as the repairs were completed.

The ladies had a chance to see their men-folk. The wounded were brought on deck to relax and enjoy the fun and the fresh air. The three ladies' maids, who had been recruited to look after the ladies on the voyage, were quick to take advantage of the weather, and brought the sewing which needed doing to a corner of the deck, to sew and flirt with the crew members working in their vicinity. Sharing the servant cabins near the staterooms around the saloon, they saw mostly the cook and the stewards. Going on deck, apart from the danger, was frowned upon during passage. So they were enjoying their freedom, whilst they may.

There had been no other serious injuries. Once bones were set and splinted, the doctor gave his patients a good chance of complete recovery. Maria had been quick to offer to help the doctor n tending the wounded, and was able to see more of Lieutenant Harman than would have been possible otherwise.

While they were in the Golfo they saw no one. That was not an indication that no-one was there. Martin was well aware that eyes were watching every move the ships made. By the time they moved, he had no hesitation in ordering that they sail due west to pick up the Peru Current to sweep them northward beyond the sight of land to the region of Valdivia where the location of the Spanish ships could be sought. Nearly five days passed as they made their way north. The weather had become dull and wet. McLean said to Godden, "This is supposed to be the bloody tropics. If I get any wetter, I'll begin to melt!"

"Trouble with you, McLean, is, you read too many books. Because of that you don't use your eyes. I told you when we anchored in the sun for those days. The moment the skipper turned west, we were for it. When we turned north we followed the weather."

McLean grumbled, stretching and wincing as the muscle twinged. "Bloody rheumatism, that's what it is."

"I don't know what that is. Does it hurt?" Godden looked at his friend warily.

"Course it bloody hurts. Always does. You'll soon know when you get it."

Tiring of the conversation, Godden got to his feet and, as he walked off, he said, "I shan't bother getting it, if that's what it does."

Mr. Watson, who heard the conversation, grinned. Turning to Midshipman James Woods, he said, "There's something for you to remember, young man. If you don't want rheumatism, don't bother getting it."

James, who had not heard the conversation, looked at the Master in bewilderment. Since he had only heard of rheumatism as a name, he had no idea what was amusing the old man. He shook his head. "Yes, sir!" He said automatically. "I'll remember."

***

They reached the island of Juan Fernandez, where they stopped to water and dry out in the returning sunshine. Soon the ships were all festooned with clothing blowing dry in the fresh breeze. The sun, absent for the past five days, had returned and there was a warm feeling in the air to lighten spirits.

For the leaders there was now the problem of intelligence. The decision was to take the biggest of the small craft, the 30ft longboat with mast and sails and make the trip to Valdivia. Alderney would escort her three quarters of the way, and wait for her return. Martin decided to command the expedition and nominated Peters, Midshipman Woods, McLean, and one other.

"I will accompany the party!" Julia Harris stepped forward. "I am the best qualified for this sort of activity, and I can speak Spanish. I do not believe any of you do?"

Martin who would have taken the Master, Jared Watson, demurred, until he realised that this woman had been an agent for Alouette before he had met her, and had been on the expedition to arrest the Colonel.

As others raised their voices to say 'no', Martin stopped them. "Julia, my profound apologies, of course you are better qualified than all of us, and Spanish? How could we manage without you? Just one thing. Where you go, Godden goes."

Julia thought for a moment. Then she nodded. "Agreed!" Thus the matter was settled.

***

Alderney towed the longboat to within easy sailing distance of the coast. Captain Hammond arranged to cruise offshore and keep the rendezvous under observation for the next two days if necessary. If there was no contact by that time, he would land the Marine contingent under Major Bristow, to come and find the party.

The longboat made land with the aid of a fisherman, who landed his catch outside the city so that he would not need to pay the taxes the city imposed. They beached the longboat in the cove over the headland from the city itself. Keeping each other in sight, they split up and drifted into the city without causing any overt interest. Julia, who now wore Spanish dress, albeit plain, was followed by Godden, who towered above her and was obviously her protector. The others were ahead and behind, Martin, with Peters in the lead, and James Woods, with McLean, following behind. The fisherman who had brought them so far, now left them to deliver his catch to his regular customers.

His warning about the Guardia was heeded, since they had been subverted by the Spanish self-styled Commodore, whose two ships dominated the politics and the trade of the coastline.

***

The harbour was now in view and it was possible to see the size of the problem faced by the expedition.

Both ships seemed in fair condition. One was alongside the quay, having repairs done to the fore-top mast which was being replaced with a new spar. The damaged spar was lying on the quay awaiting disposal. James Woods, dressed in scruffy clothing, wandered onto the quay and took a look at the spar to try and assess the reason for the damage. He was chased off for his pains, but had been able to see that the spar had been damaged by cannon fire. He had seen similar damage on his own ship.

Julia meanwhile had been to visit a small shop in the old part of the city. The clock-maker who occupied the premises, was a contact maintained through 'plain Mr. Smith'. British interest was thin on the ground on the west coast of South America and it had been through the Consular service that contact had been arranged. The small payment that retained the services of Mendoza the clock maker had made the difference between his wife spending her dying years in agony, or under the soothing influence of the drug which eased the pain and allowed her to die quietly in her sleep.

For that, Mendoza would be eternally grateful.

The visit by Julia, who was able to identify herself through password and seal, was welcomed by the Clock-Maker whose only family had been his wife. The housekeeper was his next door neighbour, and she was the only other person to enter his private rooms behind the shop, up to now.

His visit from Julia was the highlight of the day. She arranged for a visit by Martin in the evening, after his housekeeper had left for the night.

David O'Neil

Chapter twenty

One at a Time

The discussion with Alberto Mendoza was interesting. Alberto was Spanish and proud of it. He did not approve of the way the self-appointed Commodore had assumed command and control of local affairs.

"This man does not have the right to dictate the law, and order the local authority to do his bidding. This country is not his private property, but he does have the guns, and the armed men, and this means he has the power."

Martin asked "How did the damage occur to the Rosario, the ship alongside the quay at the moment?"

Alberto leaned forward and tapped his nose. "Aha! This seems to be a big secret. But I believe that the cannon from the Castillo in Conception is responsible. It seems that the Castillo refuses to acknowledge the authority of the Commodore, and at present the Commodore is preparing to attack the Castillo and bring it into his control. The local militia is under training as we speak."

"But what about the local government? Why do they do whatever this man asks? Who is this man?"

"He is of the family of Cortez, He claims to be, anyway. He claims the right of his family to rule the colonies here in America. To people such as me, this is rubbish, but to people of family it obviously means something."

"Is there no Governor?"

"Sadly the Governor is away, he went to Madrid. He was recalled for discussions one year ago, he cannot return until this Commodore has been removed. It seems that the Royal Fleet has not recovered from Trafalgar!"

"But that was over ten years ago, surely, they have other ships?"

"There was a fleet here; the Commodore is the surviving commander. To my knowledge he has sunk two of the other ships in the fleet when they refused to carry out his orders."

"When does the attack on the Castillo take place? Do you know?"

"It will be soon, possibly when the Rosario has been repaired, perhaps a week. They will need to do something to make the place secure, There is a revolution in the air. The Spanish Government has let things slip for so long, all they have done is demand the gold every year without anything in return. The revolutions in the other South American countries had brought the matter close, and our Commodore wishes to negotiate from a base of power, and that means Conception must be taken."

Martin nodded thoughtfully, he had been aware of the unsettled state of Spain's Colonies for some time, without realising how close matters were, to coming to a head.

He spoke to Alberto, "I have a ship loaded with supplies to trade. If we can get a message to the Castillo, we can offer them assistance against the Commodore when he attacks them. My supply ship can come in and deliver trade goods and accept a return cargo while the attack takes place. How does that sound to you?"

Alberto smiled, "It is true the merchants of the City would be pleased to hear this news. I will make sure they are aware that it must not reach the ears of the authorities. I will remind them of the new taxes they will have to pay if the information becomes known too soon."

Alberto Mendoza rang a small bell and a woman appeared, James Woods was stunned by her startling blue eyes, in her café-au-lait face. The girl was fifteen, perhaps sixteen, and dressed in a ragged collection of clothes. Alberto rattled off a string of words that bore little relationship to the Spanish and English used by the others.

The girl nodded and left as silently as she had appeared.

Alberto smiled at James, "She is pretty, is she not? Sophia is the daughter of a friend and enjoys her role as go-between. The message to the Castillo will be taken today."

Julia asked the question the others were wishing to ask. "What language was that?"

Alberto smiled, "My apologies, I used the local patois, it is a lingua franca that has established itself here, a mixture of the different native Indio and Spanish speech of the coast."

The party prepared to return to the boat, though Julia decided that she would stay.

For Martin it was a difficult situation, but he realised that the business of the agents for plain Mr. Smith was information, and the only way to gather and verify information was to be in place to find it. Godden and James Woods were elected to stay with her; both were skilled in melting into the background, and both were comfortable in the urban environment of the City.

Alberto welcomed Julia's decision and called the housekeeper to prepare a room for his newly arrived niece from Santiago, she was a welcome temporary addition to the household. The other members of the party disappeared before the housekeeper appeared.

Three days later James Woods encountered Sophia once more. Or to be more accurate Sophia encountered James.

***

Martin, Peters and McLean, reached the boat safely finding it undisturbed where they had left it. They were assisted by the fisherman with the launching. He had returned after disposing of his catch and was preparing to go out once more. Martin pressed a handful of coins into the man's hand as they left the shore, grateful for the help the man had given.

They made the rendezvous with the Alderney that night and were soon well on their way back to the island of Juan Fernandez and the rest of the flotilla.

Godden and James were watching Julia shopping with the housekeeper in the market.

The giggle warned James and he turned swiftly to see those astonishing blue eyes inches from his. Gone were the ragged clothes, now dressed formally in a linen and lace dress with her hair brushed and arranged her colour contrasted to the white dress. James thought he had never seen anyone so beautiful in his life. She smiled a little hesitantly and indicated the basket of flowers she was carrying. "Fiesta?" She said carefully.

James became aware of the growing sound of music from the main street beyond the market. The people around them began to react to the music, the murmur of conversation grew louder. Godden nudged him in the back, nodded to the girl and said, "Off you go, lad, I'll keep an eye on the lass."

James smiled at Sophia and she took his hand, he allowed himself to be towed off to the source of the music.

Godden watched them go and turned back to watch Julia just in time to see the two men follow the housekeeper and Julia back toward the clock-makers shop.

A watcher could have been forgiven for not realising that Godden had been there in the first place. The two followers after Julia and her companion certainly had no reason to worry, after all both were well skilled at their trade. Their first shock came when Julia turned and thrust the pistol into the throat of the nearest man.

"We have not been introduced, Senor, I am at a loss, why are you following my friend and me?"

The man found it difficult to talk as the muzzle of the pistol was pressed against his larynx. The knife in his hand was feeling slippery from his suddenly sweating hand. He did not understand why his partner had not stepped in and at least threatened the other woman. He was totally unaware that his companion was no longer conscious, in fact he was only now aware that the pistol had been cocked, and death was a very real prospect.

The knife in his hand was removed and the pistol also. Only the hand on his neck was constricting his breathing.

"Don't kill him yet, Godden, I would like to know who sent him."

"Very good, madam, his friend seems to have collapsed, will you tell this man to pick him up and bring him with us please."

Julia spoke and their dismayed prisoner collected his fallen friend and dragged him down the alley beside the shop and dumped him in the shed behind the house.

Julia lifted an eyebrow?

Godden shrugged and shut the shed door, pushing the live one through the back door into the back room of the shop.

"Now who sent you?" Julia said sweetly. She removed a small stiletto from her bag and tossed it in the air and caught it by the tip, flipped it again and allowed it to fall to the table the tip plunging into the space between the thumb and first finger of her right hand. She made absolutely no attempt to avoid the weapon, demonstrating clearly that she knew where it would land.

The prisoner was spellbound.

"Who sent you?" Julia said once more. She pulled the stiletto from the table and started flipping it in her hand.

"Major Jimenez." He said in a whisper.

"And what were your orders?"

"We were to find out who you were and where you came from." The words were strained as the tension of the situation took its toll.

"Then what?" The questions kept coming.

"Use you first and then kill you." The monotone was now sounding hopeless, as the man realised that he was as good as dead already.

"Where do we find this Major Jimenez?"

"He is in command of the la Cuartel, the barracks, in the City."

"Where does he live?" Julia asked.

The man shrugged and rolled his shoulders, "I don't know."

The housekeeper said, "He is lying, everyone knows the Major stays at the house of the Governor while the Governor is away."

***

James and Sophia found the music in the square opposite the Governors Palace. There were stalls set up and banners fluttering in the breeze and in several places there were musicians playing for individual dancers, surrounded by friends. The music was for the flamenco, favoured by the gipsy people in their Spanish homeland, and recently adopted by the local musicians because of the excitement the music generated, and the drama of the dance. Sophia spun away and started to click her fingers and stamp her heels to the wild music. The folk nearby turned and applauded as she spun and whirled to the beat of the strumming guitars, a singer was following the music with snapping fingers, her dark complexion indicating her gypsy origins.

She sang faster taking the music with her and Sophia responded, her feet tapping in time with the music, her skirt swirling as she spun to and fro.

With a flourish the guitars brought the music to a close and Sophia fell into James's arms, accompanied by the clapping of the bystanders.

"Fun eh?" The English words whispered in his ear shocked James who had not realised the Sophia spoke the language.

The feel of the nubile young body in his arms, her breath tickling his ear brought a reaction from James that was new to his young life. Up until now girls had been friends, like boys. Well, not quite like boys, but then he did not know many girls anyway. This girl with her startling blue eyes and her disturbing body was a new experience for the boy. She stood back smiling, well aware of the effect she was having on her fourteen-year-old companion.

At the age of fourteen she was more adult than many girls of the same age elsewhere. Many of her childhood playmates were already married, and two had children. She was grateful to her grandfather, who had insisted on her being educated to the extent of his own education, which had meant less opportunity to indulge in the games played by the others in her age group.

Flirting with James was fun and she was enjoying the game.

There was a murmur among the people of the crowd nearby, they were unhappy about the small group of men who were purposely pushing their way through the crowd. The mutter was of bandolera; it was the name given to the plain-clothed men used by the Major for what he called discreet operations. In a place like Valdivia there was no such thing as a discreet operation. The plain-clothed people were all known by the public. They were known as the bandolera because they tended to take whatever they wanted.

They were hated, and wherever they could be they were obstructed. In this case there was an almost immovable crowd that was preventing the Major's men from making their way through.

Looking at the source of the crowd's interest, Sophia grabbed James by the hand and whispered, "Time to go I believe." With that she was off away from the frustrated bandolera.

The crowd split to allow them through. They ran and walked for over an hour before they stopped on a hilltop at a small group of trees. There was an open stretch of grass in the sunshine, where they had a good view in all directions. There Sophia lay down on the grass in the sun and hauled James down next to her.

***

In the shop, the return of Godden meant that the two prisoners had been disposed of. Julia had a suspicion that the actual disposal was possibly permanent. While she was pragmatic she was still admittedly rather squeamish about cold blooded murder. In fact her fears were groundless. It was easier to transport the two men while they were conscious. Their disposal was accomplished by delivery to the fisherman who had brought the party into the city in the first place. He undertook to leave the men down coast where there were no roads north, and no sympathy for the Major or his men.

Chapter twenty-one

Gunfire and Politics

When James Woods and Sophia left their sunny sanctuary, his education in the relationship between men and women had been expanded. For him, the discoveries of the day had been astonishing, highlighting his innocence up to this time.

Hand in hand, they returned to the city; Sophia keeping a wary eye out for the searchers from earlier. They approached the shop with caution and were greeted by Godde, from the shadows. "Have a good time, sir?"

James stammered "Why, y-yes Godden, thank you. We had a fine time."

Godden grinned in the darkness. Having seen the girl, he guessed they really did have fun.

James and Sophia entered the shop, and found the others prepared to eat. Julia had been worried about their lengthy absence, but reassured by Mendoza, she had contained her worry.

The report about the men in the square had been disturbing but it seemed they had got away with it.

***

Martin arranged with Captain Brooks for the Castletown to sail for Valdivia with the entire party of Marines on board. Major Bristow was primed to take over the security of the city from the militia run by Major Jimenez. Through Mr. Weeks the supercargo was prepared to open trade with the local merchants in Valdivia, convinced that the goods they had brought would be welcomed in the city.

The Alderney was keeping watch to ensure the departure of the Rosario before the Castletown entered the port.

Her signal to the waiting East Indiaman was her last act before making all sail for the rendezvous with the Asterid. She shadowed the Rosario to Conception Bay just over 150 miles to the north, where the sound of the guns marked the place where the attack on the Castillo had commenced.

The Rosario approached the Sierra Nova, the 44gun frigate captained by the leader of the mutiny, Commodore Rodrigo Ramirez. The Commodore ceased fire and withdrew out of range of the Castillo's guns to confer with his associate.

Martin and Hammond had discussed their roles in the attack they were about to make, taking into account the onshore drift in the region. Asterid was sheltered at the moment behind the Punta de Fraile, the headland at the northern end of Conception Bay.

The appearance of the Alderney was a shock for the Commodore, who was unaware of any other ships or force in the area. The onshore drift was pulling both Sierra Nova and Rosario shoreward as they sat close to each other, discussing the appearance of the Alderney which was flying British colours.

As far as they were aware, there was no dispute between Spain and Britain, and certainly the British ship was not showing signs of aggression.

Ramirez decided to meet with the new arrival himself and find out what they were doing in the area. He gave orders to stand off from the shore and meet with the new arrival, leaving the Rosario to threaten the Castillo.

It was a shock to hear the guns of the Castillo opening fire as the Sierra Nova clawed her way offshore.

The Rosario had drifted closer to the shore and within range of the guns of the Castillo.

The gunfire hurt the Rosario badly. The battery at the Castillo had heated shot to use against the attacking ships and the first salvo fired at the Rosario had included the entire capacity of the heating arrangements. A total of three heated shots had struck the unfortunate ship and a trail of fire had followed the first to strike the deck, ending against the mainmast and setting the sheets tied to the fife rail alight, the flames leaped up the dried ropes to the tarred rigging at the lower mast-head, the heat melted the tar and set fire to the ratlines. The mainsail caught and the out of control wave of fire leapt skyward helped by the breeze and set the topsails alight.

The crew of the Rosario rushed about, the shouted orders of the captain ignored in the panic. The captain tried to heel the ship to allow the wind to take the stricken ship offshore and out of the range of the Castillo guns. Despite his efforts the ship drifted inexorably shoreward.

The continuing fire from the fort was causing the ship real problems, the attempts to return fire by the gun crews on the ship were becoming more and more panicky as strips of burning canvas from the sails above dropped to the deck, and in one case into a tub of cartridges which blew-up killing the gun crew, and scattering the flaming residue across the deck.

The mizzen mast fell to another strike from the fortress guns, and the Rosario, now completely out of control drifted helplessly deep into the bay, where it grounded in the shallows, still under the continued pounding from the guns of the Castillo. The surviving officers and crew abandoned her and waded ashore, where they stood and watched as the Castillo and the fire destroyed the stranded ship. As they stood and watched, a crowd assembled silently behind them. From the walls of the Castillo it was possible to see the survivors being taken.

The reception the survivors from the Rosario received was unfriendly. The local populace were dependant in part at least, upon the trade with the Castillo. And since they were protected by the guns of the fortress, they were not about to support people who were attacking their protectors.

The Commodore on the Sierra Nova was furious. He had watched impotently as his support ship was lost. His fury increasing as each part of the building disaster occurred, eventually he turned his attention to the British ship still some distance away. Noting now that despite its warlike armament it was flying a merchant ensign, which meant it was a private ship.

He swung round to his First Lieutenant, "Are the guns reloaded?"

"Yes sir, but not run out."

"Good, when we get within range, run out and crush her, before she knows what is happening."

"Yes sir!" The First Lieutenant looked at his captain warily, watching him as he turned away. Over the past few months he had seen the man change from a sensible intelligent man into the angry short-tempered person he had become. He was concerned because he believed his captain was ill and refusing treatment, making his condition worse. The Doctor in the City was wary of talking to the new authorities who had taken over the area arbitrarily. But he had confirmed that he thought, from observation combined with rumour, that the Commodore had become infected with what he guessed was syphilis.

Rodrigo Ramirez was angry, it seemed it was a regular condition these days. He could not get comfortable for some reason. Parts of his body always seemed to be causing him pain, and even lovemaking which had always been a pleasure no longer satisfied him as it once had. He gazed out at the strange ship, it was rigged and seemed armed as a frigate, but it had to be a privateer, flying a merchant flag.

As the Sierra Nova tried to close the Alderney it became apparent that the British ship was keeping her distance.

When the Asterid appeared from around the headland, it enraged the Commodore to the extent his officers feared he would have a fit.

"Get me in range of that ship," he shrieked. I'll sink her and then take the other intruder in her turn.

At this point, Hammond noted the moment of indecision by the captain of the Sierra Nova. In the Alderney, he let her head fall off the wind, and swooped down on the Sierra Nova with guns being run out, and marksmen in the tops.

Taken by surprise the Sierra Nova ran out her guns also but the move that allowed Alderney to get in her broadside was of little use to the Spanish ship, which managed to fire some of her guns, but only managed to tear two holes in the mainsail of her opponent.

The Alderney fire damaged the gun deck of Sierra Nova causing casualties among the gun crews and smashing the boats which had not been set loose as was normal when going into battle. The mayhem caused by the splintering of the boats cost the Spanish most of the people on deck. The Commodore himself was wounded as a splinter ripped down his arm and lodged in his side.

Alderney did not stay to fight but sailed off to leave the field clear for the Asterid which was approaching fast.

The result of the first strike by Alderney was decisive. The Sierra Nova captained by the bloody wounded Commodore, who was by now probably completely mad, was in no state to face the experienced well-drilled crew of the Asterid.

After the ships had exchanged two broadsides, the First Lieutenant called for the Commodore to haul down the colours. The Commodore screamed at him and raised his sword to slash at him. The Lieutenant shot his mad captain without hesitation and called for the colours to be lowered.

Looking around the bloody deck strewn with bodies and wreckage, Martin was sickened at the waste of lives, and damage to a good sound ship.

***

Anchored off the Castillo. the soldiers from the fortress took charge of the surviving crew members along with the survivors from the beached Rosario.

Martin discussed matters with the Colonel in command. As a result a company of his soldiers joined the ships for the voyage to Valdivia, to take over security duties from the militia.

The Colonel himself joined them as they sailed in company with the battered Sierra Nova the 150 miles south to the City, where they found the Castletown already moored alongside.

In the city meanwhile the Marines who had drifted ashore without attracting attention gathered up the roving patrols of bandolera, helpfully pointed out by selected friends of the Alberto Mendoza, the clock-maker.

Quietly and efficiently they patrolled the city under the guidance of the local patriots, and gathered the small groups of Jimenez's men where ever they could be found. On three occasions they found people being assaulted, which led to immediate punishment from which two men did not recover, and left several others wishing they had not recovered.

***

The major himself was in the Governor's Palace dining when Major Bristow called. Jimenez looked up at the Major's entrance, the green uniform with the black buttons were an unfamiliar sight. The remainder of the major's attire was however quite recognisable. The sword, pistol and the slung rifle, were all quite familiar and, showing sense, Jimenez did not make the mistake of reaching for the weapon he had concealed under the dining table. Realising that the servant standing behind his chair was not the man appointed to the task saved his life at that moment.

"I can smell that my servant is no longer behind my chair, so I will ask you politely, Major, who the hell are you, and what are you doing here?"

Bristow clicked his heels with a sharp click and said, "Major Alan Bristow. His Britannic Majesties Royal Marines at your service."

"Why are you here disturbing my meal?"

"I am here to place you and your militia under arrest on behalf of the Spanish government." He nodded to the sergeant standing behind Jimenez. The sergeant jerked the major from his chair and up to his feet, securing his hands behind him with a loop of rope.

The protesting major was frog-marched from the Palace and paraded through the streets to the barracks where the rest of the militia were being held. By this time there were sufficient people on the streets to make the city aware that the current regime was being replaced. The sight of the Spanish colours flying over the captured barracks was sufficient indication to the populace that the rule of law had been re-established in the city.

When the Asterid arrived with the prize, and landed the Colonel and his men, the city was handed over.

The Colonel formally took command of the town accepting the handover of Major Jimenez and his men. Major

Bristow's Marines quietly rejoined their ships, without fuss or embarrassment to either side.

The discussions between the Colonel and Martin were conducted most amicably and the establishment of trade links approved.

Mr. Weeks had been most successful with his initial trade contacts. The cargo of weaving and farm machinery brought by the Castletown was most welcome, and the purchase of tobacco, widely grown in the area and fine Alpaca wool as a return cargo was made at a very advantageous rate. In addition prepared cured cattle-leather hides were added to the cargo.

The Sierra Nova was purchased by the Chilean government at a good price for refitting and re-commissioning under the Spanish flag as protection from any other pirates that may consider moving into the area.

The Colonel gave them a laissez-passer for use up the coast, as Martin had mentioned that there were still things in the cargo of the Castletown for trade plus items from the Valdivia traders to be delivered to Santiago and Lima in Peru.

The true extent of the inhibition to trade created by the operations of the Sierra Nova and the Rosario was only just becoming apparent.

Further delays to the departure of the expedition were experienced when the Governor of the province finally returned to Valdivia. It seemed that the report of the British ships in the area had caused him to move back to keep a close eye on the local situation. His immediate reaction had been that the ships were part of the incipient rebellion sweeping the Spanish colonies. The appointment of Admiral Cochrane to command the rebel Chilean Navy was already news. When he heard that the City had been released from the grip of the rebel Commodore, he decided to risk returning and resuming his role as Governor.

For Martin the discussion with the returned Governor was interesting as the man was convinced that the current state of Chile as an autonomous Republic within the Spanish monarchy would remain. This was apparently in view of the fact that in Argentina Jose Carrera, the Chilean patriot, had been imprisoned. However Martin had been advised that an army under Bernardo O'Higgins and his anti-Carrera friend Jose de San Martin, hero of the Argentine war of Independence had set out to cross the Andes from Argentina. That army would soon be appearing. Martin had discussed the prospect with the Colonel who had been better informed than the Governor. The pragmatic Colonel had said that he would look after the Governor, until the army arrived but would guarantee no more than that.

It was thus with some relief that Martin sailed north for the visits to Santiago and Lima. The time spent on the South American coast was not comfortable though they made many good friends during their trading journey, they thankfully did not encounter Admiral Cochrane.

***

At Guayaquil in Ecuador they held a council to decide their next destination. As Martin pointed out there was more involved here than the simple decision taken by the commodore or captain in charge. Since the excursion was funded by the company, and since that meant more or less the entire company of crew and supernumeries, there was more than one option to be considered.

It was at Guayaquil that Antonio Ramos left the party to take passage on a ship to Santos where he would visit his Brazilian interests and those of his ward Maria, before returning to England and Alouette. Maria elected to remain on board with the other ladies.

Chapter twenty-three

The Wide Pacific

Striking west into the open sea, from Guayaquil the three ships, having been refurbished and stored and now fairly well stocked with trading goods, made initially for the Galapagos Islands to take on water before the major voyage to the Polynesian Islands. The decision to sail to China, thence to India, would be confirmed as they closed the Western Pacific rim. Trade would dictate their destination which could include the recent increases in cargoes of tea being carried by the East India Company.

For Martin and Jennifer the voyage was a chance to spend time together that had not been possible in the past. With their daughter Jane at home with her grandparents, they were able to enjoy each other's company. They missed Antonio but Julia, Maria and Dorothea were all lively and entertaining companions. The relaxation of formality among the ladies had affected Dorothea particularly, having for the first time in her life been in company where the inhibitions of society were of necessity ignored. The atmosphere within the ships was more like a yachting expedition than a commercial enterprise.

All four women had now learned to shoot the rifles, Julia of course was the most advanced to begin with, but Maria was soon in close competition, and though Jennifer was competent she was never in their class with the rifle she was swiftly able to demonstrate her skills with the rapier. For Dorothea, the struggle between her conscience and pragmatism was a serious handicap until they came across the ship's boat. The story told by the survivor persuaded her that there was sound common sense in learning to defend herself, certainly in the dangerous waters of the South Pacific Ocean.

Spotted in the open sea, over two hundred miles from the nearest land, they at first thought the boat empty. As they approached it became obvious that there were people lying in the partially-waterlogged craft.

Four of the people were dead, seriously sunburned but it was the wounds that they had received that were the cause of their death. Underneath two of the bodies was the girl. She had been protected by the others in the boat, though there was a wound on her leg.

The Doctor examined the survivor and announced that she would recover, her wound was probably two days old, and he had been able to clean it and dress it. Her condition otherwise was caused by shock. He would not allow any questions until the girl had rested and rehydrated. Jennifer and Maria had washed her carefully and were attending her while she was kept in bed.

Martin had transferred the survivor across to the Castletown to be looked after by the ladies, the doctor Roger Mills supervised her care personally.

***

When the girl had recovered sufficiently to tell her story, Martin was present. Her tale was not a new one. Her name was Olivia del la Cruz; she was travelling to Manila on the Spanish trading brig Porto del Oro.

Her parents were taking her to their home in the Colony, now that she had finished her education in Seville.

They were approached by a Chinese junk, though the crew spoke Tagalog, the language of the ordinary people of Manila. As they closed the brig they opened fire with their single cannon. The captain was wounded but he called to the passengers to escape in the boat that was being towed behind the ship. It was there to tighten up the seams that were beginning to gape from the effects of the sun. "Five of us managed to get into the boat as the pirates boarded the ship and my father cut the rope. There was water in the bottom of the boat but it was floating and we drifted away from the two ships. I could hear the screams of the crew who were killed and being thrown overboard.

My father said we should lie down in the boat so that the pirates would believe it was empty." She stopped for a moment the tears ran down her cheeks as she continued. "They burned the Porto del Oro, and then they came for us. I was lying beneath my mother and father, as the Junk came near the pirates fired at my father as he lay covering us. His last words were 'Don't Move'. Several bullets hit him, and my mother too, I felt them both die protecting me. There was a pain in my leg, and I fainted. That was yesterday, I was in pain from my leg and the sun was hot so I stayed where I was, waiting to die. I think I was delirious, I know I shouted to God to end it for me, then I slept, and then you came."

Olivia was brought on deck as her condition improved, shaded from the sunshine, but where the breeze cooled her skin and the fresh air brought life to her cheeks.

It also brought her the sight of the other ladies on the ship, as they trained with rifle sword and pistol. Her interest was aroused as she realised the reason for their efforts, and her admiration at the skills demonstrated was enough reason for her to join in as soon as she was able.

It was the martial games the ladies played that induced Julia to suggest that such skills were difficult to achieve dressed in voluminous skirts, and she produced the buckskin outfit that she wore in the woods, when she was in America. Using the design as a pattern and dress material instead of buckskin, the ladies with the help of the three maids produced pantaloons and jerkins that covered them from neck to ankle, and allowed them to move easily when fencing. Using spare buckskin brought for patching, McLean fashioned moccasins which were far better for moving around the deck. The ladie's shoes had rapidly became bedraggled and smeared with tar from the stopping that softened in the heat of the sun. For Dorothea, the transition from the Rectory to the quarterdeck was difficult. The presence of the other ladies helped, and though shocked at first, when she was eventually persuaded to try the modified outfit, she immediately realised the advantages of the light clothing in the tropical sunshine, and her skill with sword and rifle improved as a result.

With Martin's approval, all of the midshipmen were encouraged to practice swordplay with the ladies, earning themselves many a red face after a session with the improving Maria and the increasingly expert Jennifer.

***

Bang Lok was a successful pirate. He looked upon his base and holdings each morning with pride, from his house on the hill overlooking the harbour where his ships lay at anchor.

His position as Governor of this island had been achieved through the simple act of taking it by force, and advising the Prince who ruled the archipelago that he would resist any attempt to take the island back. While he was Governor he would ensure peace in the area, and pay a reasonable contribution to the Prince's treasury, in return for being left alone.

Thus far things had gone well, the Prince had kept his part of the bargain just as he Bang Lok, had in turn, kept his.

His number two wife entered and set down tea on the table beside him. She served it without being prompted. She was an excellent wife in all ways, and at present was occupied in addition to serving tea with a major project on his behalf, that of extending his family. He looked with approval at the burgeoning bulge that was now beginning to stretch the cheongsam, and quietly thanked her for the tea.

Since she did not immediately leave, he looked at her with eyebrow raised.

"Master there is a messenger wishing to speak with you." The pleasant sing song of her voice was most distracting, he thought.

"Send him in!" He said eventually.

She bowed and left the room.

The tramp of feet announced the presence of his deputy Captain Ramon Spiers, formerly of His Majesties East India Company, specifically the Bombay Marines.

His transition to the service of his current employer had commenced when he was in passage to China to join a Company ship that had lost members of its crew, due to pirate activity. The ship he was travelling on was raided and captured by Bang Lok who at the time was building his empire.

The loss of his sailing master in the takeover of the Indiaman was a serious matter as Bang Lok was not a navigator, and he was unhappy about sailing with a Navigator who found his way by smelling the wind and watching birds. Mr. Spiers was among the prisoners and had acquitted himself well in the fight for the ship, accounting for several of Bang Lok's men, before he had been overpowered.

It was an offer he couldn't refuse, join the pirates or join the survivors, who were already lined up for the long swim, the nearest land, as he well knew was 78 miles away. In addition the dead who had already been thrown overboard were currently shark food.

Since he joined Bang Lok, Spiers had prospered. Once he proved his worth as a navigator, and his loyalty on several occasions, he now occupied a similar house to Bang Lok, with three wives, and servants, and a standard of living he could never have achieved elsewhere.

He stepped onto the veranda where Bang Lok was seated and bowed. He was a tall fair-haired man with a pleasant, suntanned face. He was still trim and wore the uniform he had designed with flair. The sword at his side was Toledo. He was accompanied by a Polynesian, a man of the sea, who smelt of fish, and smoke, and salt. He was silent and barefoot. He bowed to Bang Lok and waited.

Bang Lok waved Spiers to a seat and said "What is this about?"

Spiers said, "Perhaps you should allow this man to explain."

Bang Lok smiled and turned to the fisherman, "Then please explain why you are here?"

The man looked up at Bang Lok and spoke in Tagalog. "I was on the island of Palau, a week ago and three big ships sailed in to the anchorage. They had been in the big storm and so had damage to repair. They are making for China as I discovered, so I thought you might be interested in one of the ships that is heavy with cargo. They will not leave for two weeks while they repair their rigging. They sail with British flag."

Bang Lok looked at his captain, "Well what do you think?"

"There were ladies with the ships." Spiers said thoughtfully.

"Does it matter to you?" Bang Lok said mildly.

"I believe it does." Spiers said, "I cannot really ignore the fact that I have friends with wives working in the East Indies. I have never enjoyed killing friends."

Bang Lok smiled, "As my friend I hope it will always be that way. I will send Chang Po, and we will see if his skill equals his boasts. I will instruct him to bring prisoners here."

Spiers rose to leave, but Bang Lok stopped him and waved him back to his seat. The fisherman left with a servant to receive payment for his news.

Turning to his friend Bang Lok said. "Ramon, let us talk a little, it is some time since we enjoyed a conversation."

He called for more tea and the two men sat and chatted, while on the other side of the island Chang Po prepared his Junks for the ambush of the three European ships that would be at his mercy soon.

Chapter twenty-three

Said the Spider

The weather changed and the three ships were treated to a violent storm which rapidly found weaknesses in rigging, and started timbers. It was wise therefore to divert to the nearest port where they could make repairs.

Palau was a pleasant island with a trading population and small shipyard that was run by an Frenchman who had served with Napoleon up to 1801, having lost his foot when his boot rotted away, and his foot was punctured by a tree root.

A former jobbing carpenter, he found that France was no longer a place where an honest living was possible, and he shipped out on an East Indiaman as carpenter in 1803, during the peace between France and England. His voyage took him to Bombay and then to Hong Kong.

There he took passage on an Island trader from Macau, seeking a place to settle. Palau was where he met his fate. He was speaking of his wife with warmth as he made the comment while discussing the work to be done on the three ships. Most would be carried out by the carpenters on the ships themselves, now they were moored in calm waters, but there were jobs for Francois Bertrand to carry out with his crew of boat builders. He was happy to accept the ship's boat, recovered from the Porto del Oro, as payment for his work.

While the ships were in the harbour they were able to restock with fruit fish and fresh water before recommencing their voyage, two weeks later.

***

Chang Po looked at his ships with pride. He thought about his childhood as an urchin on the waterfront in Nanking. The filth, scraps to eat, cold wet and hungry. Beaten, kicked and abused until finally the chance that came with the sick Englishman.

The cholera was undiscriminating, the sick man was staggering to his bungalow and Chang Po realised he could get inside the house and steal or he could kill the man and rob him. there on the pathway to the front door.

The decision made, he assisted the man into the house and helped him to lie down on a bed. He found water and gave the man water and cooled him where he could with cold water cloths. He found food and ate well for once.

"Who are you?" The man whispered.

"I am Chang Po." He replied.

"Why do you help me?" The man said, "I am dying, you can take what you want, I cannot stop you."

"It is true sir, but while I am here I can eat, I find fine clothes, and no one question me, because I look after the master."

The man smiled, "It is good, you may have everything I have when I pass. I salute a man of forethought, and happily leave my few possessions to one such as you."

Three days later the man died. Chang Po buried him in the garden of the bungalow.

He then gathered everything of value, loaded it on a cart and departed to buy a boat.

The memory was always with him, but for the life of him he could not recall whether it was compassion or just pragmatism that had driven him to do what he had done.

He stretched and breathed in. All four of his boats were sailing free, and ahead he caught a glimpse of the topsails of the ships he had been sent to intercept.

The junks were in formation and as they approached Martin guessed immediately their purpose.

If there had been any doubt, Olivia had recognised the leading craft as the ship that had attacked the Porto del Oro.

Chang Po had identified the Castletown as the deep laden ship recognised by the fisherman at Palau. He had detailed his other ships to distract the other two craft while he concentrated on the merchantman.

Captain Brooks called Major Bristow, "I believe we have a job for you and your lads."

Bristow looked at the approaching junk. "He is a big one isn't he? Are you going to show him your teeth?"

"Mr. Harmon!" Brooks said, "Let the junk know that we do not trust her."

"Gladly sir." He turned and called to the master gunner. "Remind him to knock before he comes in please."

"Aye, aye sir."

The gunner lined up one of the 24 pounder guns, then stood back. "Fire."

Chang Po was watching the single gun port rise and the gun run out. When it fired he laughed. Fools think they can.... As the cannon ball hit the bow of the junk the mast shivered as the forestays were severed. The ball went through the deck planking and smashed its way to the keel, though it did not break it. The mast was held in place by the wind filled sail though it was trembling dangerously.

Chang Po screamed at his men to secure the mast and continued toward the Castletown intent in boarding with the swarm of men crouched behind the bulwarks of the junk. As he watched he saw green clad men at the bulwarks of the merchant ship and others climbing the rigging. The green clad men were all armed and as he watched, the men fired. All along the deck wounded men cried out, others dropped dead where they crouched. Appalled at the carnage Chang Po could only stand and wait to come to grips with the enemy ship. But as he watched he realised that his attack was doomed. The full broadside from the merchantman fired at point blank range and the junk bows disintegrated along as far as the step for the mainmast. Chang Po was thrown forward into the wreckage as the junk stopped as if it had hit a brick wall. He died there, in brief agony, pierced by splinters over the entire length of his body.

Elsewhere the rest of the fleet were doing no better. The Alderney was chasing two junks that had turned to flee after seeing the death of Chang Po. Asterid had fired two broadsides and her targets were both sinking, the surrounding waters covered with the heads of frantic swimmers.

The chase was not extended. The Alderney caught the two junks with almost contemptuous ease. Both realised that they could not escape, and turned to attack their pursuer.

Since both junks depended on boarding, the cannon they had were small, and poorly served. Alderney on the other hand was well served with heavy guns and skilled men to serve them. Both junks were shattered by the guns of their opponent. The ships were left sinking with the surviving crews trying to find some way to keep out of the water where sharks were enjoying an unexpected feast day.

Captain Hammond, like Captain Harris and Captain Brooks, wasted no sympathy on the dying men. Martin had three of the men plucked from the water, so that he could find out where they had come from.

Faced with a similar fate to their companions the three men selected were only too willing to talk. They described their home port and their leader, Bang Lok who ruled their island. Catanduanes, part of the Philippines island group.

It is true that Martin had been missing the naval routine that had dominated his life up to the commencement of this voyage, but South America had been interesting and it now appeared that calling on the 'Island of the Palms,' would be needed to discuss the pirate activity with the Governor.

According to Olivia de la Cruz, her family owned property in Manila. The major city on the island, known as Luzon, was the source of the famous Manila galleon that had for many years brought the wealth of the Indies to Europe, by both Eastern and Western routes.

Chapter twenty-four

Diplomacy

The Islands appeared first a cloud along the horizon, but gradually transformed into a series of overlapping low green mounds as they neared their first destination. The Port of Dapa, taken by the pirates from Mindanao, now ruled by Bang Lok who had settled there in his private fiefdom, had anchorages offshore within the shelter offered by the island.

The arrival of the three ships, expected under the escort of Chang Po, was regarded with a certain apprehension by Bang Lok. They were reported long before they appeared, and Captain Spiers was with his employer at the time the news was brought.

"Either Chang Po missed the ships, or having encountered them, is no longer an ally to be counted upon." Spiers retorted dryly. "Perhaps this is not the time to mention the shore battery I suggested we install above the landing stage." He raised the glass he was using to examine the ships below. "Though I fear the ships are rather better armed than most and they have the look of naval craft, despite the merchant ensigns they carry."

Bang Lok looked at the busy scene around the three newcomers. They had lowered boats, and established a patrol around the anchored ships.

A larger boat was launched from the ship identified by Spiers as an East Indiaman. It stopped to take a passenger from the bigger of the two other ships and then made for the landing stage.

Bang Lok turned to Spiers. "Go and meet them and bring them here."

Spiers smiled and bowed, "As you command."

He left, and was on the landing stage when the party from the ships arrived. As the boat came alongside a dozen green-uniformed men, armed with rifles, leapt ashore and quickly spread about watchfully, whilst the other passengers came ashore.

A green-clad Major helped a lady ashore, followed by a Naval captain who accompanied another lady followed by two tall seamen.

Spiers went forward and saluted the captain. "I have been asked by the Governor to welcome you to the island and escort you to the residence. May I ask your name, sir?"

Martin returned the salute and introduced himself and the two ladies.

Accompanied by the green-clad riflemen, the party made their way to the residence where Bang Lok was seated, waiting apprehensively.

The fact that Bang Lok had secured the position of Governor of the island had given his role a veneer of respectability. When the party arrived his servants seated the ladies and the captain. The green-clad soldiers refused to be entertained and maintained their place, keeping the watch.

Acting as interpreter, Captain Spiers was seated beside Bang Lok.

Bang Lok welcomed the visitors, his words translated by Spiers.

Olivia leaned over to Martin, "He is welcoming us to the island." She said quietly. "I think he is worried."

With the welcome over, Bang Lok asked the visitors the reason for their call.

Martin said "The lady here is Olivia de la Cruz of Manila. She and her parents were returning home by ship when they were attacked by pirates. She and her parents were able to avoid capture to escape in one of the ship's boats. Even so, unfortunately they were spotted and both her parents were killed and she herself injured. The pirates burned the ship, having stripped it of its cargo and disposed of the crew and passengers.

"While we were cruising en route to China we encountered the boat with the lady still alive on board.

"While journeying from Palau Island we were attacked by pirates. Miss de la Cruz recognised the lead ship as the one that attacked and murdered her parents. My ships destroyed the pirates, but we kept some of the crew alive. When questioned they admitted they came from this island and that their chief Chang Po traded stolen cargoes here on the island."

The Governor, Bang Lok realised that he would need to be very careful with his answer regarding Chang Po.

"It is true Chang Po has a trading warehouse on the island, he is a respected businessman, his ship normally sails regularly to stock up with materials."

"It seems he will not be returning for the foreseeable future. In the circumstances, may I suggest we examine the premises owned by this man, with a view to compensating this young lady for the loss of her parents and the security that offers?"

The major walked over to the captain and whispered something to him.

Martin rose to his feet. "I understand that the premises owned by the man Chang Po have been located and are now secured by my men. Shall we take a look at the assets of the deceased pirate?"

"I have not seen proof of his death yet," wailed the Island Governor.

Martin noticed that the Governor's eyes had narrowed and the panic in his voice was not reflected in his eyes.

Spiers looked disgusted and turned to his employer and said. "Stop making difficulties, we will go now and we will compensate the lady. It will cost you nothing. Chang Po's warehouse will provide. Now let us go and do the decent thing." As he said it, he had the grace to cringe inwardly. It had to be several years since he had last done the decent thing.

Spiers had also been surprised by the reaction of his employer. Like Martin he was not entirely taken in by the panicky reactions of the man. Bang Lok had often been in tight situations before and there was an easy escape from this one. Merely by doing what was suggested without being stupid, these people with their big guns could be on their way without trouble or personal loss.

The warehouse was down the hill in the grounds of the house that had belonged to Chang Po. The group walked down together with Bang Lok and Spiers showing the way.

A large landing party from Asterid had come ashore meanwhile, and had relaxed on the quay waiting for further orders. Spiers noticed that they were all armed.

Lieutenant Gibbs stepped forward and then saluted. "Working party present as ordered, sir."

"Very good. Bring them along to that building." He indicated the warehouse. "Inventory the contents, Mr. Gibbs. We will be in the house."

Gibbs grinned and acknowledged the order, turning to the men with him. "The warehouse, lads, list the contents. Cox'on, watch them please." He turned to the warehouse door and examined the lock. Stepping back, he pointed to the lock. A big seaman stepped forward and swung the maul he was carrying. It struck the double doors at the point where the lock was situated.

The doors fell open, the lock was hanging from its mountings, both top hinges on the doors were broken and the doors sagged apart.

"Don't just stand there!" The Cox'on shouted, "Inside with you and start sorting out the goods."

The main party had stopped while this scene was played out, but once the door was opened, Martin stirred and moved over to the house door.

This was opened from within by a Chinese woman who bowed and indicated that they enter. Spiers informed the lady that they would be searching the house and told her to be available in case they needed keys or information.

She nodded and waited as they filed through the front door. Four of the green-clad Marines entered with them and the others took positions outside. Martin turned to McLean and Peters. "Start at the top and work down. You know what to look for."

The two men nodded and left the room.

Jennifer, who had accompanied Olivia on the trip ashore turned to the Chinese woman. "What should I call you? Could we have some tea perhaps?"

The Chinese lady clapped her hands and a servant appeared, there was a brief flurry of Mandarin and the servant bowed and disappeared.

The Chinese lady turned to Jennifer. Bowing she said, "My name is Jasmine, my apologies for my discourtesy I expected to be taken prisoner now my husband has been killed." She spoke English quietly, correctly and carefully.

Jennifer said, "Why would you be arrested?"

"The master does not forgive failure, my husband failed to bring your ships here as captives. His possessions are thus all forfeit."

Bang Lok was wondering what was being said, he had never really bothered to learn English. He looked at Spiers for a translation, but Spiers was not responding.

Jennifer continued her conversation. "Did your husband work for anyone here?"

"Of course everyone on the island works for the Governor."

"Please sit here." She patted the seat beside her. "Now, you speak good English. Did you learn it here?"

A look of pain crossed Jasmine's face, "I am a prize taken from my father's ship. The junk my husband sailed was owned by my father, he traded from Hong Kong where I was born and educated. Four years ago we were taken by that man," she nodded at Bang Lok, "I was given to my husband as a reward. They murdered my father and the other people on the ship. I believe I am the only survivor."

Bang Lok was becoming more and more agitated at the conversations that he could not understand. He rose to his feet and turned to Spiers. "Tell me what is going on."

Spiers rose to his feet in turn and faced him. He stood nearly a head taller than the Governor. In succinct sentences he told him what Jasmine had been saying.

Bang Lok turned pale and swung round with arm raised to strike the Chinese woman.

Spiers grabbed the arm and stopped the blow falling, gripping the wrist tightly, causing his opponent to cry out in shock. The small dagger in his raised hand dropped to the floor. Recovering he swung his other hand and punched Spiers in the chest.

Spiers gasped, looking unbelievingly at the blood that was suddenly leaking down his shirt. The pain followed. As the two men stood swaying now, Spires's left hand found Bang Lok's throat and savagely thrust his thumb into his larynx. Bang Lok withdrew his knife and stabbed him again.

The ladies scrambled back as the two men toppled to the floor, still locked in a life and death struggle. Bang Lok's face was purple as he struggled for breath. He had dropped the knife and was trying to prize the relentless hand from his throat. His efforts failed and his hand fell away, his face distorted and eyes open now fixed, looking at Spiers who was breathing badly, blood dribbling from the corner of his mouth. Major Bristow stepped forward and dragged Bang Lok's dead body aside, leaving Spiers bloody but still breathing, though not for long.

Jennifer knelt beside him, "You saved her life." She said.

Spiers grimaced, his face twisted into a smile. "Not all baddd…." The light went from his eyes, and he was dead.

McLean and Peters were there, having heard the noise and they removed the bodies, to the veranda.

Martin looked at the three ladies present. None of them showed any sign of fainting, in fact Olivia and Jasmine both looked relieved and Jennifer said, "I do believe this situation is now resolved." The servant appeared and put the furniture straight. She said in Tagalog, "Shall I serve the tea?"

Jasmine nodded and sent her off, she turned to McLean, "Behind the bed, there is a panel."

McLean produced a soft cloth bag from his belt.

Jasmine smiled and nodded, and accepted the bag McLean offered.

Martin looked at them both but said nothing.

McLean went and joined Peters beside the door. Just outside was a chest, ornately carved with brass corners and straps. The two men lifted the chest with some effort and placed it on the floor between the chairs of the seated group. The servant appeared and set out the tea things, and as silently disappeared.

Jasmine opened the chest, with a key taken from the bag that McLean had passed to her.

As the others watched Martin unhooked the clasp and raised the lid of the chest. There was a joint intake of breath as the group saw the contents. Whatever else Chang Po was he had an eye for jewellery, and gems in general. The chest was nearly full with a gold-mounted gems and un-mounted gems; in the light they flashed from the blue of the sapphires to the green of the emeralds, diamonds mixed with pearls, it was a Maharajah's fantasy.

Martin shut the lid.

Jasmine said, "Chang Po was a true thief, he stole from friend and enemy alike, much of this wealth should have been passed to the Governor, but he could not bear to pass up the opportunity to cheat. I am glad the pig is dead, and I wish you joy of the treasure he collected."

The knock on the door announced the Cox'on.

"Sir we have cleared the warehouse, there is a large stock of trade goods mainly materials, silks and stuff, though there is also a supply of barrels of powder, marked with the royal cipher.

Olivia spoke for the first time since the chest had been produced. "Please, ladies and gentlemen, in Manila I am a rich woman. I have no need of this," she waved to chest. "My parents were wealthy even in these terms. I know that they intended me to marry a man I do not know. He is of family that would be of great importance in Manila. I have been to Spain and seen Seville and Madrid. I wish to travel to England and now there is peace, to Paris and Vienna. I have no wish to stay in Manila."

Jennifer said with a smile, "Since you are not yet of age that may not be easy. Are there people who will assume control of your affairs until you of age?"

Olivia nodded, "I'm afraid so." She said sadly.

Martin said. "Surely we can do something about it. After all, Antonio Ramos became the guardian of Maria. Can we not do something similar for this lady?"

Olivia lifted her hand. "I have discussed this with my parents, we talked of the possibility of my being alone, mainly because my father travelled on business and my mother often went with him. There was no one of their acquaintance they felt they could trust. My father said that in the last resort if I found someone I could trust, by marrying, I could prevent strangers from controlling my life."

Stunned silence followed this cool statement, and Olivia sat back awaiting comment.

Chapter twenty-five

Major Bristow's Sacrifice.

The arrangements to leave the island took some days. The actual administration had rested solely in the hands of the deceased Bang Lok. By the time they were in a position to leave it was apparent that Jasmine, the former wife of Chang Po was the most suitable candidate to rule the island.

At the suggestion that she might wish to return to Hong Kong, she was adamant that it would mean that she would be soiled goods to her people and as such she would lose such wealth as she had brought and be disgraced.

There were still members of the staff to protect her, and the remaining members of the former Governor's household were pleased to accept the rule of the strong-minded lady. The head of the bodyguards came and knelt in front of her. He placed his blade in her hands and said, "The captain was our trainer and leader. He gave his life to save you, we will do no less."

***

When they sailed on the morning of their sixth day in harbour, initially for Manila, they carried the Catholic Priest from the mission church on the island. There had been problems with his health for some time and he had been waiting for a passage to get treatment in Manila. When Martin agreed to give him passage, he had no ulterior motive in mind. The fact that for Olivia, the problem of her inheritance was still an issue, made his presence fortuitous.

The solution had been offered by Major Bristow. Standing formally in the presence of Jennifer and Olivia he stated stiffly. "I am a batchelor who has up to now never contemplated marriage. The other gentlemen who might be considered, are young and such a marriage could be a barrier to them later in life.

"As things are, an unconsummated marriage can be annulled in the future. Thus I can take control of the lady's estate legally and pass it to her when we reach civilization. The worst that can result is that we share a suite, for appearances sake. In England, we can arrange for the marriage to be annulled, when her legal position has been clarified."

Jennifer looked at Alan Bristow in surprise; whatever else she contemplated, his offer was the last thing she would have expected from him. She realised it had not occurred to her that the big quiet, intrepid soldier, with the gentle manner socially, was alone because he was shy?

Olivia studied the Major; at 30 years old with fair hair and blue eyes, he was not unpleasant to look at. His six foot tall figure was trim and fit and he had a pleasant manner in company.

She spoke quietly but firmly. "Major Bristow, in the circumstanced I currently face, I would be honoured if you would consent to marry me. As you have pointed out, at the right time and place, we can amend the arrangement. I will understand also if that occurs because of your circumstances, rather than mine. "

Jennifer who was present at the conversation was surprised to notice the major blushing. It was the first occasion she had ever seen him exhibit an emotional response to anything.

Jennifer said to the couple, "Please heed me! No one must know anything about such an arrangement. Remember others know of your circumstances," she turned to Olivia, "Do not reveal this agreement to anyone, the marriage must appear to be genuine despite having been obviously arranged. You needed a husband. The Major, Alan needed a wife. Is that understood?"

Alan Bristow said, "Of course I accept what you say, but please why?"

Jennifer said quietly. "If the church feel there is any such arrangement, an annulment will not be permitted. If anyone found out and the word got out, you would be married for life."

She added with a wicked smile, "Though that may seem a worrying thought, I know of worse pairings that have been successful."

This drew a blush from both of the others and spurred Alan Bristow into action, "I have something in my cabin...." He left them hurriedly, returning a few moments later.

He approached Olivia, "People who know me would not believe our story if I did not ask you to wear this ring." He produced a rather battered blue ring box. Olivia opened it, and looked at the ring inside.

"I couldn't. this is too much." She turned to Jennifer and showed her the ring.

Alan said, "It was my grandmother's and I have no one else in mind. If you don't take it my friends will be curious. I believe—"

Jennifer interrupted. "Olivia, this is beautiful, please try it on."

Reluctantly Olivia held out her hand, and Jennifer gave to box to Alan. He slipped the ring on her finger. "There. It fits."

"But I did not intend you to provide things for me!" Olivia said, "You are already doing me a favour."

"When the time comes you can return the ring, so there would be no real problem of that sort." Jennifer smiled. "Now what may be a little more difficult is the time you will need to spend together, as the wedding will need to take place before we reach Manila. I think we should make the announcement as soon as possible. Perhaps the priest we carry will perform the ceremony.

The ships stopped and moored in the shelter of one of the many islands in the group.

In a ceremony attended by the other ship masters, Major Alan Bristow in his full scarlet Marine uniform, was married to Olivia de la Cruz. The commanding presence of Captain Sir Martin Forest-Bowers RN stood to give the bride away, and the three ladies, Dorothea, Jennifer and Maria attended the bride.

The bride and groom managed to survive the ceremony and the congratulations of the officers, with whom Alan had served for the past years.

The crew spliced the mainbrace to wish them well, and that was that.

To prevent gossip, the happy newlywed couple were accommodated in the master's cabin which comprised two cabins, a convenience for the couple in the circumstances.

***

Their arrival at Manila was low key. There were no Spanish warships in the harbour, thought there were several merchantmen loading and unloading as the three ships came in and anchored. Martin took the jolly boat ashore along with the priest, Major Bristow and his new wife. Dressed in civilian clothes Alan Bristow was looking every inch the gentleman and the attentive husband. He had been impressed by the character of the young woman he had married and was determined not to let her down in the role he had adopted.

Sensibly, Olivia had responded in public, and as they stepped ashore after the priest, they followed him with Martin to the Cathedral, where they received the blessing of the Bishop. The priest produced the proper documents confirming their wedding, witnessed willingly by Martin. They then left the Cathedral to meet with the lawyer for the Cruz family.

***

Camillo Lopez was a big man who wore a grey wig and sniffed snuff. Martin did not trust him for an instant. Olivia insisted that both men accompanied her when Lopez indicated that he wished to speak with her privately.

When informed that her parents had been killed, he looked sad and shook his head. "Senorita, I must tell you that since your parents are dead you will become a ward to a family appointed by the court. Your parent's assets will be passed to your guardian for his custodianship."

He sat down with a sigh, "Of course, if you wish, I can act as your guardian if you so choose."

"So what do I say to my husband, Senor Lopez?" Olivia asked quietly.

"Who did you say? You are married?" Lopez stood up shocked.

Olivia turned to Alan taking his hand she said, "Senor Lopez this is my husband, Major Alan Bristow. I regret he does not yet speak Spanish."

"Are you sure you are married? These Englishmen can be very devious my dear."

Martin, who had followed the conversation, stood and offered the marriage certificate. "I believe you will find that this is perfectly in order Senor, and I must point out that the major is a man of property in England and has no need to marry for fortune, so now, sir, perhaps you will advise the lady of the state of her inheritance."

"Ah of course, though I have to say that the liquid assets comprise the bulk of the value, held in the bank; the house has been rented and I am informed that the people occupying the house would be pleased to purchase it if, married to an English man you would wish to relocate elsewhere."

He shuffled the papers on his desk, "I received instruction to secure a suite for your family for your immediate occupation when you arrived." He passed over a note with the address and location of the apartments, adding. "I have paid for two weeks only, on your late father's instructions."

Martin stood, looked at Olivia who was upset at the references to her father. Turning to Lopez he said, "Please prepare a full statement of accounts for Madam Bristow. You may sell the house and forward the result to this bank in London. He passed a card over to lawyer. The bank owned by Cox and Kings had an international reputation. The account name was Alan Bristow. Major RM. "We will call for the accounts tomorrow morning if that is convenient?"

Lopez looked at Olivia, who nodded. "That will be in order, Senor?"

"I am Captain Sir Martin Forest-Bowers, RN, my ships are in the harbour I can be found through the harbourmaster."

***

Major Alan Bristow lay in bed that night, the lack of motion still a little disturbing. He was still trying to cope with the fact that he had actually married the admittedly pretty girl/woman who was currently asleep in the room next door.

As a youngster Alan had fallen in love with the daughter of the blacksmith, on the estate. She was tousle dark-haired and more grown up than her years, it was only when they had been chasing around the barn trying to catch up with the other youngsters that they had collided and tumbled all of a heap in the hay, that he realised just how grown up she was. Her name was Carol, and she stopped giggling, moved his hand to her already shapely bosom, and kissed him.

His discovery of the reason for the presence of the unspoken parts of his body was worrying, exciting and pleasurable.

Sadly her interest in him was transient, her marriage to the Innkeeper, was already arranged. So it was two lessons the young Alan learned that day.

It had made him wary. As an Ensign he had loved the captain's daughter from afar. On closer acquaintance he found her snobbish and despite promises otherwise, realised that she was also promised to a lieutenant in the Guards.

He had regarded it as an indication that his career was more important than dalliance, and concentrated on that up to now. Though not quite up to now, he confessed to himself that in the woods in America, he had been interested in Julia, now married to his friend Harris.

He turned over restlessly smiling at the thought of his sister's face when she realised he had married at last. It was only recently in fact just before they had departed England had he discovered that he was now the head of the family, and the estate at Milton in Hampshire was now his. Lady Eleanor Travis, his sister, was married to Sir William Travis, his neighbour. She had sent a letter promising to keep an eye on things during his absence. It did mean that he was now a man of real substance. The sprawling house and thousand acres on the coast meant more, strangely, than the extensive sums of prize money he had received. Though in the bank now was sufficient to more than cover the value of the estate.

He had reached that point when he finally fell asleep

***

Martin had arranged accommodation for Jennifer and the other ladies from the ships, and he had been joined ashore by the other captains.

They had until now left the trading to the man they titled Supercargo. He was a man named Jonathon Weeks. He had occupied the position and thus-far had proved himself well suited to the post. He was rapidly finding cargo to add to their trade, sugar and indigo, exotic hard-wood, and rice. Trading the cattle hides from Valdivia to local traders he rapidly filled the empty cargo spaces in the East-Indiaman, and much of the spaces in Asterid . The tall skinny Loyal American was an old acquaintance of Julia. He reported to Martin that the ships were re-provisioned and the Castletown was fully loaded.

They had been ashore four days, and entertained by the Spanish Commissioner, and interviewed by the Prince. They had been given a tour of places of interest by Olivia, and all agreed it was a pleasant place to live, but all also agreed that it was time to move on.

Olivia was beginning to adjust to having Alan around. At first she thought he would more or less be, like her father, mainly because of the age gap between them. But it soon became apparent that her close association with Alan created in her a wish to know more of the enigmatic man she had married. In passage on the Castletown Alan did not stand watches. During the day he supervised drill, training practice for his men, and the instruction of the juniors, and some of the seniors, in both rifle shooting and swordsmanship. Olivia had joined the ladies and her physique was toned with the exercise, and her swordsmanship was soon a trial to Jennifer, who challenged the best of the men at the skill.

They continued on their voyage to China, and it has to be said, Martin found things rather boring. The four day trip seemed to be endless, despite passing several junks and other suspicious-looking ships, none actually posed any threat to the trio of well-armed ships.

Chapter twenty-six

The Night of the Dragon

The port of Macau was a little piece of Portugal in the Oriental landscape. Many of the buildings could have been transferred from Lisbon, though many others were distinctly Chinese. The party made their way through the streets of the port under the eyes of both friends and enemies.

Their destination was one of the major traders of the port whose influence reached both east and west. Paulo Wing was the product of a mixed marriage. His father had established a trading partnership with the Cruz family. Between them they had created a lucrative trade in tea that by-passed the Mandarins, who controlled the Hong Kong trade. This was a source of continual irritation to the British and French interests in the region.

Not surprisingly Wing had enemies. The security at the gates of the property was alert and efficient. The party passed through without question and were escorted to the entrance hall of the house where their coats were taken, before being ushered into the large drawing room of the house.

Paulo Wing was just five feet six inches tall, with regular occidental features, and black hair greying at the temples. His smile was open and welcoming to the visitors whom he swiftly had seated and served with drinks.

Martin studied the man as he accepted the drink served by a small Chinese woman.

Wing wore a Chinese robe and chose to speak English to his guests. Only Olivia was known to him, and it was she who introduced the party. Starting with her husband Alan, she followed with Lady Jennifer, Johnathon Weeks and finally Martin.

With the guests settled, he spoke generally to them. "Macau is not a settled place at present. I am surprised that there was no attempt to accost you on the way here. I will provide you with an armed escort for your return to the ship or, if you wish, perhaps send message for your own people to make arrangements for the return."

Martin smiled, "Forgive me Senor Wing, we were in fact escorted, and we will be escorted back to the ship."

Wing turned to the man who had met them at the gate quizzically.

The man nodded apologetically, and Wing turned back to Martin. "We have all heard of your exploits during the past years, I should have realised that you did not achieve your success without forethought."

Martin smiled, "I am delighted that the people of our escort kept such a low profile. It would be a mistake for anyone to attempt to interfere with our group. I fear their reception could be fatal."

Their host turned to the rest of the group, he clapped his hands and a Chinese man appeared. "Please ask Senorita Natasha to join us." Turning to Johnathon Weeks he said. "My daughter Natasha runs the trading branch of our business. If you would care to accompany her she will take you to the warehouse where you can discuss matters more freely." While he was speaking, there was movement at the door a lady entered and the sudden intake of breath was ample warning of the impression she was making.

She was tall and slender, her face hauntingly beautiful in a pale high cheek-boned Russian-looking way. Dressed simply in a Chinese robe, her dark hair was wrapped high to keep it clear of her face, which shone in the lamplight. The low melodious voice was almost without accent. "You called for me, father?"

Paulo Wing stood and took her hand. "Ladies and gentlemen, may I introduce my daughter Natasha. She runs the trading floor of our company, I have asked her to take Mr. Weeks and discuss matters with him, Mr. Weeks, any decisions taken by Natasha you may accept without question."

Weeks rose to his feet, looked and received a slight nod from Martin and turned to Natasha "At your service, Miss."

"Won't you come this way, Mr. Weeks?" As they went through the door Martin heard her ask, "What shall I call you sir, you have my name?"

Martin nodded in approval. Paulo Wing had trained his daughter well.

***

On the journey back to the ship later that night, the party encountered many more people on the streets. The Portuguese habit of dining late and promenade had survived the journey from the other side of the world and on the occasion with shops and establishments open the residents were taking advantage of the mild evening air.

Martin noticed an odd scuffle here and there on their way to the Quay, but it was on the quay itself that there was a party of armed men.

They were silent, and as the group stepped down on the pier, the leader stepped forward and tapped the club against his other hand.

Martin stopped the group with a raised arm. "Move out of the way and you will not be hurt." He said reasonably.

The leader of the gang laughed, "Or what? Will you stick me with your little skewer there?" He indicated Martin's sword.

Martin shrugged and drew the pistol from his belt. "No!" He said. "I will shoot you with my pistol." He pointed the weapon at the man, who once more laughed. "My men will then take you and your party and they'll use the women and sell them and the other man as slaves, after we have taken your money.

Major Bristow called out. "Sergeant, shut this man up and dispose of his men.

From all around the gang came the click of weapons being cocked. Out of the darkness the Marines stepped, guns lined up and ready to fire.

From within the gang, voices were raised as the men realised they were caught and they flung their weapons down. The leader threw his club down in disgust and Martin replaced his pistol in his belt.

Major Bristow said "I did not see a police office in town?"

Martin said "There will only be the Mandarin's men to keep order. I believe we will have to let these people go."

Lieutenant Gibbs appeared to report the boat was ready, so Major Bristow called to the Marines, "Well done, men; let them go, but throw their weapons into the water first."

***

Back aboard the ship, Jonathon Weeks reported the results of his trading conversation with Natasha. "Two things I have to report, our entire cargo is traded and a full cargo of tea is promised in return, but the trade will be contingent on providing passage for Natasha to either Europe somewhere or England."

There was stunned silence at this information. "But why?" Olivia said.

Johnathon said slowly. "Her father had decided that she should be given to the owner of a competing company that had a branch in Hong Kong. This would ensure the survival of the existing company. It seems the death of Olivia's parents had created a problem with the continued financing of the trading company which depends on credit to survive."

"Does her father know she wants to leave?" Martin asked.

"No, he does know she does not want to be traded off, but it is his decision under local conditions, and she cannot appeal to anyone against his decision."

"What do you have to say, Mr. Weeks?"

Johnathon thought for a few moments, then. "She is a better trader than me. The offer she had made will give us the best possible result, however I believe that there is a problem that we will have to overcome if we wish to survive this operation, and especially if we are to keep our side of the trade. We are going to have to protect Natasha while she is ashore, and I am firmly convinced that Paulo Wing intends to hijack our cargo, and if possible our ships as well." He sat down in a stunned silence.

Alan Bristow asked the question they all wanted answered. "What makes you think Mr. Wing is going to cheat?"

"He is badly down on stock in his warehouse, and selling his daughter to a Chinese pirate." Johnathon Weeks was blunt about his instincts, and he liked Natasha. "Either we act pretty quickly or he will whisk her away and our trade will be immediately in hazard. Since we have to unload before we can take on our cargo, we will be vulnerable. The port authorities here will favour Wing."

Martin said to Peters, "Fetch McLean and Godden."

When the men appeared, Martin had a few quiet words with the two who then disappeared. They got a lift ashore from a passing sampan.

***

Natasha Wing sat in her room wondering whether the deal she proposed to Johnathon Weeks would be accepted. She desperately hoped so. Staying in Macau with her father was no longer an option. Her mother, were she alive, would have made that quite clear, and her father would not have gone against her wishes. She felt betrayed.

Thinking of her father's recent conduct – perhaps he had always been capable of such an action – she just felt stupid for never putting together many of the small acts that she now saw should have warned her. She lay down uneasily finally falling asleep.

She was asleep when they came for her. They wrapped her in the bedding, just a sheet and an overlay, with a gag to keep her quiet. The two men giggling at the task they had been given. As they carried her out of the building one of her captors was suggesting that they rape her before they handed her over to their boss. The other man said fiercely "If you wish to be hung by your testicles and suffer the thousand cuts, do not expect me to be stupid enough to join you. The boss would not be pleased, when the girl tells him what we had done."

The man in the lead heard a gasp from his partner. The body between them jerked then body was removed from his grip with a firm tug. He knew no more until he wakened in the ditch the following day.

***

McLean removed the gag from the sheet-wrapped girl. He said, "Miss, if we pop you back in your room you could perhaps pack a bag, get dressed and we will take you to our ship. Mr. Weeks said to tell you the deal has been accepted."

Natasha, still wrapped in the sheet and overlay, allowed herself to be lifted up and taken back to her room where she dressed herself, collected her private funds and her clothes, and left with her two rescuers. All the while she was wondering why she should trust these two Englishmen. She shrugged. Staying in the house was obviously not an option, what would stop the kidnappers returning? She was convinced that the kidnappers must have been there with her father's knowledge. That hurt! It had also firmly made her mind up.

The small party reached the quay and McLean lit a small lantern with a green glass panel in the side. He raised it and rotated it so that the alternate white and green lights showed out to the anchorage.

Within minutes a boat approached the quay. "Asterid?" McLean called softly. "McLean!" a voice replied and the boat slid alongside, the quay wall and hooked on. The tall figure of Johnathon Weeks stood up. "Quickly now, there is activity behind you."

The earlier uncertainties in Natasha's mind dissolved at the sight of Weeks, and she scrambled into the boat with her bags. Turning to thank her rescuers she found McLean and Godden had melted into the shadows, with other business to conduct ashore.

Chapter twenty-seven

Pier head Jump

Nothing was said when the Castletown unloaded her cargo into lighters tied alongside. The big flat-bottomed boats accommodated the cargo; when loaded fully they did not leave the ship.

Once the entire cargo was discharged, the message was sent ashore for the tea to be delivered. Eventually the line of carts appeared and the tea was sent out to the East Indiaman. As the new cargo was loaded the lighters were released one by one until the exchange was complete.

A message from Paulo Wing inviting them to a farewell reception, came aboard with the last of the cargo.

On behalf of the group Martin accepted and arranged for Captain Brooks to ensure the security of the ships, and Major Bristow the shore party. Natasha decided to stay on board and was invited with Maria and Dorothea, to join the officers on the Asterid as their guest for dinner, whilst the group led by Martin and Jennifer, with Olivia, Alan Bristow, Captain and Julia Harris. Peters and the Sergeant handled the escort. The remaining Marines were on watch throughout the ships.

The house was lit up and the sound of music was to be heard on the soft warm night. They were greeted formally as before, and ushered into the reception area where they were introduced to the Mandarin, and an anonymous Chinese lady. There was also someone who could have been related to Natasha, with the same high cheekbones and pale complexion. She was part of the Mandarin's entourage. There was a magnificent buffet for all to enjoy, and drinks both Eastern and Western for the guests. Martin was wary of the drinks, and conscious of his expanding waistline, sparing of the buffet. Whilst there, he encountered the Russian-looking lady.

"Captain, you took a chance attending this function. I trust you realise that they are taking your cargo while we dance."

"Your interest is appreciated, Madam, but if I may correct you, I think it highly unlikely that anyone is taking my cargo away. Rather, I think someone is being punished for attempting to steal my cargo."

His companion thought for a moment before speaking quietly once more. "I trust Natasha is safe. At first I thought her father had given her to the Mandarin but I hear that she has disappeared completely. That gives me hope."

"Why, Madam? Is she related in some way to you?"

"She is my daughter."

Shocked! Martin looked at her in confusion.

The lady said, "I was passed along to the Mandarin who showed an interest in me because I am not Oriental."

Martin said, "Your daughter is quite safe and if you wish to accompany her we can bring you with us."

"I would not think of abandoning my master now. Anyway my daughter does not know I am her mother. The woman she believed to be her mother was my sister. I will leave things as they are and I depend on you to keep my secret."

Martin bowed, "Of course, Madam; as you wish."

He could not get rid of the feeling that this was some sort of trap. It was confirmed by his companion and the sound of gunfire from the harbour.

Paulo Wing broke off his discussion with another guest to reassure him that there was celebration and fireworks set off everywhere tonight, as it was a Chinese holiday.

It was without real surprise that the messenger from the ships arrived and informed him that the attack by the pirates had been beaten off, and the ship they had used had been sunk. All the ladies were safe and extra Marines had landed to reinforce the party already here.

Standing on the veranda watching the fireworks, he was unsurprised to hear McLean's Scottish accent advising him that the remaining elements of the inheritance from Olivia's father, had been located and was on its way to the ship.

"Godden and me – we'll wait until we see you all into the boats before we leave this place."

Martin would have sent them both back to the ship after their efforts, but sometimes he felt it best to leave things in the hands of people like McLean. It had an annoying habit of being the right thing to do.

***

By the end of the evening everyone was waiting for the Mandarin to leave, so that they could in turn, take their leave. When he finally left, the fireworks were over and the town was settling down to darkness, even along the main streets. The party set off back to the quay. Tour of the Marines had appeared out of the darkness as the party left. Halfway down the main street to the waterfront, McLean and Godden also appeared. Hands held up, he stopped them and signalled them to step over to the wall of one of the big houses. They waited, there was a scatter of gunfire. Then the sergeant appeared, with a sheaf of swords in his hands. He passed them to the men and then on the urging of Jennifer to the ladies as well.

"There is an ambush ahead, we may have to fight a little. They are the Mandarin's men, I believe." The grim-faced Sergeant permitted himself a smile. "I think they did not expect the reception they received. Shall we go, before they get reinforced, that is?"

"Lead on, Sergeant," he turned to the party, "Let's go, you heard the sergeant, let us spoil their evening."

Down the road the party went keeping to the shadows. They encountered the ambush and went straight in to attack. The man opposite Olivia laughed in delight when he saw her, "I'll have you." He said raising his club to threaten her, Olivia lunged.

The man looked down at his punctured chest unbelievingly as Olivia twisted and withdrew. He dropped on the spot. She turned to her next opponent. The attackers did not understand women actually fighting with weapons. Julia intercepted a man aiming to stab the sergeant in the back and skewered him with her sword. Jennifer fought side by side with Martin. Olivia was looked after by Alan, but she looked after him in her turn. Her sword kept a clear area on his unguarded side. To those involved, the fight seemed to go on for a long time. In fact it was all over in less than ten minutes. Two light wounds taken by Jennifer and Alan; otherwise apart from the odd bruise the party was unscathed. The attackers left two dead on the quay and they took several other wounded away with them.

***

When they boarded the ship, the warning was already out that there were boats assembling for a sea raid. McLean and Godden returned in a borrowed sampan. They reported to Martin. "That Portuguese Paulo Wing; he was with a bunch of men at his warehouse. He was telling them to stop the ships from leaving. That is the reason for the gathering of the small boats on the other side of the harbour. This might be a good time to leave, if it is possible. We do not have room to manoeuvre here in these confined waters."

Martin said, "I agree, we'll have boats to pull the head round on the Castletown at this moment and once in line we will set sail, though the wind is light. The other ships are already prepared, and we are all on guard ready to repel boarders."

As he spoke the first of the collection of small boats loaded with men appeared in the light of the lanterns that were attached to all the moored ships. The Castletown was moving by now and the sails were dropped and tightened to take advantage of the light airs. She was moving fast enough to pace the speed of the boats of the attackers. Overtaking the two pulling boats, they managed to get the men aboard on nets dropped down the side of the ship. The tethered boats were trailed behind the ship until there was time to stop and hoist them aboard safely. Some of the attacking boats got near, and the occupants fired their muskets without effect. The Marines who fired back to discourage them made no such mistakes, their bullets slowed the boats to the point where there was no way they could catch the ship.

A junk that had moved to bar the way out of the anchorage encountered the Alderney and the Asterid; it was swiftly reduced to a shattered wreck, drifting to strand itself on the shore clear of the entrance.

Sll three ships passed through into the river leading to the open sea. Martin had been surprised at the lengths to which Paulo Wing had gone to stop them leaving Macau.

Natasha explained, "The situation in Macau is always critical when dealings with the Mandarin are involved," she said. "In the case of my father, my delivery was expected to pay outstanding debts."

Martin listened in amazement as she detailed some of the more bizarre events that had occurred since she had been old enough to be aware of what was happening.

Over the years of the control of the present Mandarin, there had been an increase in the demands for reparation of increasingly disparate types, from rental of services of family members to seizure of family members to be enslaved and prostituted without any recourse.

"So your own abduction could have led to you being sold for prostitution or being taken as a concubine by the Mandarin."

"Absolutely. I have funds but I am still at hazard in the Oriental world, as women command no respect here. Nor are we allowed to hold wealth unless we find a protector."

Thinking of Olivia, and Maria, Martin nodded his head slowly. That aspect of things was still represented in many parts of the world.

***

In consultation with his captains and supercargo, Martin agreed to sail for home. The direction would be westward. The state of the South American coastal countries made the prospect of restocking and refitting questionable, and while there were hazards enough on the westward route, there were also more friendly ports if needed.

Winning

Part two

Chapter one

The Voyage Home

The journey south down the South China Sea, for the initial part of the voyage took ten days. A squall cost Alderney a topmast spar and the repairs took time, despite the combined efforts of all three ships' carpenters. They were interrupted by the arrival of three East-Indiamen en-route to Hong Kong, entailing a necessary to-ing and fro-ing between ships to exchange intelligence and warn of hazards in both directions, and of course the need for a social occasion where the ladies from both parties were given time to socialise for one evening.

With the repairs completed, the voyage recommenced with the warnings of pirates by both parties. For the homeward ships the hazards of the Singapore Strait and the Malacca Strait had been stressed, the China-bound ships having to fight off pirates despite the strength of the three armed merchantmen.

It was with some concern that Martin reviewed their situation as the ships approached the Singapore Strait. He stood in his cabin on Asterid. Jennifer was on the Castletown with the other ladies. There was room on her to allow the ladies privacy and more stable conditions in the waters of the area. For Martin it allowed him to study the situation without distraction and that brought his thoughts back to the immediate situation. He stretched and groaned quietly, as a twinge from his latest injury reminded him that the grey hairs appearing in his otherwise dark hair was actually a sign of age. After all he was coming up to his thirty-eighth year, he was no longer the young man that started out to sea twenty-four years ago.

He decided that the best way to transit the straits would be in line ahead, with Alderney leading the Castletown and Asterid bringing up the rear.

All three ships would be worth taking, the main cargo was in the Castletown but both the other ships carried cargo as well, albeit smaller bulk but high value none the less. The profits from the trading with Valdivia in Chile were held in gold bullion on Asterid, which was chosen as the treasure ship by mutual consent. The small fleet would be a worthy prize for any pirate, and it was well worth the saving. For each of the men that had invested in the enterprise, the trade profit would be substantial, and the bounty for the removal of the Commodore and his ships would be an additional sum if it were ever paid. It was a matter that Martin had not discussed as he was inclined to think the payment would not be forthcoming.

He rose from his desk, a little wearily and went up on deck, striding the deck as he had for so many years, thinking and considering the next move in the game of survival.

***

Captain John Harris watched the thoughtful figure pacing back and forth. There was a dependability about the stolid figure that was reassuring. There seemed to be nothing that could not be overcome by the man walking the deck. He smiled to himself; Ship's Captain. albeit a merchant ship, had a ring to it. "Watch her head, Cox'n, she's wandering!"

"Aye aye, sir." The Cox'n allowed the ship to come back to her mean course.

The South China Sea was calm enough. a long wave lifting the ship without violence allowing her to cushion herself against the next in an easy motion. The moon was up and it was creating a silver sheen over the dark water and highlighting the sails of the three ships ghosting quietly through the night.

On board Castletown Jennifer was missing Martin, having been with him only two nights ago. It was something she thought was rather strange, considering her normal situation. When Martin was at sea they could be separated for up to a year at a time. She sighed. It seemed she was getting old and crotchety. It did not help much to admit she had been hoping to be with her husband on board the Asterid. She did understand why she, with the other ladies, was accommodated on the Castletown. It made sense; the cabins were here and the bunks ample, for two even, but she still wished she was with her husband, now at this moment. A tear leaked from the corner of her eye. That brought her out of the doldrums and she straightened, scolding herself for allowing herself to descend into such a maudlin mood. Touching the tear away with her handkerchief, she determinedly walked to the cabin door and went through into the saloon where Julia and Dorothy were joking with Maria, Natasha and Olivia, on the subject of men.

For Olivia, things were going as well as they expected. Alan Bristow, her husband was as kind and thoughtful a he had promised, he had made no advances that could be misunderstood, or that would prevent, the eventual annulment of their marriage. She was a little disappointed, if truth be told. Feeling that perhaps she was not as attractive as people had always told her, surely... She stopped the thought hurriedly, that was not fair, she had made the rules, and Alan was abiding by them, as any real gentleman should. She was by now aware that he was a wealthy man who had no need of her fortune to better his lot. He did not realise, as she had at first, just how attractive he was. Despite his profession, he was kind and gentle with the people close to him. She just wished he would indicate how he felt about being with her. For herself, the thought of being parted from him was something she no longer wished to contemplate.

In the Singapore Strait, the first sign of the notorious pirate threat was seen. As five ships appeared at dusk and approached the three British ships entering the Strait. All three opened their gun-ports and ran out their guns. Faced with sixty plus heavy guns, the five strangers changed course and returned to the Island of Sumatra.

Their steady progress through the strait was otherwise unchecked, their passage not bothered by the scattered fishing craft and small trading junks that speckled the waters of the strait.

The real trial came as they reached the Malacca Strait. Two ships raced out from the Sumatra shore to cut off Asterid from the other two ships. Both of the interceptors were under sail and oars and very fast. Luckily they were spotted early and the ship was already at action stations; the other ships had been warned by sounding the bell on the frigate, a pre-arranged signal. As Asterid turned to present her broadside, her gun ports were raised and guns run out.

The two attackers were obviously surprised at the speed of her reaction, but they were still bent on boarding and overwhelming the crew.

As Asterid's guns fired, the first of the ships took the brunt of the carronade blast of canister shot,that shredded the bow of the ship, destroyed the head sail, and stopped the ship in its tracks. With her bows opened to the sea, the ship began sinking casting the hordes of men into the water.

The second ship ignored the first and continued their dash to get alongside. A cannon mounted in her bows fired, and the ball clipped the rail forward and cut the jib loose. The twelve pounder broadside guns now took up the task, each aimed and fired by its crew. One by one the canister shot swept the decks of the approaching ship, each group of musket balls wreaking havoc on the crowd of men on deck waiting to board their victim.

As the guns fired they were reloaded with ball and aimed and fired to effect. Each ball hitting at this range smashed timbers, but the coup-de-gras came when the ball smashed the row of oars on the starboard side of the attacking ship. The effect was dramatic. The pirate ship heeled around to starboard and presented its exposed port side to the guns. The invitation was accepted, and the loaded guns shot direct into the side of the ship holing the waterline. As it rolled back onto an even keel the water poured in and the ship rolled over further and further before joining its abandoned companion at the bottom of the Malacca Strait.

On the Castletown, a question was answered. Olivia, bent on going on deck to watch what was happening to Asterid, was halfway up the companion stairs when the ship swing into a violent turn, caught off balance she fell down the stairs to the deck below. Alan Bristow was on his way below to reassure the ladies that all was well. He saw Olivia fall and raced down the stairs to her where she lay winded on the deck.

He lifted her gently in his arms and whispered, "Please tell me you are not hurt, my love?" As the words slipped out, he gasped at his slip. He held his breath for her reaction.

She heard his words and to his astonishment smiled and lifted her hand and stroking his cheek. "It took me by surprise." He made to help her up, but she stopped him. "Just hold me, I feel safe with you. Don't let me go!"

For a moment he was stunned, he had despaired of ever hearing her say such a thing, he could feel her trembling, and hugged her tight, "I will never let you go." He said as he lifted her in his arms. Her face turned up to him so he kissed her. Her arms were round his neck, holding him close. He carried her to her cabin and laid her on the bed. He would have risen but she would not let go. "Please stay with me, Alan."

He kissed her again and sank to the bed beside her as the kiss went on and on.

***

Jennifer and Dorothea, who had risen to help Olivia, watched the interaction between Alan and Olivia then looked at each other as Maria looked on, smiling at the incident. Finally Jennifer said, "It's about time."

Dorothea nodded with a small smile and rose to her feet. "Let us see what all the fuss is about on deck." The two women left the saloon., Maria and Natasha, mystified at Jennifer's comment followed.

While the ladies stood in a group at the top of the companion way, the activity on the moonlit water was mostly behind the three ships. The non-swimmers were gone by now and the number of bobbing heads in the water was reducing as the activity of the local aquatic life increased. Distance prevented the horrific sight being apparent to the watchers. But Captain Brooks ushered the ladies to the chairs still on deck from earlier in the day.

***

The journey along the Straits was now almost over, and the collection of houses hanging onto the shore of the island of Sumatra looked innocent enough. From around the point, the line of ships suddenly appeared, looking menacing. In Alderney, Captain Hammond did not hesitate. Already cleared for action, he called, "Guns!"

The two forward guns of the port broadside had been already charged and loaded. At the command they were run out while the gun crews of the other guns loaded their guns. The two prepared guns were aligned and the first was fired across the bows of the lead ship.

There was no reaction except for the men on deck of the strange ship, who started to shout and wave weapons at the three British ships.

The second gun was fired and it appeared to hit the first ship among the people on deck but it was difficult to see if it made any difference. The remainder of the guns were run out and the broadside fired and this did have visible effect. The lead ship staggered at the impact, and the sails shivered as the structure of the ship was threatened. It did not stop its progress, nor did it affect the progress of the following craft

That ranged from Proa's to an old looking former Portuguese frigate, which was armed with several cannon though they were not mounted in broadsides.

As Captain Harris brought the Asterid forward to screen the Castletown, Martin called across to Captain Brooks, "They are expecting to board us, so concentrate on keeping them at arm's length." Brooks acknowledged. The Marines were already deployed in the rigging and along the bulwarks and in addition, Julia, Jennifer, Dorathea and Natasha had all obtained rifles and were ready for action. Maria had received a course on the reloading procedure, and was preparing the extra rifles to be passed forward when needed. All three ships turned away from the converging pirates. There were now four bigger ships plus several smaller, all loaded with men. The lead ship was looking fragile after the pounding it was taking from Alderney. Asterid was now in range and her guns were beginning have an effect.

But the small craft were gathering around the Castletown and despite the effect of the rifles, there seemed to be an endless supply of people to attempt the climb to the ship's deck.

Asterid, using her swivel guns started to attack the boarders with grape shot as their boats started nudging the side of the big East-Indiaman. The swivels cut swathes through the crowded ranks of the would-be boarders. The Alderney then transferred her attention to the next in line. The first ship was drifting helpless in the current; the Castletown cleared the bulk of the small boats. The Marines were now using their bayonets to pry the surviving boarders from the sides of the ship. The gun-ports opened and the heavy guns were run out. The old Portuguese frigate was in range and the first broadside from the Castletown smashed into the old timbers of the ship, causing severe damage. The Asterid was able to follow with a broadside from her guns. The old frigate staggered at the impact and her guns answered with an erratic reply. Two of her shot impacted the Asterid which had placed herself between the frigate and Castletown. The damage was not great; it seemed that the gunners on the pirate were not as skilled as they might be.

The second broadside from Asterid brought down her mainmast which snapped the mizzen in turn. Both British ships then left the action to support Alderney, now threatened with boarding from several small craft.

Asterid, using her speed, raced to support her and ploughed through the small flotilla, crushing and spurning the small craft aside as she continued firing her cannon at the two remaining bigger craft. Both replied but in neither case was the gunnery effective. To Martin it seemed that the guns were there only as an encouragement to the boarding parties.

It was touch and go whether the pirates or the Asterid would win the race, but in the end the pirates lost, the mast on the lead ship fell, and despite the efforts of the rowers, the loss made the difference. The combined gunnery of the Castletown and the Asterid was too much for the pirates and both boats turned and attempted to struggle their way to the shore, pursued by Alderney and Asterid.

Martin commented to Captain Harris, as they returned to from their chase. "Whatever happens, those big ships will not be of much use from now on."

Harris looked back at the two pirates, one ashore and the other without her mast and looking very battered. They were in shoal water otherwise they would have both been sunk. Neither of Martin's ships had the draught to enter the Mangrove swamp waters on the shore of the island.

***

The voyage continued with little further incident during the Indian Ocean crossing. They had been warned of the Andaman Island pirates but had seen no sign of them. When they called at the Seychelles for fresh water, there were very few people there at the time as the fishing fleet was out with most of the men. They turned south to run between the big island of Madagascar and the islands of Mauritius and Reunion.

Martin had considered stopping at the recently secured Island of Mauritius, but decided it made sense to go straight to Capetown, where there were properly equipped shipyards to refit the ships for the last long haul north past the skeleton coast to the north and the long coast of Africa.

Having been taking exercise for the past few weeks, Martin was feeling better about himself. His period in the doldrums was just that.

***

Mooring in the bay at Capetown, the ladies could not wait to get ashore, Rooms were booked in the hotel, and the menfolk were warned that there would be time spent shopping and socialising before the journey home was recommenced.

At the threats Martin smiled to himself. They would be here for three weeks, they would then depart. That time was needed as he wished to purchase local artifacts for selling in London and the ships would need attention.

Capetown had been ceded to Britain in 1814, and he was interested in exploring the colony which to his eyes looked mostly Dutch, certainly in the design of the houses scattered over the shore of the Bay.

Chapter-two

Convoy

The stay at Capetown turned out to be a welcome break especially for the ladies. An opportunity to bring out the more elaborate of their dresses, the ladies staying in the hotel were introduced to the Governor, and invited to the ball in honour of those sailing to Britain with the six ship convoy that would be departing the following week for Britain.

On hearing this Martin decided that it would be sensible, if they could be prepared in time, for their three ships to join the six, so all efforts were to be made to meet the timetable set.

***

Fortuitously the preparations took a little longer than expected and though Castletown and Alderney were able to sail, Asterid was delayed, and sailed twelve hours later. Neither Martin nor Captain Harris were worried about the convoy, both were confident that they would catch the slower moving ships within two days at worst.

Knowing the course that was to be followed, the delayed ship set off with all sail set, to catch up with the convoy. As dusk was falling the lookout called down that there was a strange sail in sight.

"Could this be a straggler from the convoy?" Harris called.

"She is an armed ship sir, by the cut of her sails, I would say a Froggie."

Martin who was on deck at that time was approached by John Harris. "I do believe we have encountered a hopeful pirate, shadowing the convoy, do you have any ideas for dealing with her?"

Martin smiled, "You are the captain, John. Remember, I am just a passenger. I may make a suggestion but any decision for the ship has to be yours. I think we should shadow the shadow, see what she does. What have you in mind?"

"I was thinking something on the same lines. Mr. Bates, let us keep in touch with the stranger, preferably without letting him know."

Lieutenant Jackson Bates had been a master's mate with Admiral Bowers, he was a seaman from the boots up. Older than average, his seamanship was unquestioned. Harris was happy to have the opportunity to lift him from the beach. Now he answered "Aye, Sir!" and called to trim the sails and change course slightly.

The next twenty-four hours were spent playing cat and mouse with the strange ship. The second evening Harris decided to close on the stranger which was showing her stern light when darkness fell. She had been slowing each night so that she did not overrun the convoy, which in common with most convoys shortened sail each night.

Martin discussed the situation with Harris as they caught up with their quarry. There would be no moon until the early hours of the morning, "What were you intending, John?"

"I considered just keeping in place for another night, but it did occur to me that there must be a rendezvous at some point and in the circumstances it might be better to remove this ship from the equation, and take a chance on the rest."

Martin looked at Harris questioningly, "You surprised me, I had not thought of that." He shook his head and sat back thinking, then he leaned forward and said, "Pass the stranger and contact the convoy. We have no idea what ships may be involved in any attack. If the convoy is warned they will be on the lookout for trouble."

Harris looked at Martin and shrugged, "Of course you are right, that had not occurred to me." He went up on deck and spoke quietly to Lieutenant Bates. The course was adjusted slightly, and the ship ploughed on coming up to the stranger and passing her in the darkness. In the bows were extra lookouts eventually reporting the bobbing lights of the convoy ahead.

***

On the Calliope Captain Edmund Bertrand sat in his cabin looking at the bottle on the table. It sat in the fiddle designed to keep it upright despite the movements of the ship. He watched the level of the liquid within the bottle as it tilted one way and then the other, then he picked the bottle up and poured a good measure of the content into his glass. Once more he played his game, seeing how long he could watch the tilting to and fro before actually drinking the brandy in the glass.

Eventually he picked the glass up and threw the brandy back in one gulp, then he threw the glass across the cabin, where it smashed against the bulkhead.

Rising to his feet he stepped over to the bunk and carefully lay down. He closed his eyes and the memories started to creep in. The face of wife and their two children, the smiles changing to fear, then the bodies flung on a heap of others. The smiling face of his Admiral as he shot the hostages, killing them one by one, taking time to reload in between each execution.

He could hear the voice of the priest in his ears ordering the massacre of the Protestants. That voice in his head – cold, merciless, and unforgiving – coming from a man of God, from a priest. This followed by the satisfaction from the feeling as his knife slit the bastard's throat. The small smile crossed his face as he fell finally asleep.

***

Cartaret opened the cabin door quietly and conformed that his captain was asleep at last.

He had been with the captain since the beginning. When the frigate had been a part of the French navy, and the captain had been a hero. Then Napoleon had allowed that madman Admiral Parmentier to assume command of their ship among others for the suppression of the revolt by the island community.

Admiral Parmentier had slaughtered, with glee, the bulk of the population, enjoying the orders of that mad priest.

When the captain discovered the murder of his wife and children, he had become quiet. He had reported to the Admiral and asked the question. The Admiral had shouted at the captain and carried on, preparing his pistol to shoot another hostage. When the pistol had been loaded the captain had seized it and used it to threaten the Admiral, making him stand and wait, while the captain mentioned his wife and children lying in the mass grave, he had then marched the Admiral to the cliff edge overlooking the Atlantic Ocean. Making him stand and look at his future, through the mist of spray from the sea on the rocks below. The priest appeared and threatened the wrath of God on the captain if he did this dreadful deed.

His condemnation stopped as the captain's knife sliced through his throat and severed his vocal cords.

Cartaret could still picture the unbelief on the priest's face, on that cliff edge standing beside the Admiral. The pair flew, the priest dumb, but the Admiral screaming all the way down to the unforgiving rocks below.

Both lifeless bodies lay exposed on the rocks for two assaults by the waves. The third cleaned the area.

The captain had called the crew together, "We have two choices, we can continue to serve that monster who allows this sort of thing to happen, or we can take our chances as free traders, taking whatever we can from whoever we find."

The vote was a foregone conclusion. Those not happy with the idea were free to go. Nobody left, now they had three ships all well served and all former navy.

Cartaret grinned savagely, cutthroats all; all would hang one day, but meanwhile there was the convoy to attend to. There was an East-Indiaman with women aboard, Cartaret licked his lips. He was fond of the ladies, as he often put it they screamed politely when he attended to them.

When Captain Bertrand wakened they would be ready to rendezvous with the other ships and collect the convoy ahead.

***

Martin was now in touch with the Commodore. The warning was out and in the case of his three ships a plan of defence/attack was already in being. He had no doubts that the shadowing ship had friends lying in ambush somewhere ahead as his message to the Commodore pointed out. With Alderney and Asterid, the convoy had two sloops Intrepid and Rapid.

The Commodore, Sir James Hamilton, commanded a rather elderly 60 gun 4th rate ship of the line, on her last voyage, Jaipur was from the Indian station, now replaced but still a ship of force and a reassurance to the merchantmen sailing in company. Of the merchantmen, one other Indiaman, armed with twenty-four eighteen pounders, she packed a punch and was commanded by an ex-Royal Navy captain known to Martin.

All of the other ships were armed one way and another though none could be depended upon to stand against serious opposition.

***

The raiders made themselves known two days later.

Initially there was little to indicate that there was a threat. The arrival of the Calliope from astern, was innocent enough and if they had not been aware of her following, she would have been accepted without question. With a smart looking ship of 32 guns on passage to Lisbon, the charming captain spoke Portuguese immaculately in addition to French and English. Being aware and forewarned meant that the Commodore accepted the ship as extra protection, and when the other ships appeared from the west, it was sensible to send the Calliope to investigate.

As soon as the strange ships were reported the three ships under Martin's command went into action stations, signalling the two sloops to take up their position covering merchantmen. The Jaipur made sail to dominate the weather side so that she could run down on any threat, and support the sloops, both of which would be out-gunned by the three strangers.

Captain Bertrand was dismayed to see the reformation of the convoy, realising that he had no longer got the advantage he had anticipated. As things stood, any prizes taken now would cost him dear, in men and damage.

As a result he signalled his other ships to pass the convoy by, and lead the way out of sight of the convoy but close enough for him to contact within a half-day's sailing.

Both his other ships altered course slightly and raced off ahead of the slower convoy and Calliope returned to report to the Commodore, the invented details of the two ships.

The following day the Calliope also left the convoy having decided that progress was too slow.

Chapter three

The long chase

The disappearing ship took most of the forenoon to go completely from sight. On the wave-crest, Captain Hammond in the Alderney, the leading ship in the convoy, had a call from the lookout at the masthead. "Calliope is signalling sir!"

"Who is she speaking to?"

"I just caught a glimpse of the hoist sir, I could not see any other ship, but it was signal not ensign I'm sure sir."

Hammond turned to Lieutenant Gibbs. "Replace the lookout and send him to my cabin.

William Hammond was a level-headed captain, who did not jump to conclusions. The seaman who presented himself to his captain was a well-experienced man named Welland. Will Hammond said, "Tell me what you saw?"

Welland said "I was doing a horizon sweep with the telescope, thought we had lost the Calliope but you know how it is, we both must have crested at the same time. I was just looking at her last position when we rose and so did she. While I watched there was a splash of colour at her mizzen halyards, it was more than one flag sir though I could not make them out before she had gone again."

Hammond looked at the chart, open on his table, prodding the place where he estimated they were. "What would he be up to, who would he be signalling here d'ye think?"

Abel Welland smiled wryly, "Them other two mates of his perhaps, the two ships that came and went yesterday."

Captain Hammond nodded thoughtfully, "You are probably right." He straightened up, "Thank you, Welland, report back to Mr. Gibbs, and ask him to join me."

Welland straightened up, "Aye sir."

Lieutenant Gibbs was past the adolescent years and now at nineteen was already growing into the man he would become. His rather serious look was offset by the twinkle in his eye, though he was serious here with his captain. "You sent for me, sir?"

Hammond waved at a chair, "Sit down, Athol. I am unhappy at this latest sighting of the Calliope, signalling someone who is out of sight, but not far ahead from the sound of it. Welland suggested the two ships that came and went yesterday might be hanging about waiting for something, probably the convoy?"

"I'm inclined to agree with Welland, sir. I was never happy with the Calliope. To me she was still a French frigate, well found and well run, but under no flag, if you take my meaning."

"You believe she is a pirate?"

Gibbs reply was emphatic. "I think she and the other two ships are working together, and, yes, I believe she is a privateer or pirate, and in cahoots with those other ships, especially after the sighting today."

"I agree. Drop back to the Asterid I will pass on the news to Sir Martin, and let him decide what we tell the Commodore."

Athol Gibbs rose to his feet and saluted. "Aye, sir." He left Will Hammond with the chart and the problem.

***

Sir Martin Forest-Bowers was seated in the captain's cabin on the Asterid when Hammond came aboard. He had observed the approach of the Alderney from the deck but descended to the cabin to save time with whatever urgent report Hammond had to deliver.

He rose to his feet to receive the young man, and waved him to a chair. "A glass of wine, I think, and then we'll talk."

Hammond was ready to burst out with his news, but contained himself and accepted the glass, taking a tentative sip before relaxing.

"So, William, how do you like your command? It's been a rather longer voyage that any of us anticipated."

"Alderney is a fine ship sir, and as for the voyage, there are few men that can claim to have sailed around the world, I look forward to boring my great-grandchildren with my recollections."

Martin smiled, "And why not? That is something we can all enjoy, and I know my wife has found the experience exhilarating."

Will Hammond sat back relaxed, and finally gave Martin his news.

"A signal! I see, and what did you make of that?" It was typical of Martin to ask the question. So many senior officers would have dismissed him to draw their own conclusions.

"I believe the Calliope is meeting with the two ships that decided not to join the convoy, I also think that they intend attacking the convoy."

"But we are at peace with France now, why would they do such a thing?"

"Privateers, pirates, I believe they are intending an ambush, and despite the presence of the Jaipur and her two sloops, they would have had a good chance at lifting the bulk of the convoy ships. With us here there could be problems and I believe they will have to find a way to get us out of the way."

"Then we must provide them with the opportunity." Martin said thoughtfully.

Hammond kept quiet, he could not think of any way they could deceive the pirates, but he knew that this man would find an answer.

We'll take your boat over to the Commodore. You can drop me off on the way back. It will save time.

The two men conferred with the convoy Commodore in the great cabin on the Jaipur. Sir James was a cheerful red-faced Devon man with a reputation for standing his ground. "So as you say, Martin, there is no way we can be sure that these people are pirates, without dangling a little bait?" He smiled as he spoke, and Martin warmed to the man, thinking how lucky it was that he did not have to deal with some of the captains in his experience.

Sir James looked at Will and Martin quizzically, "Come on out with it, I know you have some scheme up your sleeve?"

Martin spoke first. "Well, it did occur to us that there are two ships in the convoy that are prizes, and despite their cargoes they are crewed by naval men, and commanded by naval officers. If we loaded the two ships with men, and hid them, and placed the ships where they were panicking and sailing in circles, if you take my meaning. It's possible that they would be closed and boarded, being easy prey. That would give us two things. Proof of piracy and with a little luck, two prizes."

"Damn-me, Martin, you have a devious mind. I like it." Sir James laughed.

"Just one small detail sir, it was Captain Hammond's idea. Begging your pardon sir, the men? Where do they come from?"

Sir James looked puzzled for a moment, then realised what Will was saying. His face fell. "Of course I don't have sufficient men to spare for two boarding parties."

"My men are all beached Navy as are my officers, myself included. Suppose you decided that the convoy was in hazard, and called my people back to duty?"

Sir James thought about it. "Can I do that?"

"In the face of immediate danger, I believe you can. It would mean that the men involved would be entitled a share in any prize monies, but since they would be risking their lives, that would be fair."

Sir James smiled, "So you are willing to hire your men out for a little quid-pro-quo reward."

Martin grinned, "In simple terms, I think it in our interest, for protection of the convoy certainly, and protection of the womenfolk in my ships and yours."

"Done. I'll write the orders now, and you may correct me if I go wrong. I presume you intend leading at least one of the boarding parties."

"It did occur to me." Martin smiled grimly. "How about the other party, do you have a man in mind?"

"Lieutenant Angus Cameron commanding the sloop Intrepid I think would be a good choice. He can select his men from my three ships, if you look after the other boarding party using your own men."

Having agreed between them the Commodore called Lieutenant Cameron to the flagship and introduced him to Martin.

The tall, rather severe looking Scot smiled when he met Martin, "You would not remember, sir, I served in HMS Hera as a Midshipman in the Caribbean. That was in 1811/12 if I recall/ I will be proud to serve with you again."

Martin said, "You may be aware that Lieutenant Harris is currently captain of Asterid. I am certain you may know several of her crew as they have all sailed with me many times in the past."

"I'll be happy to see them, sir, if the opportunity arises." Cameron said, "I had good friends on the Hera."

The sound of Sir James clearing his throat reminded them both of the reason for this meeting. So Martin told Cameron of the suggested arrangements and outlined the plan they had formulated.

Cameron accepted the plan enthusiastically, and shortly left to prepare his selection for the second boarding party.

***

Once back in Asterid Martin wrote orders for Will Hammond in Alderney. His task was to occupy the third pirate, whilst the boardings were under way. It entailed his being in place, close, but out of immediate range of the two vulnerable merchantmen.

The confused bait would be separated from the main convoy by several miles, with just the Alderney bustling up to shepherd them back.

All this happening under the lee of the three shadowing ships, who hopefully would be close enough to fall into the trap. The difficult part would be ensuring that the actual boarding operations were carried out simultaneously, so as not to forewarn the other ships.

What they needed now was a squall, to allow then to separate the convoy and stage their scene.

***

The Atlantic provided three days later. The extra men for each of the bait ships were sent over from the other ships standing close by. Once the men were loaded, both ships cracked on full sails to make as much distance as possible.

Close to the latitude of Dakar, the two merchantmen and Alderney cracked on as much sail as they could, while the remainder of the convoy shortened sail to widen the gap between them.

In the region of the squall, visibility between the ships was reduced to no more than a cable length. While the pirates and the convoy reduced sail, the small decoy group made up ground to a point close to the pirates' position, though still out of direct sight, but able to receive the signal from Rapid, the sloop shadowing the pirates.

Prompted by the Rapid, the two merchantmen started milling around with tangled sails and rigging. The crew of both ships were in the rigging trying to sort the tangles out. The Alderney was close, but there were the three pirates, and in the distance the remainder of the convoy milling about way out of range.

Calliope and Venger headed straight for the two merchantmen, the Garonne inserted herself between the Alderney and her charges. The two unfortunate merchantmen were grappled and the boarders on both frigates roared as they started to cross to the two merchant ships. At Martin's signal the ambush was sprung. The two parties flooded on deck and pushed the boarders back to the attacking ships. The general battle raged across the decks of the two pirate ships. The surprise had given the ambushers the edge and the initial shock impact had taken the heart out of the opposition. On both ships the boarders battled fiercely finally overcoming the pirates.

Martin was vaguely aware of the guns from the Alderney and Garonne when he looked across at the battle, he saw the Garonne leaving the area with the Alderney in pursuit. As he watched he saw the topmast of the Alderney tremble, then topple. The Garonne fled, chasing the departing squall. The approaching Asterid was still too far away to prevent the escape

Chapter four

A good day for dying.

Martin looked over to the Venger. The prisoners were standing in a depressed bunch on the main deck of the former frigate. Here on the Calliope, Captain Bertrand was lying on deck being attended by the doctor. His wounds were serious and the doctor did not expect him to survive. The doctor called Martin to speak with the wounded man.

"Well, Captain, what is it you wish to say?"

"I have little time I believe so I will be brief. In my cabin you will find a small safe." The wounded man reached to his neck and pulled-out the silver chain that was there revealing a key. There is a box with my life savings, no use to me anymore, and my wife is long dead. The safe is beneath a deck plank in the foot-well of my desk. If you do not take it may never be found, and that would be a waste," His voice wavered, and Martin thought he had gone. As he turned away Bertrand clutched his sleeve. "Beware the Sheik of Agadir; he has several ships and a greedy heart...." The dying man was looking directly into Martin's eyes, his grip slackened and as Martin watched the light in his eyes faded and Captain Bertrand died.

Martin took the key and stood up. In the distance he heard gunfire. Scanning the sea around them, the oncoming convoy and the Alderney were the only ships in sight, the squall that had hidden the retreating Garonne was still to the north of them and the entire northern horizon was now shrouded in either low cloud or mist.

The sound of guns came once more and a flash of light could be glimpsed in the gloom of the mist.

Martin called to Lieutenant Cameron. "I'm sending my prisoners over to you. Take command of the Venger and secure the prisoners but let me have as many of your men as you can, I'll take the Calliope and find out about the gunfire up ahead."

Cameron waved his acknowledgement and sent forty of his men over to join Martin, while the prisoners from Martin's prize, crossed to the other ship.

The Alderney had secured her topmast, so Martin signalled her to accompany the Calliope north to check on the gunfire. The Cox'n from the Asterid shouted for the thrown together crew to haul in the sheets. The grapnels were released and the Calliope moved away from the boarding location and turned north, accompanied by Alderney and followed by Asterid still a quarter-mile behind, the ships moved northward.

As they approached the mist bank the sound of the guns became focused to one area ahead of the ships. Asterid had caught up with the others, it was she that made contact first. Captain Harris spotted the Garonne surrounded by several galleys. Two of the galleys were looking decidedly worse for wear; all had bow mounted guns and all were in action against the Garonne. Harris did not hesitate, "Run out the guns, port broadside at the galley to port; fire as you bear."

The crash of the guns was followed by the billow of smoke that enveloped the side of the ship. The galley selected had turned half way round to face Asterid when the guns fired. The effect was dramatic, the oars on the starboard side of the galley were shattered at the cost of the lives of a large number of the slaves on the benches, the rest of the balls had struck the bows and ranged down the deck of the galley, leaving trails of smashed men among the crowd waiting to pour over onto their victim's deck. The reloaded guns now firing grape shot, caused horrific casualties among the survivors of the first volley.

The remaining oars on the galley thrashed the water, desperate to bring their craft alongside their tormentor.

The stern chasers from the Garonne now had the galley in their sights. The stern and quarterdeck of the galley disintegrated at the impact of the canister shot from the beleaguered ship.

Calliope and Alderney were now well in range and their guns started to make an impression on the circling galleys, taking the pressure off the Garonne.

But it was the arrival of the Jaipur on the scene that sent the galleys off. The heavy guns blew the wounded galley out of the water with one broadside. One moment it was there, the next all that could be seen was a mess of shattered woodwork and bodies.

The big galley was joined by the four other survivors, making eastward for the African coastline.

Guessing that the galleys were returning to Agadir. the convoy now enlarged by the addition of two new prizes, passed through the mist banks to rendezvous off Madeira.

***

The Governor was, as before, hospitable, and the ladies were able to enjoy the facilities provided whilst the crews were reorganised and returned to their own ships for the moment. The pirates meanwhile were detained in the island prison. The crew of the Garonne which lay under the guns of the fort at Funchal, was still on board and engaged in repairing the damage from the skirmish with the galleys. She was moored under the guns of the fort on the land-ward side, and the Jaipur to sea-ward. As far as Martin and the Commodore were concerned, she was an embarrassment, and neither was keen to make a decision about her at present.

In the Governor's Palace the Commodore, Martin and the Governor were discussing the attack by the galleys. The Governor was able to confirm that their origin was probably Agadir. "These galleys have become a problem in recent months. Several of the ships passing through the area between Madeira and the African coast have been attacked and I do not know how many have been taken. I have been told that there has been a rise in the number of European slaves appearing in the Moroccan slave markets, and there has been pressure on the Admiralty to do something about it.

The Commodore pointed out that the waters were international. That always made things difficult among the navies of the world.

Martin commented "I spent time with the rulers on the Barbary coast, and I understood that Morocco was part of the agreement reached. I think we should raid Agadir. Strip it of its wealth and ships, and if necessary its current ruler."

The Commodore grinned, "There speaks a man no longer bound by the constrictions of the Admiralty."

"I would like to point out, Commodore, that the chances of you retaining your position in active service are very slim. On returning home, your current command will go into ordinary. You will be without a command once more, unless you have considerable influence but my guess would be the beach, just like the rest of us.

"We could do the Governor and ourselves a considerable favour, with a good chance of increasing our respective pensions at the same time. As things are, the prizes we have may well not be brought in; remember, the war is over. My people are on this voyage to make money, I'm sure your men would be delighted at the chance to add a little to their own nest egg. I think we could lose the Garonne in the process; after all, they are mercenaries. They could take part for any booty they could find. Or we could remove the Jaipur to take part in the raid and be surprised when we found the Garonne gone, having slipped her moorings.

The Commodore nodded slowly. "That would be a better solution, I believe, and Governor, I think we may also relieve you of many of the prisoners you have. I believe they are an embarrassment to you and the Portuguese Government."

He turned to Martin, "Now, as you are aware there is no way that I can be officially linked with an attack on a sovereign country with whom we are not at war. That means that you will need to command the expedition and any auxiliaries that may join you for such a hazardous undertaking."

Martin smiled, "I understand that we will need to stay in Madeira for two weeks to recover from our exertions with the pirates.

"Meanwhile we have the Calliope, the Venger, the Asterid, and Alderney. I think with the right crews, it should be enough to remove the threat for the passing ships."

The arrangements for the crews of the ships to be involved with the raid, went forward from that time. Many of the men from the Jaipur were assembled to man the prizes. The

Alderney – with her replaced topmast – and the Asterid were already manned. Captain Brooks from the Castletown commanded Calliope with members of his own crew, enhanced by drafts from the Jaipur. Finally Sir James Hamilton, with Angus Cameron as his first Lieutenant commanded Venger.

Over the following week they ensured that all the ships were well armed and, daily exercises of the guns and sail handling were initiated to make sure all knew what they were doing in the heat of action.

On the Saturday of that week the ships set sail for Agadir.

Chapter five

The raid

Three days later, in the early dawn light, the four ships approached the town of Agadir. Essaouira had replaced Agadir as the trading port of this coast, an earthquake that had destroyed Agadir had led to the trade moving north. The small settlement that had grown in the meantime had been taken over by Sheik Amir, who had created his own sheikdom, and re-established the town of Agadir. It suited him to have the main bulk of traffic elsewhere. It kept prying eyes well away from his activities. Having acquired two ships to start with, he had proceeded to establish a lucrative trade in stolen goods and slaves, based on the passing ships trading up and down the coast of Africa.

Now with a fleet of seven ships, life was good for the Sheik. He had assembled a reasonable harem and was now possessed of a small mountain of gold and jewels in his treasury. The army of men who were subject to his rule, stood at nearly one thousand soldiers, and the trading township accommodated close to seven thousand people.

The waterfront was his. It was there he had quays for the ships to come alongside and unload. There was a warehouse which allowed the goods to be offloaded out of the sight of the ordinary people. That was the way he liked it. The less others knew, the less they could talk about.

The early morning and a low mist over the water meant that the masts of the four warships seemed to glide unaided along the surface of the layer of mist. The masts of the Sheik's ships also projected out of the layer of mist, and the gunners used these as points of aim.

The opening volley of gunfire stunned the area and the dreadful noise of smashed timber could be heard between the roar of the cannon.

A landing party was put ashore commanded by Martin. The green-coated Marines from his own ships with their rifles immediately deployed to scout the warehouse and take possession. The Marines from the naval ships, in traditional red coats and armed with muskets, assumed control of the quays. The party in green followed Martin up the hill toward the building that dominated the area, presuming that it was the home and headquarters of the Sheik. From the houses on both sides of the road people poured, aroused by the gunfire in the harbour. Martin and his marines were forced to fight their way up the hill, the increasing number of people making the battle more difficult for each foot gained. Luckily the mass of people involved hampered the defence in their effort to stop Martin and his men. By the time they finally reached the open square opposite the big building, there was a file of armed men in the way. The Marines reloaded their rifles and the withering volley of aimed shots created a swathe of dead and wounded and a breakthrough for Martin and his party. Though there were attackers still, they were mainly coming up the hill, and the width of the street they had used, constricted the crowd, and made that attack front easily defended.

The town was still waking despite the now recurring noise of the guns. At the entrance to the big building, the great doors were closed, reminding Martin of the attack at Tunis. Here there was no one to meet them, nor did he wait. He pointed to the door. Major Bristow came forward, turned the handle and swung the door open.

The dark interior was a stark contrast to the bright light of the sun reflecting from the low lying mist. Martin dashed in followed by his men. The entrance hall was big and once inside it was possible to see the double doors at the far end of the hall. The hall was quite empty. The doors closed behind them by their own weight and the silence of the great building seemed to gather round the small group. The Marines spread out, two of the men went to the double doors and yanked them open. The room beyond was lit, and the hooded lamps revealed the walls draped with silks, the window was draped so that little daylight filtered through. Perfumes scented the air mixed with an exotic odour that was familiar to Martin. It reminded him of another time and place. Martin could not identify it at first. Then it hit him: it was hashish. He had encountered the drug before in the Mediterranean. Though he had never used it himself, he knew people who did.

It explained the lack of reaction from the man lying buried in the cushions, and only now lifting his head to see what was going on. The man looked puzzled, gazing at Martin and then at the green uniform of Major Bristow.

Martin looked at the bewildered man on the cushions. "Sheik Amir, I presume?"

The man shook himself, and then asked the question. "Who the devil are you?" The accent was English and looking closer Martin realised that the man was European.

"You are obviously not an Arab. Who are you really?" Martin shot the question at Amir.

The Sheik gave a tired grin, "I suppose the accent gives me away. In fact I was captured by slavers in 14, I escaped in 16 and I was too ashamed to return home."

"Where is home?"

"Near Cookham, in Berkshire, Father was a rector with a living in the area, so I cannot return. I am already lost to dissipation.

While still looking at the Sheik, Major Bristow stepped out of the room to reappear followed by two men carrying a chest. He told Martin they had located the chest in the back room, along with a great heap of bullion and gold objects.

The Sheik started to protest when he saw the chest but went quiet when Alan Bristow flung the lid back to reveal a sparkling array of jewels. "There is a heap of gold bars and other bullion also, in the room where we found this trunk. I have put guards at the door.

The Sheik protested, "It took me a long time to collect that loot, you cannot just take it away."

"It is all stolen I believe!" Martins reply was terse.

"Well, you are stealing it too." The Sheik was swift to reply.

Whilst Martin could see the validity of the Sheiks claim, he had no intention of admitting to it in his presence. It would be taken away regardless of the ethics involved, if only to be used to recompense the men involved in the raid.

The Marine sergeant came into the room shepherding a group of young women including several of European origin. "I believe this to be the harem, sir."

Martin looked the women over, "Are all of you here, slaves?"

Two of the European women spoke, one in a very English voice. "I wondered what was going to happen when I was put in with this group. I suspected that I could expect deflowering by some desert Sheik. So far I have not been called and therefore my fate is now in your hands, whoever you are."

The spirited reply came from a pretty shapely woman, possibly under eighteen, dressed to advertise her firm body and pert breasts. Her shapely legs were visible through the gauzy stuff of her pantaloons. Her face was framed by a gauze scarf that was draped around her head and neck.

Martin took all this in before he said. "I am Captain Sir Martin Forest-Bowers RN. Your innocence will be safe from now on, by my word, Miss."

The Sheik spoke up, "I do not remember seeing you. When did you arrive?"

The woman said, "I have been here for three months I believe. I was travelling to India on the Worcester, an East Indiaman with my family. We were attacked by galleys, and brought here. I have not seen my parents since."

"What is your name?" Martin asked her.

"The Honourable Cecelia Nugent, I was on my way to join my fiancé, who is captain of a frigate in the Company Navy."

The other lady claiming to have been captured and enslaved was a little older. She wore a wedding ring. Also shapely, with an interesting face, she stepped forward. "I was travelling to join my husband in Gibraltar, I am Marian, the wife of Major Peter Hargreaves RA. He was transferred from Capetown to Gibraltar. He travelled with a naval ship. I was forced to await a merchant ship to follow with our household. I was taken from the merchantman Two Girls six months ago. I

David O'Neil

also have never been introduced to the Sheik. In fact, since I have been here the Sheik has not called for any of the ladies of his harem."

The Sheik was not looking too happy and Martin noticed he was beginning to sweat and show signs of stress. He suspected that the man's dependence on hashish was seriously out of control. It must have been for some time, if what the women were saying, was true.

People dependant on hashish lost interest in other things including sex. Having seen the harem he would have been very surprised at any red blooded man ignoring them all without very good reason.

He turned to the Sheik. "How much control do you still have over your people?"

Amir looked at him in puzzlement. "Why, they obey my every wish."

"Then who gives the orders, day to day?"

"Achmed is my major-domo. He looks after things on a day to day basis."

"Does he supply the hashish?" Martin asked.

"Why yes, he keeps control of it on my behalf."

"Where can I find him?"

Amir now on his feet although holding the door frame for support, pointed to a door half hidden behind some drapes.

Martin nodded to Major Bristow, who went to the door and turned the handle. He flung the door open and stepped back. There was a room largely taken up with a desk. On the desk there were stacks of bags of coins and from behind the stacks a man's head appeared.

"Achmed, come and explain the system to these gentlemen here. Stop skulking behind those sacks of money; we have no time for nonsense, our lives are at risk here. Tell the captain about how we run the business here."

Achmed walked slowly from the office, his face impassive but his body language unwilling. Martin was immediately aware of his hostility. He turned to Sheik Amir, "Either this man cooperates or he becomes one of the casualties of this raid. I did not come here to play games. My ships are demonstrating that fact at this time. It was only then that he

- 240 -

realised how quiet it was within the walls of this building, no wonder the Sheik had not been wakened by the attack. Apart from the effects of the hashish the insulating qualities of the building were astonishing."

The Sheik looked at Achmed, and Martin saw a strange thing, his eyes blazed at the Arab, Achmed wilted in front of him.

Achmed turned and with head lowered he started to speak. "Here we run the entire operation from within this building. There are points where we can speak and the people outside can hear us. Depending where we speak, that is which place we use. We can issue orders with a roar, or a whisper. The followers do what they are told they are frightened of the Sheik who has the look that can melt a man's heart."

Martin guessed that the look was what had decided Achmed to cooperate.

Martin thought for a moment. "Tell the people to disperse and go to their homes. Where can I see the effect of the orders?" Achmed pointed to the other corner of the room. There was another door. A Marine opened the door, revealing a stairway. In a room at the top there was an observation place consisting of a lattice through which the square could be viewed, without the viewer being seen from below. The crowd that had gathered were still there, but in response to an order, the crowd dispersed as Martin watched.

He ran down the stairs, looked at the Major who nodded. Then he turned to Achmed. "I want a cart to carry the treasure to the quay."

Achmed, thoroughly cowed by now, went to a talking point and spoke into it. One of the Marines went up to keep an eye on the scene, and he reported that a cart had been wheeled to the door of the building and left there unattended.

Martin turned to the women, "I will be returning to my ship in a short while. My next port of call is Gibraltar, and then England. I will take any or all of you if you wish, Though I believe many of you come from other places, Sadly I am aware that for many of you there is no going back, the mere fact that you are here as part of a harem will be sufficient for you to be abandoned as spoiled goods by your own people. Any of you who wish to stay in the town here may do so. I will give you money to establish a home. Those who would rather start again in Gibraltar, or England, gather your things and prepare to accompany us to the harbour."

Marian Hargreaves translated to the women who spoke no English. Not surprisingly all decided to accompany the party in the ships.

Chapter five

Homeward bound

The African coast slid past the starboard side of the ship, a long vista of sand and rock, with the occasional settlement of white houses.

The treasure had required a second cart. There was more than Martin had anticipated. Apart from the women, there had only been two prisoners taken from Agadir: the sheik and his man Achmed. The smashed galleys had produced slaves, many dead. Several British and Frenchmen had been released along with the other slaves. When the four ships left the harbour, the Europeans – mainly Spanish and Italian, though there were also forty surviving Englishmen – elected to sail with Martin. The several hundred remaining slaves decided to organise themselves. Martin was not optimistic about the impending fate of the townspeople.

The Europeans had been scattered through the ships to make up the shortages in crews. Losses from the skirmishes they had been involved with over the past months, a place on the British ships must have seemed an easy option after the life they had been facing on the rowing benches.

The women had created problems, but between Jennifer, the Hon Cecelia, and Marion the women were accommodated in the saloon in a series of hammocks rigged and demonstrated by selected seamen amidst an excess of hilarity as some of the ladies insisted on falling out, requiring assistance from the willing seamen, and flirting with them outrageously. The appearance of the Bo'sun was needed to curtail that activity.

By now most had gained their sea legs and the Castletown deck seemed alive with colour and the chatter of the women, ranging in skin colour from Circassian white to Nubian black.

One benefit Martin noticed was the efforts made by the seamen to smarten themselves up when coming on deck.

In their cabin, Jennifer asked, "So, Captain Forest-Bowers, how do you like sailing under merchant colours?"

Martin thought about it, "It has been interesting; at least this voyage has been interesting. But I would point out that in many ways this voyage has not been a typical trading enterprise. So far we have fought several actions in addition to trading, and we have diplomatically managed to upset relations between Britain, Macau and Hong Kong, and also Portugal and Britain. On the other hand we have rid the seas of three separate pirate strongholds, and in addition sunk several pirate ships in passing. I do recognise that this can fall into the present definition of mercantile trade, but I still maintain that this voyage has not been typical and therefore I reserve judgement until there is more realistic evidence forthcoming." He stopped at that point, realised how pompous his speech must have sounded and turned to face his wife, who was doubled up trying to suppress her laughter.

Martin lifted his hands high, in exasperation. "Well, you did ask!"

Jennifer exploded with laughter and Martin couldn't help joining in. He was again reminded how lucky he was, to be married to this beautiful intelligent woman.

***

In Gibraltar the ships moored in the still waters of the harbour. The mighty rock dominated the area. Martin went ashore, accompanied by Jennifer, the Hon Cecelia and Marion Hargreaves. Captain Hammond and Major Bristow followed in another boat with an escort and the two prisoners.

They were received by the Admiral's Flag Lieutenant, who assured them that the Admiral would be with them directly. As tea was being served, Dominic Gordon walked in and greeted the party politely. He was introduced to the two rescued ladies; he was, it seemed, already acquainted with the Honourable Cecelia.

Excusing himself for a moment pleading government matters, he took Martin to one side. To Martin he said, "A grateful Spanish Government has sent their thanks and an honorarium; it awaits you in London. Happily, it arrived before Admiral Cochrane and the infamous O'Higgins raised a revolution in Chile, evicting the Spanish Governor and subverting the Spanish troops in place to the Republican cause. It seems they are losing their influence in the South Americas, as Chile, Peru and Argentina are all in turmoil, all bound for an independent future." This message was delivered with a smile, and Martin wondered whether his part in the removal of the Commodore in Valdivia had made the rebel take-over that much easier.

Back once more with the ladies, Dominic chatted for a few moments before taking the Honourable Cecelia away to be lodged with friends of the family before her eventual onward journey to her fiancé in India.

***

In the Admiral's office Martin was well received, Phillip Newman had been a contemporary of Martin, albeit senior, in his earlier years as a Midshipman. Now the news he had was not so happy. It appeared the loss of the ship that was bringing Marion to join her husband had been reported several months ago and since no ransom demands had been received, it was presumed that she had been lost. The major did not grieve for long, in fact it seemed that his mistress here in Gibraltar, had become pregnant and the major had moved the lady in. A sailor from the lost ship was produced who swore he had seen Marion fall to a shot through the head, and his word was accepted after he produced a ring that the major identified as his wife's as confirmation of his story.

The major had then married his mistress. Phillip Newman added, "It seems that the mistress is leading the major a merry dance. The child is a by-blow of some other association, obviously not the major's progeny."

Martin raised an eyebrow.

Newman said, "He's dark skinned and black haired, looks like a Spanish gipsy. His mother is a red-head, pale skinned; the major is a fair-haired Yorkshireman." He smiled, "I saw his lady Marion, and I cannot help thinking, she is well rid of him. Were I not happily married myself I confess, I would be happy to call upon her."

Martin laughed, "From my knowledge of the lady, limited though it is, I would say she will be a prize for any man. I presume you wish me to let her know her current situation. Oh will she be able to marry again?"

"I did inquire, I understand from the Bishop that, in the circumstances, an annulment can be arranged. It will take an act of Parliament, which I understand your friend Dominic Gordon has undertaken to have passed."

At the words 'your friend' Martin was surprised, but if it worked for Marion Hargreaves, so be it.

Martin rejoined Jennifer and Marion. Major Bristow and Captain Hammond had come to meet them. As the two men chatted to Marion, Martin took Jennifer aside, "Marion's husband has re-married on proof of Marion's death." In a few words he explained what Phillip Newman had told him.

Jennifer nodded, "Let us go to the hotel, and we will have this matter out properly among friends, in private."

***

The meeting in the suite in the hotel was interesting. Marion had been wondering why her husband had not appeared to claim her. Believing he was possibly on detachment on the other side of the rock, or perhaps posted away, she had been waiting to be told the situation. The actual news of her husband's remarriage was a shock. At some level she had been prepared for rejection because of the harem, and perhaps a natural suspicion that she had been tampered with, but the rush to prove her dead, and the marriage to his mistress?

As the others watched they saw no grief, no sorrow, they saw anger. Marion drew herself up and turned to William Hammond. "Tell me, Captain, in the circumstances, would you have acted as my husband has?"

Taken aback he blurted out, "Madam, were I married to you, hell would freeze over before I would act in such a way."

Startled by his vehement reply Marion suddenly realised that Hammond had spoken from the heart. Looking around at the others, she realised that they saw what she had seen. Martin had a small smile on his face.

The anger drained out of Marion as she realised that it meant that she was no longer tied to the selfish man she had been resigned to tolerate for the rest of her life. She smiled and the tension in the room relaxed. Will Hammond sighed with relief as he thought he might have upset matters with his unthinking outburst.

Marion turned to Hammond as the others all started chatting in the more relaxed atmosphere, "Did you really mean that?" She asked quietly.

Will Hammond still pink-faced, "I meant every word, Madam."

"My name is Marion. It is William, is it not?"

Will nodded.

"Then please," she touched his hand, "If I may call you friend, please call me Marion."

"Of course Marion, I would be honoured."

"And I will call you Will."

The ever vigilant Jennifer observed the quiet exchange with approval.

***

A carriage drew up outside the home of the major and his wife. The Cox'n presented a note and waited while the personal possessions of the former Mrs Hargreaves were produced and loaded into the carriage.

The current Mrs Hargreaves was absent at the time which was perhaps as well, since she had laid claim to many of the things that were despatched with the Cox'n. It gave the major some satisfaction to know that his wife would be upset, but then he was still angry at being deceived over his so-called son.

***

The three ships of the original enterprise sailed from Gibraltar, with the prize Calliope, manned mainly by the recovered slaves from Agadir, commanded by Lieutenant Angus Cameron, by order of the Admiral, who disposed of several of the spare officers collected at the Gibraltar for various reasons. And with the added presence of Dominic Gordon, who had decided to take passage on the Castletown having done his duty in Gibraltar. He had arranged the onward transmission of the Hon. Cecelia who, while sad to leave her new found friends, was committed to her fiancé in India. Marion Hargreaves was also aboard and looking forward to a new life back in Britain.

***

The arrival of the ships in Portsmouth was an occasion for celebration. The cargo in the Castletown was being fought over while the ship was being brought alongside. The contents of the holds of all three ships were off loaded into a warehouse and left in the competent hands of Mr. Weeks, who happily settled down to several days of haggling on behalf of the company.

For Martin, Antonio brought a message from the Admiralty with a post carriage. His hurried departure was a disappointment to Charles and Jane, and daughter Jane, who was compensated to some extent by the arrival of her mother and Maria Diaz, with their new friend Natasha Wing. Midshipman James Woods, now bursting out of his uniform at fifteen years old, promised to follow the party to Eastney when his new uniforms were ready, the following day.

Antonio's wife, the Countess Alouette, had taken an apartment in Portsmouth and insisted on entertaining Captain Harris and his wife Julia on their first night ashore. There was an ulterior motive that she confessed unashamedly. With her husband in London, she could de-brief Julia without the reproving looks that her work sometimes evoked.

Major Bristow had invested his prize monies with advice from his bankers, and one of the investments had been the upkeep of his family estate. It was therefore his intended destination upon their arrival in Portsmouth. Not having been accustomed to the ways of the women in the world, he discovered his sister had anticipated his arrival and despatched his own carriage from his Milton home. As he escorted his bride ashore he was astonished to see Lady Eleanor, his sister, waiting to greet him. For once in his life Alan Bristow was struck dumb, not so Olivia, who guessed that this was the sister that Alan had mentioned to her. "Lady Eleanor? How lovely to meet you at last, Alan has spoken of you, though I fear he is overcome for the moment. I am Alan's wife, Olivia."

"Wife? Oh I did not realise. I am so happy for you both. I am Eleanor, and I thought to surprise my brother after his voyage around the world."

Alan finally gathered his wits and broke into the conversation. "What a surprise! As Olivia has told you, we were married some months ago on the way to the Philippine Islands, and as you may have noticed, we are expecting an addition to our family."

Olivia placed her hand on her growing waistline, causing Eleanor to smile, and Alan to blush

The driver was instructed to drive to Eastney they were invited to stay for the welcome-home celebration. Lady Eleanor was staying in Portsmouth with friends, but was invited on the spot by Jennifer who had observed the entire meeting.

Marion Hargreaves joined Jennifer at Eastney, as did Captain Hammond, who would otherwise have lodged in the Inn in Portsmouth. Jennifer had insisted, that since there was ample room at Eastney, he could make up the numbers. As Marion had no escort, he could do duty in that capacity.

Because Martin had been taken off to London, the plans for the homecoming celebration had to be transferred to the house in Ovington Square. After three days of local activity the entire party transferred in a convoy of coaches to London.

***

For Martin there was an unexpected series of interviews awaiting him in London, including, an interview with the Duke of Wellington, who was currently Master-General of the Ordinance. The Duke was particularly interested in the activities of Admiral Cochrane, whose activities were receiving attention in London and throughout the western world. To many, the operations in South America was giving hope to the Republicans in Europe.

Sadly none of the interviews were related to his being given a sea command. So it was with a heavy heart he prepared the London house for the influx of guests.

His friend Antonio Ramos commiserated with him, "Martin, my friend, you can sail anywhere you wish, at any time. The sea is still there."

"Antonio, as you well know, going to sea with a purpose is not the same as going on a yachting trip!" With that Martin ended the conversation and threw himself into the preparations for the celebration and the ball to follow.

Soon enough the house was alive with the activities of the various people staying there. Maria and Natasha were staying with Antonio and Alouette in their nearby house, and the arrival of Neil Harman was imminent.

At the Forest-Bowers residence, James Woods, a little stiff in his new uniform, was enduring the attention of Jane; his impassive face giving little away, but his patience in the situation was noted and appreciated. As Jennifer observed to Martin, "Jane assures everyone that she will be marrying James when she is of age, and he does not turn a hair."

Martin said "What does that mean? I know he likes Jane and that they used to play together when I first brought him home, but are you saying he is ready and willing to marry her in some four years' time?

"It means exactly that." Jennifer answered seriously. "Would you not approve of the match?"

Martin looked at his wife helplessly, "Of course I would approve but…"

"But what?" Jennifer was smiling.

Martin shrugged helplessly. "You mentioned the other situation, that of Marion Hargreaves…"

"Oh yes, Will Hammond is undoubtedly prepared to marry Marion the moment she is free once more. I know she is aware of it, I just hope she does not make a mistake once more."

Martin looked up at his wife keenly, "Mistake? You think it would be a mistake for her to marry Will?"

"No I do not, at least, not if she loves him; but if she does not? That would be a mistake."

Martin smiled, "I see, yes, now I understand." He did not really. The entire conversation with his wife convinced him that there was an aspect of the character of women that was completely beyond his understanding and he realised that this was a good subject to steer clear of – leave the entire matter to Jennifer.

***

The party with all their friends present, was a great success. The ball given by Dominic Gordon was also. The announcement of the engagement of Neil Harmon and Maria Diaz was made at the ball.

Jennifer smiled at the announcement, and Martin noticed and whispered, "I suppose you knew?"

Jennifer looked at her husband pityingly, "Everyone knew, darling."

***

At home during the days after all the celebrations were over, Martin was plunged into an accounting nightmare. Johnathon Weeks arrived from Portsmouth with the results of the trading and the outcome of the sale of the ships they had returned with.

The Calliope had been sold to the Swedish Navy, Asterid and Alderney were purchased by the Royal Navy. The Castletown had been retained by the company owned by Martin, Antonio and Captain Brooks. It was already loading cargo for India, and Dorothea, was having the captain's apartment refurbished, since it was going to continue to be their home for the next two years at least. Patrick and Dorothea Brooks had been present in London for the party and the ball, though both had now returned to Portsmouth to look after the ship.

Martin was getting the look in his eye when Jennifer knew he was contemplating a sea voyage.

She found him seated in the garden behind the house where the ground was largely dedicated to vegetables. It was quiet here which was the reason he had chosen the seat, away from the noise and chatter.

"I wondered how long you could survive the pace of life in London." Jennifer's voice was soft and understanding. "We will go to Eynsham tomorrow with little to distract us, there are things waiting to be done on the estate. There we can talk in peace."

"I'm sorry, my love. I find I am missing the feel of a deck beneath my feet, and the more of the London life I 'enjoy', the more I miss the sea. I will be calling upon the Admiralty tomorrow, with little expectation but high hopes."

Jennifer sat on his knee and faced him. "You know I will miss you, but I know it makes you happy, go if you must but I still pray that I will have you for a little longer. Do you realise that only by travelling around the world with you have I managed to spend more than one year with you in our entire married life."

Martin was silent. The truth was exactly as she had put it. He loved his wife but his life was at sea.

"Tell me, Jennifer, when Alan Bristow offered himself as husband to Olivia, you knew it would be permanent."

"In truth I did not, but I had a feeling that it would work out that way." I knew that Alan was a gentle man and I knew she could trust him. More importantly she guessed it as well, so by being in close proximity, they actually got to know each other without pressure or obligation, I hoped it would happen for both their sakes, and it did."

***

At the Admiralty the following day, as he predicted, there was nothing available for Martin to do. The possibility of a sea appointment was remote because of the reductions in the size of the fleet. In addition, despite his celebrity, the fact was that the Admirals now firmly entrenched in office were a new breed with a different circle of friends.

Martin had always been aware that the time would come when he would be forced to give up his naval career. In the carriage on his way back to Knightsbridge contemplating his future, it seemed that the time had come. He shrugged. He had always recognised that life was a series of challenges. He had wealth, he had Jennifer, a beautiful daughter, and wonderful friends. Though his naval career may be no longer possible, there were plenty of other challenges to face, and battles to win. Looking back, he seemed to have made a habit of winning.

When he returned from his visit to the Admiralty he was greeted by an excited Jane with the inevitable James Woods in tow. "Come, father, we are packed and ready to visit Eynsham. Mother is in the drawing room with Marion and Captain Will."

He allowed himself to be towed to meet the others, by his excited daughter.

At Jennifer's look, he shook his head, squared his shoulders, and – with a wry smile – said, "Well, what are we waiting for? Let's get going."

~~~~~~

Also by David O'Neil

Action/Adventure/Thriller series
Counterstroke # 1

Exciting, Isn't It?

O'Neil's initial entry into the world of action adventure romance thriller is filled with mystery and suspense, thrills and chills as *Counterstroke* finds it seeds of Genesis, and springs full blown onto the scene with action, adventure and romance galore.

John Murray, ex-Police, ex-MI6, ex management consultant, 49 and widowed, is ready to make a new start. Having sold off everything, he sets out on a lazy journey by barge through the waterways of France to collect his yacht at a yard in Grasse. En route he will decide what to do with the rest of his life

He picks up a female hitch-hiker Gabrielle, a frustrated author running from Paris after a confrontation with a lascivious would-be publisher Mathieu. She had unknowingly picked up some of Mathieu's secret documents with her manuscript. Although not looking for action, adventure or romance, still a connection is made.

An encounter with Pierre, an unpleasant former acquaintance from Paris who is chasing Gabrielle, is followed by a series of events that make John call on all his old skills of survival to keep them both alive over the next few days. Mystery and suspense shroud the secret documents that disclose the real background of the so called publisher who is in fact a high level international crook.

To survive, the pair become convinced they must take the fight to the enemy but they have no illusions; their chances of survival are slim. But with the help of some of John's old contacts, things start to become... exciting.

Counterstroke # 2....

Market Forces

Market Forces, Volume Two of the Counterstroke action adventure romance thriller series by David O'Neil introduces Katherine (Katt) Percival, tasked with the assassination of Mark Parnell in a hurried, last-minute attempt to stop his interference with the success of the Organization in Europe. As a skilled terminator for the CIA, Katt is accustomed to proper briefing. On this occasion she disobeys her orders, convinced it's a mistake. She joins forces with Mark to foil an attempt on his life.

Parnell works for John Murray, who created Secure Inc that caused the collapse of an International US criminal organisation's operation in Europe, forcing the disbanding of the US Company COMCO. Set up as a cover for money-laundering and other operations designed to control from within the political and financial administration, they had already been partially successful. Especially within the administrative sectors of the EU.

Katt goes on the run, she has been targeted and her Director sidelined by rogue interests in the CIA. She finds proof of conspiracy. She passes it on to Secure Inc who can use it to attack the Organization. She joins forces with Mark Parnell and Secure Inc. Mark and Katt and their colleagues risk their lives as they set out to foil the Organization once again.

Counterstroke # 3....

When Needs Must...

The latest action adventure thriller in the Counterstroke series opens with a new character Major Teddy Robertson–Steel fighting for survival in Africa. Mark Parnell and Katt Percival now working together for Secure Inc. are joined by Captain Libby 'Carter' Barr, now in plain clothes, well mostly, and her new partner James Wallace. They are tasked with locating and thwarting the efforts of three separate menaces from the European scene that threaten the separation of the United Kingdom from the political clutches of Brussels, by using terrorism to create wealth by a group of billionaires, and the continuing presence of the Mob, bankrolled from USA. An action adventure thriller filled with romance, mystery and suspense. With the appearance of a much needed new team, Dan and Reba, and the welcome return of Peter Maddox, Dublo Bond and Tiny Lewis, there is action and adventure throughout. Change will happen, it just takes the right people, at the right time, in the right place.

**Young adult action/adventure/ romance
thriller series
Donny Weston & Abby Marshall # 1**

Fatal Meeting

A captivating new series of young adult action, romance, adventure and mystery.

For two young teens, Donny and Abby, who have just found each other, sailing the 40 ft ketch across the English

Channel to Cherbourg is supposed to be a light-hearted adventure.

The third member of the crew turns out to be a smuggler, and he attempts to kill them both before they reach France. The romance adventure. now filled with action, mystery and suspense, suddenly becomes deadly serious when the man's employers try to recover smuggled items from the boat. The action gets more and more hectic as the motive becomes personal

Donny and Abby are plunged into a series of events that force them to protect themselves. Donny's parents become involved so with the help of a friend of the family, Jonathon Glynn, they take the offensive against the gang who are trying to kill them.

The action adventure thriller ranges from the Mediterranean to Paris and the final scene is played out in the shadow of the Eiffel Tower in the city of romance and lights; Paris France..

Donny Weston & Abby Marshall # 2

Lethal Complications

Eighteen year olds Donny and Abby take a year out from their studies to clear up problems that had escalated over the past three years. They succeed in closing the book on the past during the first months of the year, now they are looking forward to nine months relaxation, romance and fun, when old friend of the family, mystery man Jonathon Glynn, drops in to visit as they moor at Boulogne, bringing action and adventure into their lives once again.

Jonathon was followed and an attempt to kill them happens immediately after his visit. They leave their boat and pick up the RV they have left in France, hoping to avoid further conflict. They are attacked in the Camargue, but fast and accurate shooting keeps them alive. They find themselves mixed up in a treacherous scheme by a rogue Chinese gang to defame a Chinese moderate, in an attempt to stall the Democratic process in China.

The two young lovers, becoming addicted to action and adventure, link up with Isobel, a person of mystery who has acquired a reputation without earning it. Between them they manage to keep the Chinese target and his girlfriend out of the rogue Chinese group's hands.

Tired of reacting to attack, and now looking for action and adventure, they set up an ambush of their own, effectively checkmating the rogue Chinese plans. The leader of the rogues, having lost face and position in the Chinese hierarchy, plans a personal coup using former Spetsnaz mercenaries. With the help of a former SBS man Adam, who had worked with and against Spetsnaz forces, the friends survive and Lin Hang the Chinese leader suffers defeat.

Donny Weston & Abby Marshall # 3....

A Thrill A Minute

They are back! Fresh from their drama-filled action adventure excursion to the United States, Abby Marshall and Donny Weston look forward to once again taking up their studies at the University. Each of them is looking forward to the calm life of a University student without the threat of being murdered. Ah, the serene life.... that is the thing. But that doesn't last long. It is only a few weeks before our adventuresome young lovers find that the calm, quiet routine of University life is boring beyond belief and both are filled with yearning for the fast-paced action adventure of their prior experiences. It isn't long before trouble finds the couple and they welcome it with open arms, but perhaps this time they have underestimated the opposition. Feeling excitement once again, the two youths arm themselves and leapt into the fray. The fight was on and no holds barred!

Once again O'Neil takes us into the action filled world of mystery and suspense, action and adventure, romance and peril.

Donny Weston & Abby Marshall # 4....

It's Just One Thing After Another

Fresh from their victory over the European Mafia, our two young adults in love, Abby Marshall and Donny Weston, are rewarded with an all-expense-paid trip to the United States. But, as our young couple discover, there is no free lunch and the price they will have to pay for their "free" tour may be more than they can afford to pay, in this action adventure thriller. Even so, with the help of a few friends and some former enemies, the valiant young duo face danger once again with firm resolve and iron spirit, but will that be sufficient in face of the odds that are stacked against them?

And is their friend and benefactor actually a friend or is he on the other side? The two young adults look at this man of mystery and suspense with a bit of caution. Action, adventure and romance abound in this, the latest escapades of Britain's dynamic young couple.

Donny Weston & Abby Marshall # 5

What Goes Around...

Just when it seems that our two young heroes, Donny Weston and Abby Marshall are able to return to the University to complete their studies, fate decides to play another turn as once again the two young lovers come under attack, this time from a most unsuspected source. It appears that not even the majestic powers of the British Intelligence Service will be enough to rescue the beleaguered duo and they will have to survive through their own skills. In the continuing action adventure thriller, two young adults must solve the mystery that faces them to determine who is trying to kill them. The suspense is chilling, the action and adventure stimulating. Finding togetherness even among the onslaughts, Donny and Abby also find remarkable friends who offer their assistance; but will even that be enough to overcome the determined enemy?

Donny Weston & Abby Marshall # 6

Without Prejudice

Donny Weston and Abby Marshall, on their way to park their beloved boat *Swallow* in Malta to be ready for the summer, encounter the schooner *Speedwell* at La Rochelle, where problems arise for Commander Will and his wife Mary Pleasance. Tom Hardy and Lotte Compton, both from the *Speedwell* join forces with Donny and Abby to oppose the threats to the Commander. From Valetta the four follow up the threat, only to find themselves faced with a plot to use a famous mercenary in an assassination that will rock the foundations of the Euro community, and the western world. Backed by Russia and with the tacit approval of the head of

MI6, a rogue CIA operative has set things up for a public shooting at a Euro summit.

The four foil the plot and the assassination fails, but ironically the CIA agent, is credited with foiling the coup and promoted. He wants revenge, and comes after the four with blood in his eye and his guns loaded. The outcome is decided in a action-packed shoot-out in high speed boats in the cold waters of the Thames estuary.

Sea Adventures

Better The Day

From the W.E.B. Griffin of the United Kingdom, David O'Neil, a exciting saga of romance, action, adventure, mystery and suspense as Peter Murray and his brother officers in Coastal Forces face overwhelming odds fighting German E-boats, the German Navy and the Luftwaffe in action in the Channel, the Mediterranean, Norway and the Baltic – where there is conflict with the Soviet Allies. This action-packed story of daring and adventure finally follows Peter Murray to the Pacific where he faces Kamikaze action with the U.S. Fleet.

Distant Gunfire

"Boarder s Away!" Serving as an officer on a British frigate at the time of the French Emperor Napoleon is not the safest occupation, but could be a most profitable one. Robert Graham, rising from the ranks to become the Captain of a British battleship by virtue of his dauntless leadership, displayed under enemy fire, finds himself a wealthy man as

the capture of enemy ships resulted in rich rewards. Action and adventure is the word of the day, as battle after battle rages across the turbulent waters and seas as the valiant British Royal Navy fights to stem the onslaught of the mighty French Army and Navy. Mystery and suspense abound as inserting and collecting spy agent after spy agent is executed. The threat of imminent death makes romance and romantic interludes all the sweeter, and the suspense of waiting for a love one to return even more traumatic. Captain Graham, with his loyal following of sailors and marines, takes prize ship after prize ship, thwart plot after diabolical plot, and finds romance when he least expects it. To his amazement and joy, he finds himself being knighted by the King of England. The good life is his, now all he has to do is to live long enough to enjoy it. A rollicking good tale of sea action and swashbuckling adventures.

Sailing Orders

For those awaiting another naval story of the 18/19th century, then this is it. Following the life of an abandoned 13 year old who by chance is instrumental in saving a family from robbery and worse. Taken in by the naval Captain Bowers he is placed as a midshipman in his benefactor's ship. From that time onward with the increasing demands of the conflict with France, Martin Forrest grows up fast. The relationship with his benefactors family is formalised when he is adopted by them and has a home once more. Romance with Jennifer the Captains ward links him ever closer to the family.

Meanwhile he serves in the West Indies where good fortune results in his gaining considerable wealth personally. With promotion and command he is able to marry and reclaim his birth-right, stolen from him by his step-mother and her lover.

The mysterious (call me merely Mr Smith) involves Martin in more activity in the shadowy world of the secret agents. Mainly a question of lifting and placing of people, his involvement becomes more complex as time goes on. A cruise to India consolidates his position and rank with the successful capture of prizes when returning convoying East-Indiamen. His rise to Post rank is followed by a series of events, that sadly culminate in family tragedy.

While still young Martin Forrest-Bowers faces and empty future, though merely Mr Smith has requested his services????

Quarterdeck

Following the highly successful introduction of Martin Forrest-Bowers into the Royal Navy in the best-selling sea adventure, **Sailing Orders**, David O'Neil, the UK's hottest selling author, presents another daring tale of Martin and his valiant men in a stirring story of war and sea, romance and action, valor and courage.

Now married and a decorated Captain himself, Martin returns home to find his wife Jennifer at death's door. Prompted by his safe return, her recovery is assured and is followed by the necessity of returning to work for 'plain Mr. Smith' with clandestine excursions and undercover trips to France. . At sea once more, he is involved not only with preventing treasure ships from falling into French hands, but also with events on the east coast of America in the run-up to the war of 1812.

Action, battle, romance, adventure and thrills abound in O'Neil's latest venture into the world of sea battles with France, Spain and American pirates.

Adventure thrillers

Minding the Store

O'Neil scores again! Often favorably compared to America's W.E.B. Griffin and to U.K.'s Ian Fleming, and fresh from his best-selling action adventure, "Distant Gunfire," O'Neil finds excitement and action in the New York garment district. The department store industry becomes the target of take-over by organized crime in their quest for money-laundering outlets. It would seem that no department store executive is a match for vicious criminals, however, David Freemantle, heir to the Freemantle fortune and Managing Director of America's most prestigious department store is no ordinary department store executive and the team of ex-military specialists he has assembled contains no ordinary store security personnel. Armed invasions are met with swift retaliation; kidnapping and rape attempts are met with fatal consequences as the Mafia and their foreign cohorts learn that not all ordinary citizens are helpless, and that evil force can be met with superior force in O'Neil's latest thriller of adventure and action, romance and suspense, mystery and mayhem that willl have the reader on the edge of his seat until the last breath-taking word.

The Hunted

David O'Neal, UK's answer to W.E.B. Griffin and Dean Koontz strikes again with his newest suspense thriller filled with action, adventure, romance and danger. When the Russian Mafia joins forces with other European and Asian gangsters to take over a noted world-wide charity organization to smuggle guns and drugs into unsuspecting nations and begins to kill innocent people, one man – Tarquin Gilmore – Quin to his friends – declares war on the Mafia. To achieve his goal of total destruction of the criminal gangs, he surrounds himself with a few dangerous men and beautiful women. But don't be fooled by their beauty, the girls are easily as deadly as any man. On the other hand, there are a lot more gangsters than Quin and his friends and it's a battle to the finish. A stirring tale of crime and murder, mystery and suspense, passion and romance, guns and drugs... but that is war!

The Mercy Run

O'Neil's thrilling action adventure saga of Africa: the story of Tom Merrick, Charlie Hammond and Brenda Cox; a man and two women who fight and risk their lives to keep supplies rolling into the U.N. refugee camps in Ethiopia. Their adversaries: the scorching heat, the dirt roads and the ever present hazards of bandit gangs and corrupt government officials. Despite tragedy and treachery, mystery and suspense while combating the efforts of Colonel Gonbera, who hopes to turn the province into his personal domain, Merrick and his friends manage to block the diabolical Colonel at every turn.

Frustrated by Merrick's success against him, there seems to be no depths to which the Colonel would not descend to achieve his aim. The prospect of a lucrative diamond strike comes into the game, and so do the Russians and Chinese. But, as Merrick knows, there will be no peace while the Colonel remains the greatest threat to success and peace.

Meet our Author

David O'Neil

Frequently compared favorably to noted author, W.E.B. Griffin, O'Neil is an avid student of military history, especially during the time of sea battles and political uprisings. A native of the United Kingdom, artist and photographer David O'Neil started writing seriously with a series of Highland guide books. His boyhood ambitions were to fly an airplane, and sail a boat. As a boy he and his family were bombed out of their home in London. He learned to fly with the Royal Air Force during his National Service. He started sailing boats while serving in the Colonial Police, in Nyasaland (Malawi). He spent 8 years there, before returning to UK. Since then he lived in southern England where he became a management consultant, for over twenty years. He returned to live in Scotland in 1980, and became a tour guide in1986. He started writing in 2006, the first guide book being published in 2007. A further two have been published since He started writing fiction in 2007 and has now written five full length novels. A student of history and formerly military, O'Neil has been compared favorably with the UK's Ian Fleming and is frequently referred to as the "W.E.B. Griffin of the United Kingdom" due in a large part to his insightful recounting of exciting military exploits and his unique ability to develop credible characters.